AFTER MIDNIGHT

BOOK YOUR PLACE ON OUR WEBSITE AND MAKE THE READING CONNECTION!

We've created a customized website just for our very special readers, where you can get the inside scoop on everything that's going on with Zebra, Pinnacle and Kensington books.

When you come online, you'll have the exciting opportunity to:

- View covers of upcoming books
- Read sample chapters
- Learn about our future publishing schedule (listed by publication month *and author*)
- Find out when your favorite authors will be visiting a city near you
- Search for and order backlist books from our online catalog
- Check out author bios and background information
- Send e-mail to your favorite authors
- Meet the Kensington staff online
- Join us in weekly chats with authors, readers and other guests
- Get writing guidelines
- AND MUCH MORE!

Visit our website at
http://www.zebrabooks.com

CONTENTS

RED MOON RISING

Carol Finch

One

Colorado Territory
1859

The wind howled and swirled, pelting the jutting peaks of the Rocky Mountains like invisible drumming fingers. The red moon blazed in the night sky, showcased by the shadowy archway of the cave, flanked by the roiling clouds of an approaching thunderstorm.

It was the worst kind of night—the kind that Seth Tremayne dreaded, resented.

He always had. He always would.

Restlessly, Seth paced the oppressive confines of the cavern that had been his home for the past twenty years. The craving he fought to control was at peak intensity when the red moon was on the rise. For years—a couple hundred of them—Seth had battled his bestial "condition," constantly searching for methods to control the cravings, hoping one day to find a permanent cure. But curing the torments of the damned seemed to take as long as extinguishing the fires that sizzled in hell.

The flutter of wings—hundreds of them—prompted Seth to step outside his cave. The bats that shared his living quarters flooded out, filling the darkening sky. Their silhouettes streamed across the red moon like a rippling ribbon as they soared off to feed in the darkness.

Seth lingered on the stone ledge, watching the creatures of the night succumb to their instincts—and felt the maddening urge to feed his own craving. He knew none of the remedies he applied would be potent enough to counteract his ageless hunger. After years of scientific experimentation, he had come to the depressing conclusion that the vials and test tubes of potions he had concocted would bring only minimal relief—when that cursed red moon was on the rise.

Muttering, Seth strode back inside the cavern and snatched up the vial of green liquid. He downed the dose of foul-tasting medicine, then braced himself for the fierce reaction that usually knocked him off his feet.

Sure enough, it did.

Gasping for breath, Seth crawled to his hands and knees, then staggered to his feet. The hazy confines of the cave swirled around him as he struggled to orient himself. Still, the craving caused by his affliction prowled through him, demanding to be fed.

Damn! This last potion he had mixed hadn't had time to ferment properly, he mused. Either that or he was beginning to develop a tolerance to the potion. He would have to begin new experimentation—or surrender to the cravings.

A sardonic smile twisted his lips as he braced his hand against the stone wall for support. He was a fool to think he could cure the curse of being born the seventh son of a seventh son. His studies in alchemy in England's famed Oxford University hadn't enabled him to control this raging beast within him. He, like the bats that shared his bleak existence, was a creature of the night, unable to enjoy the bright warmth of sunlight.

Seth had remained on the fringes of civilization, moving deeper into the interior of the country when humanity crowded his space. He had led a gypsy lifestyle, traveling from France to England then to America. And never once in the past two hundred years had he grown older a day past thirty-two. Ah, what he wouldn't give to see a gray hair on his head, to know he had grown older normally instead of being stuck in time until the end of eternity.

His life had become a complex lie comprised of dozens of deceptions and false truths. The friendships he had allowed himself to form over the decades had been superficial and temporary. The family who had raised him was long gone. He had become a loner by necessity and habit, a revenant who couldn't truly live—or die.

Seth had investigated all the myths and legends circulating about lost souls who suffered from his condition, hoping to find a shred of truth in the superstitious lore that might end his torment. Over scores of years he had experimented and studied every word of hearsay. But as far as he knew, nothing could cure his cursed affliction—except a stake through the heart . . . or a pure and decent woman who remained willfully by his side until dawn . . . or performing a purely selfless act that would save his tortured soul.

Seth grimaced at the first prospective solution to his problem, then laughed at the irony of the last. How in hell could he perform a totally selfless act while harboring a purely selfish motive? And how could a woman remain pure and untouched if she lay beside *him* in bed? Ah, the great paradox of the undead!

Lightning flashed and thunder rolled through the labyrinth of plunging ravines nestled between the rugged mountain peaks. Seth winced at the panoramic sights and amplified sounds that offended his keen senses. Mother Nature's eye-catching, ear-splitting spectacle served to remind him of just how lonely and tormented he was. He had donated several fortunes to scientific medicine, but he still wasn't in command of his own soul—the one thing he needed to give his life meaning. He had spent two centuries borrowing life from his victims, but he had never had a life of his own.

Although Seth's restless cravings had been temporarily appeased by his potion, he still felt the need to venture from the musty confines of his cave to breathe in fresh air—and hope that feasting on the meat of a hapless rabbit would pacify him for the night.

"Damn that red moon rising," Seth scowled. The Indian summer moon always played the worst kind of hell with his self-control.

Seth stopped in his tracks when his exceptional night vision zeroed in on the shapely silhouette of a woman. She stood on an outcropping of stone that overlooked the V-shaped valley below. Where the blazes had she come from? No one lived in the ghost town in the valley below his cavern. Two years earlier, when word came down the pike that a mother lode of gold ore had been discovered to the north, the miners had packed up and swarmed off to seek their big bonanza.

So what was this woman doing out here all alone, standing on the edge of a cliff, her arms upraised to the descending storm—as if she intended to end it all?

The alarming thought sent Seth scrabbling down the steps of stone that led away from his cave. Even as he raced toward the windswept precipice, he felt the hope rising inside him that rescuing this suicidal female from certain death would bring an end to his lifelong curse.

But there it was again, the cruel paradox: Even his supposedly selfless act held a selfish, ulterior motive.

Seth skidded to a halt, staring in amazement as electrically-charged particles of air flashed like pale-blue diamonds around the woman's outstretched fingertips. The panicky realization that the woman was attempting to turn herself into a human lightning rod, and that she was about to be struck by a thunderbolt, put Seth in motion again. Frantic, he surged toward her, taking her legs out from under her a split second before a sizzling bolt speared down from the clouds.

The deafening clap of thunder threatened to blow out Seth's ultrasensitive eardrums. Dazed, he clutched the woman to his chest, straining to see through the silver-white flash of light. He forced himself to breathe, in spite of the burning, prickling sensations that clogged his nostrils. While his face was mashed against the woman's throat, the wild urge to feed nearly overwhelmed him; then his eyes watered and the urge to sneeze overtook him. He turned his head away to sneeze—and glimpsed the falling limb of the pine tree that was crashing toward him at blazing speed. Lightning had struck the tree and he and the woman were about to be crushed!

With the woman clamped tightly in his arms, Seth rolled the only direction he could—away from the ledge that dropped into nothingness. Yet, he couldn't move quickly enough to dodge the falling limb. Although he protected the woman with his own body, the branch lanced off his head and the world turned pitch-black.

Matilda Shaw squirmed out from under the fallen branch and cursed the bad luck that kept following her like her own shadow. "Mishap Mattie," her family called her. It seemed that no matter how far west she migrated, and despite her benevolent deeds, the nickname still applied.

After Mattie accepted the job as restaurant cook in the mining town a few miles north of this ghost town in the mountains, she was certain her luck had changed. The prospectors in the community known as Slapout praised her cooking and respected her ability to heal their injuries with her poultices and potions.

And now this! Chagrined, Mattie stared at the sprawled form of the man who had taken it upon himself to save her when she hadn't needed to be saved. It seemed her string of bad luck had rubbed off on this good Samaritan who came rushing out of nowhere.

As lightning glared and the storm clouds engulfed the full moon, Mattie studied the man who was dressed completely in black. It had to be the legendary Seth Tremayne, the hermit who was reported to be the sole inhabitant of this ghost town that was tucked against the mountainside.

Of course, Mattie had heard the wild rumors circulating about the recluse who rarely mixed with civilization, the man who was reported to guard his bonanza in the mountains like a fire-breathing dragon. Obviously, the rumors were the product of the active imaginations that ran rampant when miners congregated in saloons to swap tales and douse their woes in whiskey. But there seemed to be more to Seth Tremayne than the legend claimed. This kind, good-hearted man had tried to save her life—and he'd suffered a serious blow to the head because of his heroics.

Despite the pounding rain and grumbling thunder, Mattie grabbed hold of the branch and dragged it away from the unconscious man. He lay on his back, his arms outflung, his long legs spread-eagle on the ground. He was a muscular, ruggedly handsome individual who had a knot the size of a hen egg right between his eyes.

"Oh dear me, what have I done now!" Mattie gasped as she crouched beside Seth, appraising his waxen features.

His face was alarmingly pale, his breathing so labored that, for a moment, Mattie feared that he wasn't breathing at all!

Hurriedly, Mattie dug into the pocket of her gown to retrieve the cure-all potion of herbs that she kept on hand for emergencies. She smeared the waxy stuff on Seth's bloodless lips, then touched her index finger to his tongue. Several apprehensive seconds passed before Seth gave the slightest reaction to the medication. To Mattie's dismay, the brawny man's eyes opened momentarily as he sneezed loudly, then he collapsed.

Mattie frowned, bemused. Every injured miner from

Slapout had reacted favorably when receiving a drop of the strong potion. Why not this particular man?

Apparently, the blow to Seth's head was so severe that nothing fazed him. Alarmed, Mattie glanced around her. She had to transport her would-be rescuer to her cottage in Slapout if she was to properly tend his injury. She had to ensure that he didn't develop complications after being exposed to inclement weather.

Raising her arms skyward, Mattie closed her eyes and begged for the strength needed to transport Seth to her cabin. Her newest patient needed to be tucked in bed and nursed back to health, and she wouldn't be satisfied until he was back in the healthy condition he had enjoyed before performing his heroic deed on her behalf.

Seth awoke to agonizing pain. It was blinding—and so was the streaming light that poured through the curtained window in the bright-yellow bedroom where he lay. He seemed to have no strength, no energy to move.

Where was he? How had he gotten there? And, he thought with a leaping sense of panic and alarm, *who* was he? For the life of him he couldn't even recall his name.

Beyond the bright yellow door that boasted etchings of colorful butterflies, he heard something clatter to the floor and break in a thousand pieces. Voices—and there must have been a dozen of them—yammered all at once. The loud noise caused Seth to wince.

And what was wrong with his eyesight? he wondered as he squinted against the shafts of sunlight. The light seemed intolerably intense to him, making him consider pulling the quilt over his head. He wanted to crawl from bed to close the curtains but he couldn't muster the strength to rise.

Confused, miserable, Seth studied the bright-colored patchwork quilt that covered his naked body. He felt like death warmed over, surrounded, ironically, by every cheerful color in a rainbow. He was definitely out of place, though he wasn't certain how he knew that.

Seth groaned when the voices beyond the door grew louder, more intense. His sensitive ears tingled and he wondered why the racket of voices disturbed him so greatly. Was that normal?

Despite the anticipated pain, Seth propped up on his elbow and shouted: "Hello!" He grimaced when the sound of his own voice ricocheted off one side of his skull, then slammed into the other.

Groaning, he glanced sideways to see a mirror reflecting sunlight, then he squeezed his eyes shut against the blinding glare. When he heard the door creak open, he suddenly forgot to breathe. There, standing before him in a bright orange satin gown was an angel. Long, red-gold hair tumbled around her shoulders and flowed over the bodice of her gown in a riot of ringlets and curls. Eyes as green as a pine tree glistened in the sunlight.

For a dazed moment, Seth wondered if he might actually be in heaven. The scenario fit his perception of the glorious hereafter—all gleaming sunshine, vivid colors, and his own personal angel to attend to him. He must have done something right in his life to receive this eternal reward.

When Seth remembered the loud voices that had

suddenly died into silence, he glanced around the angel's shoulders, then frowned curiously at her. "Is there a conference of some kind being held in the other room?"

Mattie swiveled her head around to glance over her shoulder at the vacant room, then she smiled kindly at Seth. "No."

"No?" he repeated, bewildered. "But I swear I heard—"

The dainty-looking pixie swanned toward him, waving her arms as if to shoo away his concerns. "You need your rest, Mr. Tremayne. And let me say that I am dreadfully sorry about your mishap, truly I am. I hope you're beginning to feel better."

"Tremayne?" he repeated, dumbfounded. The name didn't ring a bell. But then, nothing rang a bell in his mind, except for the sensation of sledgehammers driving spikes through his skull.

Mattie stopped short, then stared down at the handsome man who occupied her bed. Clearly, the blow he'd sustained had clouded his thought processes.

"You say my name is Tremayne?" he asked.

The poor dear man looked so eager for information that Mattie felt the urge to hug him tightly, reassuring him that he would be all right and that she would take perfect care of him. Alighting beside Seth on the bed, she wrapped her arms around his broad shoulders and patted him comfortingly.

"You mustn't worry, Mr. Tremayne . . . Seth . . . if you don't mind my sounding so informal. You needn't worry about a thing. I intend to see that you are back on your feet in no time at all—"

When he sneezed suddenly, causing his head to thrust

forward, his jet-black hair flopped across the discolored knot on his forehead.

Mattie frowned in concern. "You must have caught a chill last night in the rain. I have something that will make you feel better." She bounded to her feet, then scurried into the kitchen to fetch a potion of herbs specifically designed to counteract sniffles and sneezing.

"Here," she said, as she poured the syrupy medication into a spoon. "Take this. It will make you feel better."

"Who are you—?"

When Seth opened his mouth to speak, Mattie gave him the dose of medication. To her shock and dismay, Seth gasped for breath, then choked on the medicine. When he wheezed and sputtered, she whacked him between the shoulder blades.

"My goodness, none of my other patients have suffered that kind of reaction to this potion. Are you all right, Seth?"

All right? Seth wasn't sure he'd be all right ever again. The sticky goo this angel of mercy crammed down his gullet set his throat aflame then exploded in his empty stomach like blasting powder. The woman's home remedy obviously wasn't working, because he felt the urge to sneeze again.

"Uh . . . chew! Uh . . . uh . . . chewwww!"

"Mercy me, you must need a double dose," Mattie diagnosed.

When she wheeled away from him, his need to sneeze instantly subsided.

"What I need," Seth insisted in a wheezy voice, "is to know who you are, what I'm doing here and where I belong. Obviously, I am not a permanent resident of this house or you wouldn't be calling me Mr. Tremayne. I can't seem to recall a blasted thing about myself, or my past, since the moment I woke up this morning. And if you don't mind, ma'am, please shut the curtains. The sunlight is giving me more of a headache than I already have."

Stunned, Mattie stared at the disoriented man who lay in her bed. "Sweet mercy! Do you mean to say that I am not only responsible for your atrocious headache and your symptoms of the grippe, but I have also caused you to lose your memory?" She slumped, dispirited, on the foot of the bed. "I'm terribly sorry about this, Seth. Why, if it wasn't for me, you wouldn't have suffered this accident. You would still be up in your cave, digging for gold."

Seth blinked, startled. "I live in a cave?"

When she nodded, red-gold curls danced around her shoulders. "That is what I've been told. The local miners claim that you're a hermit who doesn't mix with society. Not that I blame you," she inserted hastily. "The greed for gold makes men vultures and criminals. I'm sure you have had no choice but to protect your treasures from theft. In fact, I took certain measures to ensure your cave wouldn't be disturbed during your absence. So don't fret about anyone ransacking your belongings to steal your fortune. I am certain everything in your cave will remain just as you left it last night."

Seth frowned pensively. "What did you mean when you said you were responsible for my accident? What accident? And who the blazes are you?"

Mattie squirmed awkwardly, then met those mesmerizing blue eyes that peered so intently at her. Stared *hypnotically* at her, she mused. To date, she had never met a man whose very gaze had had such a startling impact on her.

Seth Tremayne was a wildly attractive man, despite the rumors that made him out to be some sort of demon who haunted the rich gold bonanza located in the mountain peaks above the ghost town. Although his skin was alarmingly pale, his lips—though bloodless at the moment—were full and sensuous, his hair as black as a raven's wing.

Mattie tamped down the effect his mystifying stare had on her, cleared her throat and smiled tentatively. "My name is Matilda Shaw. My friends and family call me Mattie. Last night I was wandering around in the mountains. I presume that you thought I intended to leap to my death, because you rushed out of nowhere to save me from the oncoming storm. When lightning struck a tree, the falling branch landed on your head," she explained. "If not for me, you would be perfectly fine right now. But rest assured that I will provide all the care and attention you'll need until you are back on your feet."

"That is very kind of you." He glanced toward the window. "Do you work in this mining town?"

"I cook at Wild Boar Saloon." Mattie smiled proudly. "The patrons claim that I serve the best food in the territory. I will make certain that you're served extra portions until you regain your strength."

When Mattie rose gracefully and approached him to press her palm to his forehead—presumably to check his temperature—Seth's eyes watered and he sneezed.

"I'm going to mix a stronger dose of medication to battle your symptoms," she said, before she whirled away.

When the door closed behind her, Seth stared pensively at the ceiling. Try as he might, he couldn't conjure up a single event in his past life, not even that moment the previous night when Mattie claimed he had been hit by a lightning-struck tree limb.

He was a recluse who protected a gold mine? He lived in a cave? If he'd acquired staggering wealth, why was he living in some remote mountain range on the outskirts of civilization? And how had he acquired the reputation of a vengeful demon who frightened off would-be claim jumpers? What kind of man was he? What bitter, traumatic experiences in his past had made him the man he was rumored to be?

Seth inched toward the edge of the bed, then eased cautiously to his feet. Using the night stand for support, he approached the window. Cupping his hand over his sensitive eyes, he stared down the rutted street of Slapout, watching miners, mules, and wagons pass by. Two men halted in front of the window, gaped at him in surprise, then scurried away.

Unless Seth missed his guess, Mattie Shaw was about to become the brunt of fast-flying gossip. No doubt the miners would spread the word that a bare-chested man—stark naked actually—was staring out Mattie's bedroom window. Her reputation would be in tatters.

Seth staggered back to bed to lie down, shocked that he had so little energy. For Mattie's sake, he had to leave her house before his presence caused her shame and embarrassment. And he would leave—as soon as this blasted headache eased up. He would find his way back to the cave where Mattie claimed he resided. Maybe familiar surroundings would prompt his memory.

Although Seth had every intention of catching a quick

cat nap before making his departure, a feeling of lethargy overwhelmed him. Without understanding why, he slumped into a deep, motionless sleep that lasted for hours.

Mattie scooped the iron skillet off the stove and carefully transferred the juicy steak onto a platter. She garnished the meat with her secret recipe of spices, put a few slices of fried potatoes on the side, then handed the plate to the young man who waited tables at Wild Boar Saloon.

"Is something wrong, Clem?" she asked when the lean waiter with carrot-red hair continued to stand there, staring speculatively at her.

"As a matter of fact there is," Clem Horton said, frowning in concern. "Two miners came in an hour ago, claiming they spotted a man staring out your bedroom window. Word around Slapout is that you've taken up with that loony hermit from the mountains."

"I haven't—"

Clem held up his free hand to silence her. "You don't have to explain to me, Mattie. You know how I feel about you, but I know that doesn't give me any right to object to the company you keep. Me and the other menfolk in town have become mighty attached to you, you know that. You're the only woman in town, other than that fussy old Widow Pruitt who runs the dry goods store. We like having you around. You're the closest thing this town has to a doctor, too. And well, we're extremely partial to you. Your cooking and your healing potions have brought dozens of us pleasure and comfort. Nobody wants to see you come to harm."

Clem's words put a sentimental mist in Mattie's eyes. For the first time in her life she felt wanted, needed, appreciated, respected. It was a far cry from the belittling treatment she often received from her family. The entire brood of Shaws was constantly clucking at her, spouting advice, and making her so nervous that she dropped things, tripped over her own feet. Although Mattie was too kindhearted to come right out and tell her parents and older siblings that their repeated taunting and badgering had transformed her into "Mishap Mattie," it was the truth.

"Now I've made you cry," Clem mumbled apologetically. "Didn't mean to do that. It's just that the citizens of Slapout are very protective when it comes to you."

"And I am extremely fond of all the friends I've made here," Mattie replied, dabbing at her eyes with her kerchief. "But there is no need for any of you to be concerned about me. Seth Tremayne was injured while trying to save me from a nasty fall. Now he is my patient and the least I can do is to tend his injury while he recuperates. I would do the same for any other man in town, wouldn't I?"

Clem frowned darkly. "Seth Tremayne is not any other man in Slapout, Mattie. He has a reputation of being lightning fast on the draw, a man who has the deadly instincts of a predator. I've heard it said that he is one of the toughest hombres in the territory. Most decent folk are afraid to tangle with him. Some of the men feel uneasy just having him in town, not to mention having him in your cottage. We don't want him to take advantage of the situation."

Mattie smiled reassuringly, then turned Clem around and aimed him toward the dining hall where dozens of hungry prospectors awaited their meals. "Never fear, my friend, I am perfectly capable of taking care of myself. I have been doing it for years. Besides, Seth Tremayne is nothing like the unflattering rumors circulating about him. If he were, he wouldn't have rescued me last night in the storm, now would he?"

Clem glanced over his shoulder. "Just what were you doing out in that storm in the first place? It's dangerous for a woman to be wandering around alone at night."

Mattie grinned impishly. "How can it be dangerous when you just assured me that the menfolk are watching out for me?"

Clem braced his feet when Mattie tried to shove him out the door. He turned to stare somberly at her. "Mattie, there are times when even the best of men get these hankerings to be with a woman, especially one as kind and pretty as you. You have to be careful about gadding around alone. I'm not even sure I would trust myself alone with you in the moonlight, miles away from protective, watchful eyes. As for Seth Tremayne, he is all man, too, and not the best kind of man to be lounging in your bed. Now you be careful around him, hear me?"

Mattie nodded when Clem refused to leave without her promise. The dear sweet man was concerned about her welfare. Although she knew Clem harbored tender affection for her, she looked upon him as a friend, a brother.

Despite all the places she had been, and the men she had encountered along the way, no man had left a lasting impression on her—until she had stared into Seth Tremayne's mesmerizing silver-blue eyes and felt an unfamiliar stirring deep inside her. Mattie wasn't sure what there was about that handsome mountain man that attracted her, aside from his arresting good looks, but something compelled her to him.

There was something about the way he had risked personal injury in order to save her that touched her heart, something about the vulnerability she sensed in him when he learned he had lost his memory. Despite the uncomplimentary rumors, she knew, *sensed*, that Seth was a man of character and honor. And it was her responsibility to restore him to health. After all, she was the reason he couldn't remember who he was or where he belonged. He needed her. . . .

A flash of forbidden memory raced across her mind as she turned back to the stove. Last night, when Mattie had undressed Seth and eased him into bed, she had viewed, close-hand, every muscled inch of his virile body. She was thankful Seth had been too oblivious to notice the profuse blush that had flamed her face, and she was ever so thankful he had been too disoriented this morning to inquire as to how she had managed to get him down from the mountain, into town, and into her bed.

Harboring thoughts of a man who probably wasn't aware of her fascination for him, Mattie picked up the waiting order and hummed a soft ballad while she cooked. Perhaps she had accidentally stumbled across the kind of man she had searched for all her life—not the kind of man her parents and siblings insisted she marry and settle down with in the expected Shaw fashion. Mattie believed there would be a lot less squabbling in her family if her brothers and sisters had been a bit more selective of their mates.

Mattie smiled mischievously while she cooked. She could almost hear her father's booming voice claiming:

"This is the way it has been done in the Shaw family for generations, my girl. No need for you to break a perfectly good tradition."

And from her mother: "That's right, dear. There are simply certain things expected of the Shaws. This family doesn't need a black sheep, a nonconformist, a rebel. You will be much better off when you accept your legacy and get on with your life."

Well, Mattie was determined not to be one of the flock that followed obediently at each other's heels. She may have been the youngest of thirteen children, stigmatized by the nickname of "Mishap Mattie", but she wasn't going to flaunt any family legacy, though the Shaws constantly maintained that she should prevail upon the power of her position because of her family name.

Oh certainly, Mattie could, at any given moment, trade this simple existence in the mining camp for a life in the lap of luxury. She could indulge in selfish pleasure, cruise around the world to revisit the seven wonders. But Mattie Shaw was holding out for more than just the superficial pleasures life had to offer. She wanted substance, a meaningful, rewarding existence. She wanted to enjoy the feeling of satisfaction derived from helping mankind, wanted to be her own person.

Mattie Shaw was going to live life her own way, by her own rules! If the powerful Shaw family didn't approve, that was just too bad. She could withstand the family pressure. She had done it for years!

Two

Seth awoke to find the same fascinating angel of mercy sitting on a chair beside the bed. A heaping tray of steaming food waited on the night stand. Groggy, Seth glanced around, trying to orient himself. The blazing sunlight that aggravated his headache had melted into the shadows of darkness. He had slept the day away, it seemed. And for some reason, he felt more relaxed now that the sun had ducked its head.

"I was beginning to worry about you," Mattie said, smiling cheerily at him. "I nudged you three times before you roused. When I came to check on you this afternoon, I couldn't make you wake up, not even when I passed a plate of food under your nose. Since you haven't eaten all day, you must eat everything on the tray."

Although Mattie didn't let on, she had been gravely concerned when she had been unable to rouse Seth from sleep when she came home earlier to feed him. Tonight she had added a heaping dose of herbs and spices to his meal, in addition to the medicinal potion designed to provide energy for her sluggish patient.

Mattie set the tray of meat, vegetables, and fruit on Seth's lap. "Eat," she ordered, in her most authoritative voice. "I'm not going to be able to live with myself until you are your old self again."

Obediently, Seth ate. The food was absolutely delicious, especially the juicy steak, which was cooked rare. Whatever spices Mattie had added brought out the full flavor of the meat and vegetables. With each bite, Seth felt himself gaining energy.

Mattie Shaw was not only a bewitching female, but her cooking was out of this world. Seth imagined every miner in Slapout had set his cap for this gem of a woman. If Seth had been in the market for a wife, he would certainly entertain thoughts of courting Mattie. Just having her in the same room with him stirred a need that this succulent food couldn't satisfy.

And that reminded him of a question that had drifted across his mind earlier in the day. "Did you have one of your miner friends undress me after they toted me to your cottage?" he asked between bites.

Mattie could feel her face blooming with color. She had hoped to avoid that question. "No," she murmured, staring at the carpet beneath her feet.

One thick brow rose as his mystifying eyes zeroed in on her, commanding her to meet his penetrating gaze. Mattie squirmed awkwardly.

"Well then, I seem to be at a distinct disadvantage, don't I?" He chuckled softly when the heat of embarrassment spread from her face to leave red blotches on her neck.

His laughter was a rich, infectious sound that had Mattie smiling impishly. "Fact is that I have treated dozens of patients in various states of undress," she confided.

"I see."

"My only concern at the time was for your health and welfare," she was quick to add.

"I'm disappointed to hear it."

Mattie glanced up, meeting those devilish, silver-blue eyes that lured her into their sparkling depths. "You have a magnificent body," she heard herself say before she could bite back the words.

Realizing what she had said, Mattie stared at the far wall, but Seth's good-natured laughter filled the room— filling the lonely depths of her heart. As if he silently called to her, she turned to meet his engaging smile. Something strong and intense and wildly arousing coiled inside her. This, Mattie realized suddenly, was the kind of reaction she had wanted to feel all her life. This man touched her in some elemental way.

It could work, she told herself. Seth wouldn't have to know all the family secrets, wouldn't have to be given the rigorous interrogation prospective husbands and wives underwent before joining the Shaw family. Mattie wouldn't let them chew Seth up and spit him out—so to speak.

"I appreciate your honesty, Mattie," Seth murmured in a voice like velvet. "I see why the miners worship the ground you walk on. Like them, I find myself bedazzled, entranced."

Though Seth knew he was being too forward, he felt

himself moving magnetically toward the lovely pixie in orange satin. The moment his gaze dropped to her heart-shaped lips, desire coursed through him like a rock plunging down a mountainside. In that instant, Seth could think of nothing he wanted, or needed, more than to taste her, experience her. He felt as if he had been lonely for years and just now knew the meaning of completeness.

When Mattie didn't retreat into her own space, just stared at him the same way he was staring at her, Seth slanted his lips over hers—and felt himself come to life, felt hungry need intensify with each pulse beat. He experienced the strangest urge to devour her, to tilt her head back and make a feast of the satiny skin of her throat . . . .

The appalling thought startled him and he withdrew before the peculiar craving got the better of him.

"Oh, my . . ." Mattie wheezed, as her thick lashes fluttered up.

Here was the kind of kiss Mattie had waited all her life to experience! It spoke of gentleness, yet she sensed a burning need for more, sensed something wild and hot and explosive awaiting her.

The magical moment shattered when a loud rap sounded on the front door. Mattie wobbled to her feet and hurried across the room, pausing at the bedroom door to steady herself and inhale a deep breath.

Seth reached for his clothes that had been laundered and neatly folded on the end of the bed. He couldn't be certain, but he didn't think he was the kind of man who was accustomed to being caught without his breeches, and he had no intention of changing that policy now. A man without a memory was vulnerable enough as it was.

When Seth wobbled unsteadily across the parlor, he saw Mattie standing on the stoop, squared off against two dozen men holding torches and looking like a lynch mob. Seth's keen sight enabled him to pick out two familiar faces—the faces of the men who had seen him standing at Mattie's bedroom window. The same two men he remembered seeing in the ghost town below his cave . . . .

The thought caused Seth to blink in amazement. He was beginning to remember fragments from the past. That was a good sign. In a day or two, if he was lucky, he would have his memory back.

"Are we about to have some sort of town meeting here?" Mattie questioned the cluster of men.

"Not exactly," one of the men called out from the center of the mob.

'Then what is this powwow all about?" She wanted to know.

The crowd stepped back a pace when Seth loomed behind Mattie like an ominous shadow. But the mob, feeling safety in numbers, refused to disperse. The shabbily-dressed miner who elected himself spokesman for the group thrust back his thick shoulders and took a bold step forward.

"Tremayne," Otis Whitmyer said with a curt nod. "We don't want no trouble here in Slapout. If you don't know it yet, folks around these parts are mighty fond of Miss Mattie. She's patched up more than half of us since she came to town. We want to make sure she's all right."

Seth scanned the crowd of admirers. He presumed

he was expected to give a statement that reassured this leery mob. Trouble was, he wasn't sure that his intentions toward his lovely nursemaid were all that pure and noble, especially after that kiss they shared in the bedroom. This delightful woman had ignited a fire in him and it was burning still.

But if reassurance would appease these men, then reassurance they would get. "I owe Mattie a tremendous favor," he announced. "I am not a man who forgets a favor, gentlemen."

He was going for effect here. He was in no condition to take on Mattie's protective brigade. One blow to his sensitive head would likely render him oblivious again.

Seth's speech was met with the kind of skeptical silence that forced him to continue. "In fact, I was preparing to go back where I belong when you showed up."

"You can't do that!" Mattie protested. "You are in no condition for traveling yet."

Seth sensed the tension draining from the crowd. Clearly, the men were pleased that he was making his departure and wouldn't be spending another night in Mattie's bed.

"Now see here," Mattie lectured the crowd. "Though I am touched by your concern, I am not in the slightest danger. I have always followed the policy of tending to injured patients, no matter who they are."

"Yes, Miss Mattie, we know that. But we want Tremayne to know that we protect our womenfolk here in Slapout," Otis insisted.

When the crowd wandered off, Mattie frowned at Seth. "You are not going to go traipsing off to the mountain. It is a four-mile walk."

"I'll rent a horse," he insisted.

Mattie planted herself squarely in front of him. Though she only stood a couple of inches over five feet, and Seth towered four inches over six feet, she boldly stood her ground.

"I refuse to let you ride off alone. There is no guarantee that the slightest exertion won't send you into a relapse. You have only taken two doses of medication and that is nowhere near enough. And furthermore, those well-meaning but meddling miners are as bad as my family when it comes to trying to run my life! I will not have anyone dictating who stays in my house and who will go!"

"Your family hovers over you to the same extent as these prospectors?" Seth questioned.

Mattie nodded. Red-gold curls bounced around her face. "You would not believe the mandates my family tosses at me. No one seems willing to accept the fact that I am my own person, that I can take care of myself."

Seth smiled at her vehement tone of voice. Mattie certainly was sensitive on the subject of overprotectiveness. And truth be told, her delicate appearance tended to bring out a man's protective instincts. Seth made a mental note not to ruffle her feathers by treating her like a helpless female.

Bowing gallantly, he took Mattie's hand and pressed a kiss to her wrist. Then he immediately sneezed.

It ruined the whole effect. When he gazed down at her, he noted the look of disappointment that etched her beguiling features.

"My goodness," she murmured, withdrawing her hand from his. "It has just occurred to me that you might not be suffering symptoms of the grippe at all."

She stared at him, horrified. "Mercy me, I think you might be allergic to *me!*"

Her sultry voice hit a squeaky pitch. Seth's ears twitched and pain thrummed through his sensitive skull.

Mattie retreated another step. "You sneezed the moment you latched onto me before lightning struck last night. You sneezed when I leaned over you this morning!"

Seth's heart sank. Could she be correct in her diagnosis? Now that he thought about it, he did recall sneezing when he caught a whiff of her flowery perfume. But he hadn't suffered an allergic reaction when he kissed her. React, yes he'd definitely done that. Allergic? No, absolutely not.

Mattie looked so miserable and disappointed that Seth felt compelled to say something—anything. "If I recall, the kiss we shared was nothing to sneeze at."

Mattie grinned in spite of herself. She liked that about Seth—his ability to make her smile. His dry wit appealed to her. His smile dazzled her.

Perhaps a change in perfume would cure his sneezing attacks. She would rush over to Pruitt's store first thing in the morning to purchase a different fragrance of soap and perfume.

"Well," Seth said belatedly, "I better be going before your protective roosters return to crow in objection."

"I'm coming with you," Mattie insisted.

When Seth opened his mouth to object, Mattie hurried on. "I'll meet you outside of town so the snoopy citizens of Slapout won't think you have cast some sinister spell on me and lured me to your cave."

When Mattie whizzed toward the back door of her cottage, Seth frowned pensively. Cast a sinister spell?

Why did the comment stir something deep and foreboding inside him, making his belly tighten in a knot?

Must be the healing potion he suspected Mattie had sprinkled on his food, he decided. He had detected a slight undertaste in the potatoes, despite the savory seasoning. He was sure she had slipped him one of her home remedies without informing him.

Certain that his activity was being closely watched, Seth strode to the blacksmith shop to borrow a horse. Within a few minutes the sturdy roan mountain pony was saddled and the reins dropped into Seth's hand. He could almost hear the collective sigh of relief breathed by the citizens of Slapout as he rode away. He wondered what he had done to draw the animosity of the miners.

Maybe he *was* some sort of dangerous villain. When he happened to glance skyward, a strange feeling of restlessness and hunger rushed through him. The moon hung in the cloudless sky like a flaming red-orange ball. Discomforting sensations pelted through him, making him shift in his saddle. The horse sidestepped and pricked its ears, as if sensing the change that overcame Seth.

Seth broke out in a cold sweat while he stared unblinkingly at the moon. Instinctively, he reached up to unbutton his shirt, letting the cool evening air bathe his heated skin. He breathed slowly, deeply, battling the restrictive sensation that spread from his throat to his chest.

The horse broke stride beneath him, stepped skittishly, then threw its head. Seth shook his own head, trying to clear his thoughts—which were spinning like a carousel. Then suddenly, his heartbeat decreased and the tension subsided.

Seth's rented horse settled into a leisurely walk, but the animal began to act up again when he rounded the bend to make the steep uphill climb into higher elevations. It occurred to Seth that he knew exactly where he was headed, though he hadn't been consciously aware of his destination.

A murmur of voices—at least he thought he heard voices—caught his attention. Seth stared toward the clump of pines on the towering ridge above him. Had the mob of miners decided to bushwhack him? Automatically, he reached for the revolver that hung on his hip, waiting for the oncoming attack.

To his surprise—and relief—Mattie Shaw stepped into view, spotlighted by the glow of the moon. He stared up at her, bewildered. "How did you get here?"

"In a hurry," she said, smiling impishly down at him. "I was gathering more herbs for my healing potions."

"In the darkness?" he asked dubiously.

"I knew exactly what I was looking for and where to find it," she assured him. "I've been here many times before."

When Mattie disappeared from sight, Seth expected to see her waiting for him when he rounded the second horseshoe bend, but Mattie was above him on the moonlit path, kneeling to gather plants that grew beside the road. The woman was amazingly fleet of foot, he decided, and in excellent physical condition. Why, she wasn't even panting for breath after what must have been a brisk uphill hike.

"Don't you have a horse?" Seth asked, as he stared down the mountainside to view the winking lights from the mining camp.

"No, horses and I don't get along all that well," she

explained as she set a swift pace. "For some reason I make them as nervous as they make me. I haven't ridden a horse since I was a child, and I discovered that being bucked off was not an experience I cared to repeat."

Seth glanced down at his horse, noting the way the animal pricked its ears and tossed its head. Damn, something strange seemed to be going on here. The horse didn't appear to be comfortable around either of them.

When Seth reached the stony ledge where lightning had struck the tree, an odd sensation rumbled through him. It was as if he had returned to the site where he had left his past behind, the location where previous thought and memory had vanished. Before he could wrack his brain and retrieve even a small fragment of his past, Mattie gestured toward the shadowed entrance to the cave on the ledge above them.

"Does this place look familiar to you?" she asked.

Seth peered up the rocky footholds that led to the cavern. For a split second he sensed a familiarity, but he couldn't imagine what had possessed him to hole out in this cave when there was a perfectly good hotel in Slapout. He must be an odd sort of individual, he mused as he dismounted.

His senses came to instant alert when he heard the flutter of wings and glanced up to see a half-dozen bats soaring from the mouth of the cave.

"You share your home with bats?" Mattie chuckled in amusement as she led the way up the tumble of boulders. "No wonder the miners have attached superstitious rumors to your name. None of the miners have the slightest appreciation for those rodent-like creatures."

Mattie pulled a candle from the pocket of her cloak

and lit it from her tinderbox. Stepping boldly forward, she held up the candle to scan the interior of the cavern. "Oh my . . ." she breathed in surprise.

The shadows receded to reveal a cozy room, complete with a table and chair, a cot padded with quilts and an expensive Oriental rug.

"This is nothing like what I expected," she admitted. "You have furnished your cave dwelling exceptionally well, Seth."

"I have, haven't I?" Seth studied the furniture that looked like heirlooms from previous centuries. In a far corner sat a hand-carved bookshelf lined with beakers and test tubes. He frowned, wondering what potion he kept in those bottles.

"You must be some sort of scientist," Mattie murmured in awe. "A man after my own heart! I have tremendous interest in herbal curatives and remedies. . . . Oh dear, you may have come upon some kind of revolutionary cure and I have stripped you of your memory and knowledge! Dear Lord, what have I done!"

Mattie felt mortified. Because she was accident prone, she had stripped Seth's memory away! "Do you suppose you were conducting scientific experiments with the bats?" she asked.

"I don't have the foggiest idea," Seth mumbled.

His head was beginning to ache ferociously again. His legs wobbled, as if he were losing strength by the second. His face must have gone chalk-white, because Mattie grabbed hold of his arm to lend additional support.

"I knew this wasn't a good idea," she muttered, as she ushered him toward the stately Windsor chair that sat beside the table. "You have overexerted yourself." When she had Seth settled comfortably in the chair, she reached into her pocket for the syrupy cure-all she had brought along—just in case a situation exactly like this arose.

"I'm going to administer a double dose," Mattie told him. "You don't look well at all."

Seth accepted the bottle Mattie offered him. After two swallows of the foul-tasting goo, he shivered, then broke into a cold sweat.

"Lay your head back for a moment," Mattie instructed, refusing to venture too close, for fear of setting off an allergic reaction that might complicate his weakened condition. "Now, breathe slowly, deeply. Give the medication time to take effect. This potion is designed to revive your energy."

Mattie glanced over her shoulder toward the decorative trunk that sat at the end of the cot. "While you're recovering, I'll rifle through your belongings to see if I can find anything that might prompt your memory."

Seth didn't accept or reject the offer—he couldn't. The offensive potion seared his throat, then dripped into his belly like acid. It was all he could do not to gag on the awful taste. And worse, the putrid smell of it clogged his nostrils, making it difficult to breathe.

To Seth's amazement, the moment of discomfort passed. After several minutes he began to feel much better. The unexplained tension ebbed. He could feel color returning to his face. He didn't have a clue what ingredients were in Mattie's remedy, but the home-brewed medication curtailed the odd feelings that had assailed him since that moment he glanced up at the Indian summer moon. Earlier, he had felt the ridiculous urge to howl like a coyote. Now, he could rise to his feet without swaying and collapsing in an undignified heap.

"Good gracious," Mattie exclaimed as she rummaged through the ornately carved trunk. "You have the most amazing collection of artifacts that must date back at least two centuries! Look at this ring!"

She upheld the gold band that was embedded with priceless rubies. Seth blinked in astonishment. That stunning item of jewelry belonged to *him?*

Or had he stolen it? He couldn't help but wonder, but when Mattie slid it on his finger it seemed a perfect fit.

"It must be yours," she murmured, staring at him. "And this . . ." She handed him a diploma from Oxford that was dated more than a century earlier. "Apparently, you were named after one of your ancestors who was an accomplished alchemist. No wonder you dabble in scientific experimentation. You obviously come from a long line of learned men."

Seth crouched down beside the trunk to study the certificate, then set it aside to dig deeper into his past. He found newspaper clippings that reported the deaths of several Tremaynes who had lived nearly two hundred years before him.

When he noticed a golden pendant, inlaid with diamonds, dangling from a heavy chain, he scooped it into his hand. A shard of forgotten memory leaped at him, a deluge of baffling emotion bombarded him. Terror, grief, bitterness, and desolation converged on him at once, overwhelming him. Seth sank to the floor, clutching the pendant as if it were his lifeline.

"Seth? Are you all right?"

When he didn't respond, Mattie wrapped a support-

ing arm around him and hoisted him to his feet. Though
he sneezed twice from close contact, she held onto him
tightly. It was more than obvious that the potion she
had given him had worn off. Hurriedly, she rummaged
through her pocket, then pressed another small bottle
to his ashen lips.

"Drink this, all of it," she instructed. "The combination of thin mountain air and your fragile condition
are draining you. First thing tomorrow, I am going to
brew a potion to counter these attacks you keep having."

Seth wheezed to catch his breath and fought the
oncoming sneeze. He would not succumb to this allergic
reaction! He savored Mattie's nearness, her gentle
touch, her concern for him. He would be damned a
thousand times over if he let something as insignificant
as a sneeze-attack prevent him from sharing such a con-
tented moment.

And then suddenly, like a bolt from the blue, his
breathing returned to normal, the dryness in his throat
abated, his erratic heartbeat thudded to a predictable
pace in his chest. The uncomfortable moment had
passed. The stifling air seemed to cool by several degrees
in less than a minute.

Seth stared down at the pendant resting in his palm.
He wished he could understand the fierce connection
he felt to it, wished he could remember why he had
saved that aging diploma that belonged to his ancestor.
But none of the objects in the trunk spurred thoughts
of his past. The man he had been was still a mystery to
him.

Mattie stared toward the tunnel that led deeper into
the interior of the mountain. "According to local gossip,
you discovered a rich vein of gold and have fiercely

protected it from poachers. Do you suppose you stashed your treasure in the tunnel?"

Seth chuckled as he cuddled Mattie against his chest. "Ironic, don't you think? I might be the wealthiest man in the territory and I haven't the vaguest notion where I keep my money."

"I have never put much stock in money," Mattie confided. "I consider love and friendship much more rewarding and long-lasting. My family is wealthy beyond imagination, but I cannot honestly say that many of them are happy."

Seth smiled wryly. "I suppose you are some sort of duchess from royal breeding who came west for the thrill of adventure."

When she returned his grin, her green eyes sparkled like polished emeralds. "Not precisely, though I do have very powerful connections. Yet, I choose to meet life on my own terms, armed with my meager skills and talents. After all, what is the worth of a resplendent castle, mansion, or sprawling plantation unless your life has meaning and purpose?

"My family is spoiled from the luxuries at their fingertips and they fail to appreciate life's simple pleasures. They take entirely too much for granted, to my way of thinking."

"What simple pleasures are you referring to?" Seth murmured as he lost himself in the sparkle of inner spirit that glistened in Mattie's eyes.

"The pleasure of your kiss, for instance," she whispered.

Her open honesty, her tenderness, stirred him deeply. Although Seth couldn't remember what motivated the man he had been before the past was lost to him, he knew what pleased the man he was now. Mattie pleased him greatly. When everyone else in Slapout shooed him on his way, Mattie remained loyal, steadfast, and caring. And she didn't seem to care about the dark rumors surrounding him or his supposed stash of gold. She seemed to like *him,* seemed to enjoy his company. She was straightforward enough to say so, and that pleased Seth, too.

He drew Mattie into his arms and tasted her deeply, marveling at her eager response. When he kissed her hungrily once again, she begged for more, encouraged his advances. Her slender arms wound around his neck, holding him as he held her, savoring the magical moment, feeding the fire that burned between them . . . .

And then that odd craving bombarded him again, that insane, inexpressive need to tilt back her head, brush away the mass of red-gold curls and feast on the delicate flesh of her throat.

Seth released Mattie abruptly, leaving her stumbling for balance. He was appalled, shocked by the ravenous need that boiled up inside him. What kind of vile brute was he? Had he made it a habit of ravishing women in his past life? How could he want with such uncontrollable intensity? How could he even think of taking more than Mattie offered him? He wanted to share the mystical moment, not greedily force himself upon her.

"Seth?" Mattie peered up at him. "What's wrong? Are you feeling ill again? Are you having another allergic reaction to being near me?"

Seth shook his head, then raked trembling hands through his hair. What in God's name was the matter with him? These unseemly feelings betrayed the tenderness he wanted to communicate when he held Mattie in his arms. It was as if he were fighting his worst enemy—and that enemy was himself! He had the unnerving feeling there were two entirely different men housed in his body, each one battling for supremacy.

"I think it's time to administer the potion I usually reserve for extreme cases," Mattie insisted, as she watched the color ebb from Seth's rugged features. "You look anemic. It is a condition caused from a diet lacking fresh meat and the nutrients of vegetables. According to the studies I've read on the subject, there are a number of herbs that can improve the condition, in addition to supplying more nourishment to meals. In fact," she added, "I intend to gather the necessary herbs before I return home this evening. I think I should treat your condition very aggressively so you won't have to suffer prolonged bouts of discomfort."

She grabbed his hand and pulled him up beside her, amazing him with her strength. It was just as he thought: Mattie was in exceptional physical condition.

"Though I don't approve of your sleeping in this gloomy cave, without proper ventilation, I think it's time you got some rest."

When she led him to his cot, Seth lay down obediently. In the dim candlelight, she reminded him of an angel hovering over a lost soul, guarding him from harm, comforting him. If anyone had ever treated him so kindly, so gently, in his life, he didn't remember it. This dainty female was as close to an angel as Seth would probably ever come. It horrified him that he harbored such beastly urges when he kissed her, held her. He would never hurt her, couldn't bear the thought!

Mattie doubled at the waist to brush her lips over his

forehead. "I'm going to give you a sedative to help you sleep. I'll be back at dawn with a new potion."

"I'll accompany you back to town," he insisted. "You shouldn't be alone at night—"

"No," she cut in, smiling down at him. "I'm perfectly capable of making the jaunt myself. And I would never forgive myself if you suffered another dizzy spell while trying to be gallant. No need to fret about me, Seth. Just rest, and I will see you in the morning."

Seth dutifully accepted the baked morsel that reminded him of a miniature cookie. It tasted like mint—and something else he couldn't name. The taste was pleasant and the potion apparently worked, because he felt himself slump on the cot. His eyes drifted shut and the sight of Mattie's infectious smile was the last thing he remembered before peaceful sleep overtook him.

Three

Mattie glanced up when she heard the crackle of twigs in the near distance. She knew who had followed her into the darkness. After all these years, she could sense her parents' presence easily.

"I do not approve of this little episode with that cave-man," Horace Shaw snorted as he stalked forward. "Your mother and I have tried to be patient with you, and your insistence on performing all these humanitarian deeds, but this is simply too much! You have your reputation to consider!"

Mattie stared at her father. He was a broad, bulky, intimidating man who preferred to dress in formal attire, no matter what the occasion. Even if he decided to ford a river, Mattie expected he would do it wearing his favorite cloak, top hat, and Hessian boots. Although Mattie did admit that her father's manner of dress and full, booming voice gave him an additional air of authority, she didn't cower beneath his gimlet-eyed stare.

"Your father is quite right," Abigail Shaw chimed in as she stepped up beside Horace. "This association, or whatever you call this relationship with that Tremayne fellow, is inadvisable. You know that as well as we do. There simply can be no future in it. I sense that you have grown entirely too attached to the man."

"I already explained that I am personally responsible for the accident that zapped Mr. Tremayne's strength and destroyed his memory," Mattie replied, as she met her mother's disgruntled glance.

Abigail lifted a delicately arched brow and tossed her head, sending a cloud of blond hair floating around her shoulders. "Merely an excuse," she said dismissively. "Your father and I can detect the difference in the way you treat that Tremayne fellow, compared to your behavior around these bumpkin miners whom you have taken it upon yourself to feed and nurse. This is entirely different."

"Entirely," Horace harumphed, then flicked the leaf from the cuff of his expensive cloak. "Your mother and I have made an extensive search to find you a suitable mate. The man I refer to comes highly recommended and has all the right connections—"

"We are not having this conversation again," Mattie cut in impatiently. With basket in hand, she faced her parents, her chin uplifted at a defiant angle. "You can follow me around for the next five years if you wish, tossing beaux at me who bear your stamp of approval, but I will not budge. I have seen the matches you've made for my brothers and sisters. Most of the so-called couples spend more time apart than together."

Abigail and Horace shifted uncomfortably, unable to argue the point.

"I am growing very tired of these family conferences and mandates," Mattie continued. "And I do not mean to sound ungrateful, but I am satisfied with my life, just as it is. As for Seth—"

"Seth?" Horace gasped. "You are on a first name basis with him already?

Abby shook her head in dismay. "I'm afraid you are making a disastrous mistake during this rebellious phase of your life, child."

"I'm not being rebellious, merely independent," Mattie clarified.

Abby strode over to curl her arm around Mattie's shoulder. "You must realize that we are concerned about you and that we know things will never materialize between you and Mr. Tremayne," she murmured softly. "Granted, the man is an attractive specimen, but he isn't like us. He simply wouldn't fit in. All sorts of accommodations would have to be made for him. And eventually you will wind up being hurt if you let yourself care too deeply for him. Please, Mattie, spare yourself the inevitable heartache that I know is coming your way."

Mattie retreated a step, then knelt to pluck up the plants that provided medicinal juices for her healing potions. For a long moment she didn't speak.

"By damn, you're falling in love with the man, aren't you?" Horace erupted, aghast. "That's why you're being unnecessarily stubborn, isn't it?"

Yes, Mattie supposed she had fallen in love—practically overnight as it turned out. The touch of Seth's hand, the whisper of his lips, and the sparkle of his smile warmed her heart. And there was that hint of vulnerability about him that made him irresistible to her.

Despite the uncomplimentary rumors about him, Seth had proven himself to be every bit a gentleman. He had proven that twice when she had felt his desire for her consuming him. Yet, he withdrew without forcing his masculine needs on her ... even when Mattie was eager to discover where the tantalizing sensations of passion led.

"Well, at least have the gumption to admit you've fallen for that ne'er-do-well miner," Horace muttered.

Mattie looked up at her father who towered over her. "Yes, I have," she admitted.

When Horace growled and wheeled away, his dark cloak swirled around him like a whirlwind. Mattie watched her father wear a path in the grass, smashing the plants she intended to pick.

"Now, Horace," Abby cautioned her fuming husband. "Don't let your temper get the better of you."

"I should whisk Mattie as far away from that prospector as she can get. Better yet, I should give that rascal a shove off a cliff!"

"You will do no such thing," Mattie insisted as she bolted to her feet. "I want you to stop following me around, cease interfering in my life. When you are breathing down my neck, it makes me so nervous that I drop things, fall over things, cause mishaps!"

There, she had said it outright in a fit of temper. Well, maybe it was time her family encountered the truth.

Horace lurched around, his distinguished features frozen in a look of disbelief. "Are you saying that your mother and I are responsible for your mishaps?"

"I have pretty much been mishap-free since I came to Colorado Territory. These surprise visits, especially when you call in the entire clan to badger me, are extremely upsetting to me. I have tried to be courteous and respectful to you, but blast it! I need my own space, need to make my own decisions, rather than have decrees and threats hurled at me."

"Now see here, young lady," Horace blustered, wagging his forefinger in her face. "There are certain rules that Shaws must follow. And like it or not, which you obviously do not, you are a Shaw who is entitled to prestige, power, and all the special privileges that come with that position. Even if you have taken a fancy to that caveman, we Shaws still must maintain our dignity among our peers."

These disagreements always came to this, Mattie reminded herself. Her family was caught up in tradition, determined to keep up appearances, to wield their power and influence in society.

Mattie smiled ruefully at her parents. "I know this is difficult for you to understand and accept, but I yearn for the simple life. I don't want to settle for an imitation of affection. I want to feel as if I truly belong somewhere, to someone. In all our travels and vast experiences, that feeling has never been appeased."

She stared directly at her mother, then focused on her father. "The two of you were fortunate to find that special feeling in each other. You travel far and wide, hand-in-hand, always together."

Mattie knew she was finally gaining ground when her father stared down at Abby from his lofty height. Mattie could see the lifelong affection glowing in his green eyes. Horace Shaw, domineering and intimidating though he could be, would try to fly to the moon or kneel humbly at Abby's feet if she asked him to. Through thick and thin, he had been at Abby's side— and never left her while she bore him another child. He shared her happiness, her sorrow, her pain, as if it were his own.

"You see, Papa," Mattie murmured as tears misted her eyes. "I want to find that special man who will always look at me the way you look at Mama. Would you deny me the happiness you have? Would you have me settle for less than strong, enduring love?"

Horace gathered his wife in his arms and tucked her against his heart. "You hit me right where I live, my girl, and you damned well know it." He smiled concedingly at Mattie. "All right, child, you made your point. You leave me no room for argument. But this caveman of yours had best be honorable and respectful when it comes to you. If he turns out to be something less, I will not take it kindly. We do understand each other, don't we, Matilda?"

Mattie understood perfectly. Her father had agreed to compromise—up to a certain point. He would back off and allow her a short grace period. Mattie shuddered to think what Horace might do if Seth decided he had no further use for his nursemaid after he fully recovered from his injury. Horace Shaw could bring down the thunder when he completely lost his temper. Mattie had seen her father in action twice in the past. Neither time had been a pretty sight.

"We will leave you in peace," Abby promised as she slid her hand into her husband's. "But we will never be far away."

When her parents disappeared into the darkness, Mattie resumed her selection of plants and herbs. By the time she had gathered all the necessary ingredients, the first rays of sunshine were peeking over the horizon.

"Yoo-hoo!" Mattie called as she stood outside the gloomy cavern. "Seth?"

Mattie frowned in concern when Seth appeared a moment later to lean heavily against the wall. Although she knew he must have slept through the night—because she had given him a potent dose of sleeping potion in the shape of a small cookie—he didn't look well rested. But Mattie had arrived this morning with picnic basket in hand, determined to see that Seth received a medicinal dosage of sunshine and mountain air. Living in a cave simply was not good for the man!

Seth took one look at Mattie, who was garbed in a vibrant purple gown and smiling that disarming, dimpled smile, and he felt considerably better than he had when he dragged himself from bed. He inclined his head toward the reed basket dangling from her fingertips. "More potions?" he asked in a gravelly voice.

"No, a picnic lunch," Mattie informed him. "I thought an outing might be good for you. We could walk down to the mountain stream to share lunch, a little exercise, and wholesome fresh air."

Seth decided to give her remedy a try. What could it hurt? he asked himself. Moping around in his cave, sporting this nagging headache, and struggling to reclaim memories from his past were wearing him out. A distraction might do him a world of good.

The instant Seth stepped out into the sunlight, he was practically blinded. He shielded his eyes with his arm as he followed Mattie down the winding path, then breathed an appreciative sigh when he saw the rippling stream that cut its way through the rocks to form lazy rapids that sparkled like diamonds in the morning light.

He headed for the shade provided by the trees that flanked the stream. Direct sunlight left him with a wilting feeling, but sitting in the shade provided relief.

"Now then," Mattie said cheerily. "Would you like to go wading first or would you prefer to eat?"

Wading? Seth couldn't recall if he had ever waded through a stream. Surely he must have when he was a child. But perhaps the activity would prompt childhood memories.

When he reached down to pull off his boots, Mattie sank down in the grass beside him. "Simple pleasures," she murmured. "A walk in sunshine always does wonders for the spirit, I always say."

Hers maybe, thought Seth.

"Splashing through a stream is refreshing and invigorating," Mattie added as she took off her slippers.

That, Seth mused, *remains to be seen.*

He watched in amusement as Mattie tied the trailing hem of her skirt to the satin sash at her waist. Dressed in her makeshift breeches, she bounded to her bare feet and offered Seth her hand. He folded his hand around hers and surged to his feet.

While Seth led the way to the shady shallows of the creek, a feeling of contentment washed over him. It amazed him that the mere touch of Mattie's hand could stir his emotions.

Seth yelped when Mattie scooped up a handful of water and splattered him in the face. The playful elf intended to engage in a water fight, did she? Well,

Seth was game. If he couldn't revisit his childhood in memories, maybe he could make a few memories to replace the ones he had lost.

For several minutes, Mattie and Seth did battle. Water flew like sparkling jewels in the sunlight. Mattie's laughter sent Seth's spirits soaring. The gloom and doom of his cavern were forgotten. The frustration of living without a past no longer concerned him. For a short time, there was nothing more important and enjoyable than sharing the company of a woman whose antics brought joy and laughter to his life.

"Enough!" Still giggling, Mattie raised her arms in surrender. "You have soaked me to the bone." She tugged the mop of wet hair from her face, then squeezed out her soggy clothing. "You win."

Seth stood there, his helpless gaze riveted on the bodice of her gown, watching her full breasts rise and fall with each breath. Before he could stop himself, he reached out to brush his knuckles over one pebbled peak, then the other. He heard Mattie's breath catch, saw the flicker of desire in her eyes. Need pounded through him, accelerating his heartbeat. Mattie was as potent as her potions. Indeed, she was the best medicine for everything that ailed him.

Giving way to impulse, Seth drew Mattie into his arms, then bent his head to trace a row of featherlight kisses over her shoulder. The urge to nip, to taste her flesh, rose up inside him, but he refused to succumb. He didn't want to frighten Mattie away, didn't want to destroy the trust she placed in him. He simply wanted to pleasure her as much as touching her pleasured him.

Mattie nearly swooned when Seth's lips skimmed over her flesh. He was handling her with such delicate care that she felt herself melting beneath his touch. When his fingertip grazed the clinging fabric that covered her breasts, a coil of fire blazed deep inside her. Breathless, aching, she arched into his hand, felt the bold evidence of his need pressed against her belly.

She heard Seth moan as he gathered her tightly in his trembling arms. She was tempted to close her eyes and give herself up to the indescribable sensations Seth aroused in her. Did she dare yield to newly discovered passion? Did she dare risk her heart? Everything inside her longed to take a chance, longed to discover what it was like to become intimate with a man.

Mattie didn't know if she was disappointed or relieved when Seth moved away, then nuzzled his forehead against hers. But she did experience a sense of loss as she felt the radiant heat ease by degrees.

"I'm sorry, Mattie," Seth whispered unevenly. "I had no right to touch you. But the fact is that you're hell on my willpower. Forgive me?"

Mattie kissed his cheek lightly. "There is nothing to forgive. Truth is, you show a great deal more willpower than I. Surely you realize that I find you irresistible."

"That is not the appropriate comment to make to a man who is having a devil of a time controlling himself."

"No?" She stepped back to peer earnestly at him.

Seth shook his head as he led her from the stream. "Definitely not. The entire male population of Slapout would have my head if I overstepped propriety with you. I wouldn't be surprised if there were spies lurking about to ensure I wasn't taking advantage."

Mattie glanced around the secluded area, then muttered under her breath. She wondered if she would ever be able to outrun the protectiveness of her family and friends. Blast it, she did not need protection. Why couldn't everybody accept that?

When Seth plunked down in the grass and towed the picnic basket toward him, Mattie studied him covetously. His wet clothing accentuated every lean muscle and the broad expanse of his chest. She well remembered how he looked when she undressed him and put him in her bed.

A rush of color surged through her cheeks as she speculated on how it would feel to learn his muscled contours by touch and taste . . . .

"Mattie? Is something wrong?"

Mattie snapped to attention immediately, cursing her wayward thoughts. "No, not at all."

Liar, she scolded herself silently. She was falling so deeply in love with this charismatic man that she was already visualizing herself lying in his arms—heart to heart, flesh to flesh, as one . . . .

Seth grinned wryly when Mattie continued to stand there staring at him. "Memory lapse?" he asked.

"No, wild imagination," she admitted, as she sat down beside him. "I believe I better enjoy eating my early lunch and leave it at that."

Seth decided she was right. If she kept staring at him like that, he wasn't sure he could keep his hands to himself. He had dared too much already, and he enjoyed Mattie's companionship far too much to let unruly desire destroy the fragile bond developing between them. He had to proceed slowly; it was the respectable thing to do with a very respectable woman.

Have patience, man, Seth lectured himself as he munched on his meal. *Don't spoil your only touch with pleasure and happiness. Mattie deserves to be treated like the angel she is.*

Bearing that in mind, Seth finished off his meal, then thanked the powers that be for granting him the will-power to back away from Mattie before he compromised her. Until he regained his memory, he wasn't certain what he could offer a woman. If it turned out that he truly was some sort of criminal who hid out in the mountains, he couldn't consign Mattie to that kind of life. She deserved better.

Seth hoped he wasn't the devilish sort that the prospectors from Slapout made him out to be. All his secret dreams would come crashing down around him. If he knew nothing else, he knew he was developing the kind of fond attachment for Mattie that wasn't going to be satisfied much longer with an occasional kiss and caress.

And he would sincerely like to know what there was about her that made him want to sneeze. It was embarrassing! Even while he held her in his arms in midstream he had battled the urge. It was the damnedest thing!

Seth awoke, roused by the swarm of bats that descended into the cave like a breath of cold air. What kind of man would share his home with these ugly-looking creatures? And what kind of man kept certificates and diplomas of a relative long-dead? What was his connection to the Seth Tremayne who graduated with honors in England more than a century earlier? And what was the importance of the newspaper clippings about Count Tremayne from France . . . and the kinsmen from London . . . Philadelphia . . . and another relative who had lived in Charleston . . . San Antonio?

Did he have relatives scattered across Europe and America? If so, what the hell was he doing here in a cave carved into the stone peak that overlooked a ghost town?

Seth had been asking himself the same questions for the past two days and hadn't come up with a single answer. He simply couldn't remember why he led this lonely existence or if any of his relatives cared where he was or what he was doing.

When the racket of the bats swirling into the tunnel subsided, Seth swung his legs over the edge of the cot. He felt considerably better this morning. The miniature carpenters who had been driving nails into his sensitive skull the past week appeared to have packed up and moved on. Although he still felt a bit sluggish, and the light outside the anteroom of the cavern made him squint uncomfortably, his dizziness was gone. He stood up to see how well he functioned with his legs under him. Thankfully, he didn't stagger or sway. From all indications, the miracle cures Mattie had been administering each time she came to visit were showing promise.

A muffled noise caught Seth's attention. He suspected Mattie was about to pay him a call. She must be making her assent up the ladder of boulders to the cave.

Mattie . . . Seth smiled in anticipation. The woman did wonders for his attitude. He almost dreaded the day she would pronounce him physically fit. Then he would have no excuse to share every minute she could spare him, in between her job as chef and resident nurse in Slapout.

Soon, he would begin to court Mattie properly, Seth decided. He intended to keep seeing her, if she was agreeable. Maybe he hadn't been particularly respectable in the past, but he damned sure would be now. He could change, he told himself. Even if there were dark secrets in his past that he couldn't recall, he would turn his life around and acquire a respectable reputation in Slapout.

A shadowy figure moved outside the cavern and Seth broke into a greeting smile to welcome Mattie. To his dismay, he found himself staring down the spitting end of three shotguns.

This was not, he realized, a social call.

Three scraggly mountaineers stepped into view. Seth recognized them immediately. He had seen these scroungy mongrels hovering at the back of the mob that stood outside Mattie's door earlier in the week. No doubt, these scavengers had put their heads together and decided to take advantage of Seth's weakened condition. They had come to steal the gold he was rumored to have stashed in the cave.

"Stand easy, Tremayne," Harley Baker growled, as he raised his shotgun threateningly. "If you behave yerself, me an' my boys might let you live."

Seth cast Harley's "boys" a quick glance. Each chip off the Baker block stood six feet tall and weighed a solid two hundred pounds. The odds were not in Seth's favor, especially since his pistol lay on the floor beside his cot.

"You're after the gold," Seth presumed.

"Yer memory must be returning if you remember you've got a cache of gold nuggets hidden hereabouts," Harley smirked. "So where is it, Tremayne?"

"I have no idea," he said honestly.

Harley snorted skeptically. "I'll bet you don't." He

gestured his shaggy head toward the "boy" on his right. "Alvin, check that trunk for bags of gold."

Seth stayed where he was while Alvin galumphed over to the trunk. "You're wasting your time, there's no gold in there."

"We'll let Alvin see for himself," Harley grunted.

While Seth remained at gunpoint, Alvin dug through the trunk and came up empty-handed. "There's nothing here but a bunch of papers I can't read, Pa."

"Then Tremayne must have stashed the gold in the tunnel. Charlie, grab that torch and see what you can find—"

"What is going on here?"

Seth cringed when he heard Mattie's voice echoing through the cavern. Dear God, if she landed in harm's way, he couldn't bear it! The thought of his angel of mercy catching a ricocheting bullet had Seth cursing under his breath. He had to send her racing away from danger before these scoundrels used her as leverage against him.

"Run for it, Mattie!" Seth bellowed as he launched himself toward Harley.

Startled, Harley staggered back, swinging his shotgun into firing position on his shoulder. Seth ducked low and plowed beneath the swerving weapon. He buried his head in Harley's soft underbelly, making the older man grunt in pain. Charlie squawked when Seth's forward momentum caused Harley to stumble backward. Charlie's shotgun exploded accidentally. Buckshot zinged around the stone walls, prompting Alvin to sprawl on the floor before he was hit.

Seth felt an unexplained burst of strength as he reared up to bury his fist in Harley's whiskered face. Although

the punishing blow caused Harley to wilt on the floor,
Charlie came up fighting. Snarling, the buck-toothed
miner swung the butt of his shotgun at Seth's head.
Before the weapon collided with Seth's tender skull, he
snaked out his hand to block the oncoming blow.

For several frantic seconds Charlie and Seth battled
for possession of the weapon. Seth felt himself gaining
ground, heard Charlie screeching and cursing . . .

And then pain exploded in the back of Seth's head.
Alvin had come to his brother's defense, Seth realized
as his vision blurred and queasy sensations pooled in
his belly. Willfully, he fought to remain conscious, but
he fought a losing battle.

"Run, Mattie!" he wheezed.

The second thump on Seth's head caused him to
slump helplessly over Harley's barrel-shaped belly. Try
as he might, Seth couldn't twist around to disarm Alvin.

Seth had no concern for his own welfare. His last
thought was of Mattie's mad dash to safety. No matter
what became of him, Seth hoped—prayed—that the
one person in this world who took the time and made
the effort to get acquainted with him, to help him when
he was injured, would survive. Seth would roll over in
his grave a dozen times if these brutal scavengers laid
a hand on Mattie Shaw.

Four

"Seth? Can you hear me? Seth?"

The carpenters were back, hammering in his head. Something cool and wet flitted over his brow, bringing him a step closer to conscious awareness. Groaning, he pried open one eye—and saw two images of Mattie, dressed in a bright pink gown, hovering over him.

She was safe, thank God. She had managed to hide until the Bakers slithered off like the snakes they were. Seth didn't care if they found his stash of gold, he was simply relieved to see Mattie unharmed. Or at least he hoped she was. His vision was too blurry to determine what condition she was actually in.

"Are you all right, love? The Bakers didn't—?"

"I'm fine," she whispered, as she eased down beside him on the cot. "You took an awful chance by attacking those brutes when you were outnumbered and unarmed. You could have been killed, damn it!"

Her concern for him was evident in the rising pitch of her voice. Seth smiled in satisfaction. Mattie cared about him. It was comforting to know that the woman who had captured his interest returned it.

"All that concerned me was providing the distraction that enabled you to make a run for it," Seth rasped.

"And I keep telling you that I can take care of myself, Seth Tremayne," she snapped at him.

Now *that*, Seth mused, was not experienced confidence speaking. That was unfounded folly. Mattie Shaw was a dainty female who was no physical match for three armed men who might try to have their way with her. This woman was too accustomed to looking for—and expecting to find—the good in all mankind. She was too pure of heart to believe anyone would purposely harm her.

"I have spent my day off from the restaurant experimenting with new remedies that might get you back on your feet, once and for all, and you go and pull your daring heroics!" she sputtered in exasperation. "You idiotic man! Don't you realize that the thought of you being injured or killed is agonizing to me? . . . Seth . . . ?"

Mattie gasped in alarm when Seth's face turned milkwhite and he slumped onto his pillow. His breathing became so shallow and irregular that she could barely find the pulse beat on his neck. My God! The man had collapsed and she was snapping at him because he had scared her half to death. The dear sweet man had admirably tried to spare her from danger and she hadn't behaved appreciatively. She should be thanking him for taking her welfare into consideration, not scolding him.

Hurriedly, Mattie dipped the cloth in the water she had carried up from the mountain stream, then she dribbled droplets over Seth's ashen cheeks. Gently, she turned his head to tend the cut caused by the forceful impact from the butt of Alvin's shotgun.

Ripping cloth from her petticoat, Mattie wrapped a makeshift bandage around Seth's head. When she pressed the vial of medication to his lips, he didn't respond. He needed the potion she prepared for him, but he was too oblivious to ingest it.

Mattie traced the thick substance over his lips with her forefinger, then waited an anxious moment. Nothing. There was naught else to do but force the medication down his throat and make him swallow.

Tipping up the vial, Mattie gave Seth a strong dosage, then massaged his throat. She sighed in relief when he reflexively swallowed. When he made an awful face, she smiled in amusement. Even though he was semi-conscious, he objected to the chalky taste of her remedy.

Seth lay there motionless, looking frighteningly vulnerable, undernourished, near death. Mattie's heart twisted in her chest. Twice, this man had tried to save her life. She was beginning to think she was more of a curse than a blessing to him. But somehow she would compensate, she promised herself. Even if Seth couldn't return the tender affection she felt for him, she would be by his side when he needed her.

Perhaps, she thought as she gazed adoringly at him, it wasn't so important to be loved as it was to love unselfishly, unconditionally. Even if her feelings for Seth were one-sided, she had experienced something deep and satisfying. This man had made the difference.

"I love you," Mattie whispered for the very first time in her life. "If I know nothing else to be true, I know that I love you . . . ."

* * *

After what seemed a century-long nap, Seth opened his eyes. His throat felt like the parched sands of Death Valley and his stomach boiled like a vat of acid. When he licked his bone-dry lips, the residue of Mattie's home remedy encircled his tongue, nearly gagging him. Those foul-tasting potions had better cure him—before they killed him!

Glancing sideways, Seth watched the tapered candle flickering, casting shadows on the cavern wall. Fascinated, he watched the dark images float around like lost spirits. He levered onto his elbows, stunned as memories that linked him to his forgotten past cascaded through his mind, overwhelming him.

He had expected that regaining his lost memory would come as a relief, but the opposite was true. All his dreams and expectations of forming a lasting bond with his angel of mercy ended in an anguished groan.

Seth remembered why he had saved the diploma and certificates that were stashed in his trunk. *They were his!* And so was the ring that the king of France had presented to him in return for a favor. Seth remembered it all—every year, every decade of his hopeless entrapment.

He recalled those strange, appalling urges that assailed him while he held Mattie in his arms, tasted the honeyed sweetness of her kiss. He had very nearly succumbed to the cravings of his affliction. If he hadn't managed to control himself, he would have sentenced Mattie to the kind of hell he'd endured for centuries.

The thought shook Seth to the very core of his being.

Mattie ... Her name echoed through his tormented mind as he shot up from his cot. Where was she?

Frantic, Seth wobbled toward the mouth of the cave. Three lizards scurried out from under his cot and he frowned in annoyance. Wasn't it enough that he shared his primitive abode with bats? Next thing he knew, rattle-snakes would take up residence with him. Well, it was no better than a creature like him deserved, he thought with a self-deprecating snort.

"Mattie!" Seth called into the darkness that blanketed the mountains.

He listened intently, but no sounds alerted him to her presence.

Hopefully, she had the good sense to return to her cottage, to leave him where he belonged. Seth could risk no further association with Mattie, not when he had nothing to offer her but a bite on the neck and eternal misery.

The dismal prospect of never seeing Mattie again intensified the feeling of desolation that had been his constant companion. For Mattie's sake, he had to send her away and make it understood that he wouldn't be calling on her. This budding romance was doomed to disaster.

Despair and regret overwhelmed Seth as he lingered on the towering ledge that overlooked the V-shaped chasm. Damn, he wished he had never met Mattie. Now that he remembered what he was, she was forbidden to him, and the ache of longing became even more difficult to endure.

For a week, for one glorious week, he had known what it was like to be a man. He hadn't carried the oppressive weight of his curse on his shoulders. He had *lived*, truly lived.

And now he was back in hell . . . .

The rustle of branches on the ledge below brought Seth's sharp senses to full alert. He could see a cloud of golden curls reflecting in the moonlight, see that angelic face lifting toward him.

"So you are up and around," Mattie called to him. "I knew that new potion would do the trick."

"I'm feeling much better," Seth said stiffly. "You better head back to town so you can rest before your shift at the restaurant."

Mattie halted her climb up the footholds of rocks and frowned at the remote tone in Seth's voice. There was something about his stance, his very presence, that seemed unfamiliar. Eyes that once glimmered with wry amusement burned down on her with an emotion she couldn't decipher.

It appeared Seth had awakened in the foulest of moods. Of course, that shouldn't surprise her. The poor man had barely had time to recover from one brain-scrambling blow to the head before Alvin Baker had pounded on him.

Wearing a cheery smile to counter Seth's gloomy stare, Mattie pulled herself onto the outcrop of stone. "If you're hungry, I brought along—"

"No, I'm not hungry," he cut in gruffly. "You need to leave *now.*"

Although his abrupt dismissal left her pride smarting, she tried to ignore the hurt. "Well then, I'll leave several doses of medication for you—"

"I'm fine," he rapped out.

She surveyed the haggard lines of his face in the

moonlight, noting the lack of color, the circles under his eyes. Dear God! Her remedies seemed to be having the reverse effect on him! In her effort to heal, it looked as if her potions were killing him, bit by bit.

Sweet mercy, what had she done now? Maybe she had been wrong in blaming her family for making her accident-prone. Maybe she was well and truly plagued with mishaps—mishaps that were affecting Seth's health and well-being.

Seth felt a sneeze coming on when the wind carried Mattie's scent to him. He battled the tickling sensation in his nostrils—and lost. After three consecutive sneezes he directed her attention to the ladder of rocks. "Go home, Mattie. Just go away."

Her heart dropped to the soles of her feet. The finality in his voice told the tale. Seth was tired of her companionship. His interest in her had been short-lived. He was ready to return to his isolation.

"If that's what you wish," she whispered brokenly.

"That is what I wish." He turned and walked away. "Go tend to the miners who worship the ground you float over. The less you see of me the better."

Mattie had the sinking feeling that what he wanted to say was: The less I see of you the better. But Seth chose not to be that cruel. He was ending their friendship, making a quick, clean cut.

"One question before you go, Mattie."

His voice rolled from the cavern and Mattie pivoted, seeing nothing but darkness and shadows looming before her. "Yes?"

"Why were you trying to kill yourself that night I met you?"

Mattie winced uncomfortably. Although she was

pleased to realize Seth had recovered his memory, she wasn't eager to discuss that particular night with him— or anyone else for that matter. It was personal and private.

"That is not what happened that night," she insisted.

"No? That's what it looked like to me."

Mattie wheeled away. "Well, it doesn't really matter now, does it? You have made it clear that you prefer your own company, now that you recall who you are and what you're about."

Blinking back her tears, Mattie eased over the boulders. She really shouldn't let Seth's standoffish attitude affect her. She should march back to his cave and let him know that she much preferred the man he had become when he was oblivious to his past. She had seen his vast potential for kindness. She shouldn't have let him crawl back in his dark cavern and live in lonely isolation. He needed her, damn it! She was good for him, even if he didn't realize it.

She should help that troubled man, even if he resisted and resented her intrusion in his life. She *should*, but her feminine pride was bruised and being cast aside left her spirits scraping rock bottom.

Mattie made her way to town, chanting all the consoling platitudes, but nothing helped. She had whispered her love for Seth while he was unaware—which was a good thing, because he would not have been the least receptive if she spoke her affection out loud. Nobly, she assured herself that one-sided affection was better than never experiencing those feelings at all. But her heart kept whispering that she had lost a very precious part of her life.

Fact was, Mattie was hurting, all the way to her bones.

She couldn't explain Seth's abrupt, unapproachable attitude. She supposed she had witnessed the natural reaction of a man who had tired of a woman's company and had come to his senses—literally.

Seth propped himself against the face of the cliff, watching Mattie's slow decent from the platform of stone. Twice, he had to stop himself from calling her back to apologize, stop himself from explaining the tormenting truth.

The damnable truth would frighten her away. Seth couldn't bear the thought of staring into that enchanting face and seeing horror and revulsion fill her eyes. He despised what he was, was ashamed of his affliction. He couldn't stand to see those same emotions staring back at him when he looked at his lovely angel of mercy.

Angel ... The word whispered around him. Now there was another irony—the worst kind, in fact. He was Mattie's diametrical opposite. *She* would spend her well-deserved eternity equipped with a pair of gossamer wings and a halo shining above her head. *He* would be wandering around forever, a revenant, the undead, the unliving. What a pair they would have made! She, the pure of spirit and epitome of kindness and he, a creature of darkness who had no soul to call his own.

When the sound of lizards scurrying across the stone floor gained his notice, Seth muttered sourly. He wished the scaly creatures would slither off and leave him to wallow in his misery.

Seth couldn't force himself to mix and measure chemicals, either. What good would it do to continue his experiments in alchemy? There was no cure for his morbid affliction. He'd spent years trying to concoct a vaccine—and to no avail. He could spend another hundred years searching in vain.

He would never find a remedy that would make him the kind of man Mattie Shaw needed and deserved, a man who could laugh in the sunshine with her, not a prowling predator of darkness.

Seth stared down at the ring on his tight-fisted hand. He would give anything if this valuable, jewel-studded ring could buy him freedom from this hell where he lived, could make him a whole man. He would give all the gold crammed inside the niches of the tunnel . . . .

The thought prompted Seth to spin on his heels. Without bothering to light a torch he made his way through the labyrinth of tunnels to retrieve the pouches of gold nuggets. Although Mattie insisted she had no need for wealth, his fortune would be hers. If he was lucky, she would take the gold and move back to civilization, away from the raucous mining camp, back to society where she would encounter a gentleman worthy of her laughter and affection.

When she was miles way from him, perhaps Seth could accept his dismal fate, perhaps he wouldn't dream up excuses to catch a glimpse of her, wouldn't long to hold her in his arms one last time . . . and then one more time again. He couldn't risk knuckling under to his desire for her, couldn't let himself cast caution to the four winds and indulge his secret whims. For if he dared to seduce Mattie, there was the chance that—in the heat of the uncontrollable passion he knew he would discover with her—he would surrender to the ravenous monster inside him and all would be lost.

Seth pried loose the rounded stone that concealed the pokes filled with gold nuggets. In determined strides he marched from the tunnel. He would go to Slapout and present Mattie with a gift of gold. And then he would confine himself to this cavern with its tenants of bats and lizards.

He would see Mattie one final time. It would be a brief, impersonal visit, and then he would be gone.

Seth scrambled down the steep incline and took off in a brisk walk to retrieve the mountain pony he had penned in the box canyon. He ignored the dull ache at the base of his skull, the wilting feeling that came from depriving himself of nourishment. He mounted up and rode off into the night, carrying the pouches of gold in his saddlebag.

If he dared to tell Mattie the truth about his affliction, would she bristle at his noble attempt to protect her from dangers beyond her wildest imagination? She balked at being protected, he reminded himself. He could never let on that he was trying to save her—this third and final time—from catastrophe.

It was far better for her to think he had lost interest in her, to let her assume that he didn't want a nursemaid hovering around him. Mattie was resilient, he assured himself. She would recover from his cool dismissal. Besides, there was a passel of men eager for her attention. The woman had more admirers than a tree had pine cones.

Mattie bolted up in bed when she heard the sharp rap at the back door. Blast it, that better not be her parents paying a late-night call to check on her. But then, what else did they have to do while they were practically camped out in her backyard, avoiding contact with men they referred to as "bumpkin miners." Heaven forbid that the Shaws emerge from their well-furnished campsite to mingle with the common man!

To Mattie's stunned amazement, she saw Seth standing on her porch. The makeshift bandage still encircled his head and his eyes glowed like silver in the faint moonlight. In the dark shadows he looked as formidable as her father!

"I brought these to you," Seth announced without preamble. "Take them. Use the gold to make a better life for yourself, as far away from this primitive mining town as you can get."

Mattie frowned, disconcerted. "You know perfectly well that I put no stock in gold. It certainly hasn't enriched your isolated life, has it?"

Seth didn't react to the insult, and Mattie mentally kicked herself for resorting to sarcasm. She had promised herself years ago not to reduce herself to the same level as her siblings when they made games of mocking her clumsiness.

"No, gold isn't going to make any life-altering changes in my life," he replied. "But it might be your blessing. You could establish a hospital for the ill and injured. You could purchase medication and supplies. I'm offering you the opportunity to pursue your calling."

Mattie was ashamed of herself for letting wounded pride speak for her. Seth was making a generous offer, and she was behaving like an ungrateful shrew. But confound it all! The sight of him cut so deeply that her heart bled.

"That is very kind of you, but my place is here, until the miners move on to the next potential gold field."

"Damn it, Mattie, if you care anything about me at all, you will take the gold," Seth said.

"And if you cared for me in the slightest you wouldn't offer me gold when you know that I want no part of it!"

When Mattie raised her chin stubbornly, Seth called upon his powers of silent suggestion. To his dismay, Mattie simply frowned at him and didn't outstretch her hands to accept the gold. That was odd. He had applied the technique dozens of times to discourage people from venturing too close to him. He must have lost his touch.

"Good night, Seth," Mattie said, as she closed the door in his face.

Seth walked off into the darkness, waited several minutes, then tiptoed back to the porch. Leaving the pouches of gold behind, he made his way up the winding path to his cave. Whether Mattie liked it or not, the gold was hers.

For several hours Seth ambled around the summits— as had been his habit before he had suffered a memory lapse. He hunted and feasted on wild game like the other predators in the mountains. When he had revived himself, he returned to the cave to share his space with the bats and those pesky lizards that were scrambling over the two sacks of gold that sat on the stone floor.

Seth frowned, realizing Mattie had returned the gold. So much for his attempt at generosity. Anyone else would have taken the gold nuggets and run with them. But not Mattie. The word stubborn had been coined to describe her.

Seth had the uneasy feeling that when the red moon was on the rise again, he would have to chain himself to his cot to prevent seeking Mattie out. That would be the time when his defenses were practically nonexistent.

Sighing bleakly, he lay down on his cot and closed his eyes as the spectacular rays of dawn colored the sky. Damnation, all the years he had presumed hell had nothing new to teach him.

Turned out he was wrong.

Mechanically, Mattie went about her duties of preparing meals at Wild Boar Saloon. She lacked her usual enthusiasm. She was also careless. Twice, she had dropped the skillet, catapulting food on the rough-hewed walls. The clatter had sent concerned miners pouring into the kitchen to check on her. It seemed clumsiness was catching up with her again. She couldn't blame her parents and family, because they had been noticeably absent since she asked them to back off.

Clem folded his arms over his chest and watched silently as Mattie shoved boiled potatoes and hoecakes onto waiting plates. "You're not yourself lately, Mattie," he observed. "What's bothering you?"

Mattie graced the waiter with a breezy smile. "Nothing is bothering me. I have simply been working longer shifts to accommodate all the hungry men. When I'm fatigued I become careless, that's all—"

Clem pounced at her, snatching the boiling pot from her hands before she spilled potatoes on the floor. Setting the pot aside, Clem clasped her hand in his and ushered her to the chair at the table. "Sit," he requested.

Reluctantly, Mattie sat.

"I think you need a day off," he declared as he assumed her duties at the stove. "The patrons in the dining hall don't rave about my cooking, but they'll survive while you rest."

Mattie thought it over for a moment, then nodded. Perhaps she did need to slow her pace. She had been unable to sleep, too restless to stay in bed at night. Maybe a short nap would revive her.

Once inside her cottage, Mattie sagged heavily against the door. It was time she ceased pining for a man who made it clear that he was ready to get on with his life—a life that didn't include her. She had seen nothing of Seth since he showed up on her doorstep with gold in hand. After she returned the pouches to his cave he must have accepted the fact that she didn't want his fortune. Furthermore, Seth hadn't even bothered to step outside his cavern that night to say so much as hello and good-bye forever.

"He's gone for good. Get used to the idea," Mattie said to herself, as she stretched out on the bed. But it was the bed where *he* had lain, where *he* had smiled up at her, where *he* had kissed her and made her feel sensations she had never experienced. His memory still lingered. That, Mattie suspected, was why she had trouble sleeping. Her hopes and dreams had gone up in a puff of smoke, and she couldn't make her aching heart accept it.

To Mattie's relief, sleep did overtake her—eventually. Darkness cloaked the room when she was jostled awake by the sound of fists banging on her front door and her name being called urgently.

Mattie bolted off the bed the instant she recognized Clem's voice. Something was wrong!

"Mattie, we need you," Clem panted. "One of the mine shafts collapsed. There are a dozen men trapped inside the mountain!"

Wheeling around, Mattie snatched up the satchel of bandages and medication she kept on hand for emergencies. Heart pounding, she jogged along beside Clem as he crossed the street to reach the wagon that was filled with picks, shovels, and blasting powder.

A group of somber-faced miners sat atop their mules and horses. No one spoke a word. Apprehension and concern vibrated in the night air.

When Clem assisted Mattie onto the seat, she stared grimly at the silhouette of the mountain peak to the north. This was the first time since her arrival in Slapout that massive calamity had struck. She had heard grim tales of hapless miners buried alive, of help arriving too late. But she had no first-hand experience, only the willingness to assist, to comfort, and to heal.

Serenaded by the clatter of hooves and creak of the wagon, the rescue brigade ascended into the mountain. A fog of dust hovered in the night sky, marking the location of the disaster.

Mattie wished Seth would come down from his mountain and offer his assistance, proving to the miners that he shared their concern for the men trapped in a sepulcher of stone.

The thought provoked Mattie to swivel on the wagon seat and stare toward the jagged peaks to the west. "Come down from your mountain," she chanted softly. "Lend a needed hand and accept the hand of friendship that awaits you."

"Oh God!" Clem chirped as he drew the team of horses to a halt.

Mattie stared at the tumble of rocks that blockaded the entrance to a half dozen tunnels that had been carved into the mountain. Several men had already arrived on the scene and were attempting to pry boulders from the entrance. The new arrivals scrambled from their mounts to retrieve their picks and shovels.

Muffled voices rose from inside the stone jaws of the mountain, begging for help, praying for deliverance.

Mattie grabbed her satchel and bounded off, unnoticed. She knew as well as the rescue party that the men trapped beyond the barricade of rock were running out of time . . . running out of precious air to breathe . . . .

Seth moved aimlessly around the cavern. Scowling, he stared at the pesky lizards that had a peculiar habit of perching on the sacks of gold that still sat inside the mouth of the cave. He gave one of the reptiles a nudge with the toes of his boot. The little beggar wouldn't budge.

When the bats swooped from the tunnels, Seth ambled outside to stare into the distance. A flume of dust swirled around the mountain peak to the north. Seth felt a sense of impending doom settle over him. He knew what that fog of dust indicated. He had seen it before—when unstable mine shafts collapsed inside the mountains.

Instinctively, he knew Mattie would race off to administer first aid and home remedies to survivors. She would be in the very thick of things, despite the dangers of becoming the victim of a rockslide.

The uneasy thought sent Seth scurrying along the shelf of stone, taking a shortcut across the ridges that connected the mountain range. Although he had vowed not to interfere or complicate Mattie's life again, never to risk the temptation of being near her, he couldn't live with the thought of her being injured in her attempt to save the prospectors. He had to know that she was safe from harm, that she wouldn't take unnecessary risks.

Not take risks? Mattie? Seth smiled grimly at the thought. That was a contradiction in terms. If she dared to stand up against the mob of miners who wanted to tar and feather him and run him out of town while he was injured, she would risk personal injury to rescue the men who had become her friends and occasional patients.

Seth could visualize Mattie, garbed in her customary bright-colored gowns, clawing at the rocks and rubble until her hands were raw. She would work tirelessly until she collapsed in exhaustion, making every effort to save the miners' lives.

Perhaps Seth's assistance wouldn't be well-received by the miners who were leery of him, but his cursed affliction did have several beneficial side effects. Besides keen sight and acute hearing, he possessed extraordinary strength—the kind that could literally move mountains—one boulder at a time. He would dig up the whole damned mountain, if he had to, if it would save Mattie from harm.

Moving with a sense of frantic urgency, Seth scrabbled down the face of the wind-swept cliffs. He could see the glow of lanterns and torches below him. He heard the rescue brigade scurrying around, calling out instructions to each other. He picked up the scent of lighted fuses and cursed under his breath. The miners were planning to blast a hole in the mountain to provide entrance and possible air pockets for the trapped miners. Damn it, they would likely cover themselves with a pile of rubble! One disaster was about to avalanche on another, and Seth was terrified that Mattie would find herself buried alive!

Five

Seth darted down the slope toward the group of men, frantically scanning the area. Mattie had to be here somewhere, but he didn't see her working alongside the rescue brigade.

A deafening explosion rumbled through the ground beneath his feet. Damnation, he hadn't arrived in time to discourage the men from setting off explosives!

Fragments of rock catapulted through the air. Horses screamed in terror, miners scrambled for their lives as a fog of dust swirled in the lanternlight. Sounds reminiscent of thunder echoed through the ravines as a shower of dirt and rock settled on the mountain.

Seth plunged toward the miners who staggered back to their feet. Maybe he wasn't wanted here, but he was needed. Murmurs of surprise swirled through the cluster of men as he dashed forward, halted directly in front of the rubble, then hoisted up a boulder that a normal man couldn't budge. When he heard the wailing cries inside the mountain, he heaved another boulder from the mouth of the mine shaft.

Gradually, the startled men surrounded him to lend assistance. And each time Seth hurled another armload of rock out of his way he drew more astounded attention from the miners. He was past caring what anyone thought of him. He was doing what Mattie would want him to do, what she would do if she were physically able.

Mattie . . . Seth glanced over his shoulder, scanning the area, looking for colorful clothing among the congregation of rescue workers.

"Where is she?" Seth's booming voice overrode the sound of metal picks clanking against rock.

The freckle-faced young man beside him tapped him on the shoulder. The instant Seth looked into Clem's face he knew he wasn't going to like what he was about to hear.

"We think Mattie is inside with the trapped men," Clem reported.

"What? How the hell did she get in there?"

Clem shrugged. "We aren't sure. We were setting up to carry off rock, and we looked up to see Mattie on the ledge above us." He gestured toward the moonlit platform of rock twenty feet above the clogged mine shaft. "She must have located a small opening to crawl through. After we heard another rumble deep inside the tunnel, we decided to use blasting powder."

Sickening dread overwhelmed Seth. The prospect of Mattie being buried under a pile of stone unnerved him. He attacked his task with fiendish urgency.

"Sure glad you showed up to help us," one of the

miners called to Seth. "If the rest of us had your strength we would have this rubble cleared away in no time at all."

The comment was seconded by the entire congregation of rescue workers. The men, Seth noted, were regarding him with something akin to admiration, respect, and gratitude, rather than the customary wariness. He was no longer the unwanted outsider surrounded by legend and superstition. He was working alongside the men in an urgent, common cause.

An unfamiliar sense of pleasure provided Seth with another burst of energy. He hadn't experienced the feeling of acceptance since he was a child playing in his family's palatial estate in France. He had been granted another taste of it when he encountered Mattie Shaw, had reveled in those sensations of being cared for, concerned about . . .

Seth refused to let himself ponder that which could never be with Mattie. He had to learn to be content with the memories of those golden moments. It was all he had to counter the years and decades of his dreary existence.

Though Mattie was lost to him forever, Seth vowed to make damned certain she wouldn't lose her life in this suffocating rubble of rock—if it wasn't too late already!

He had to know that she would live and breathe and laugh again, that she would spread the radiance of her dimpled smile and lift the broken spirits of her fellow man. The world deserved, needed, all the Mattie Shaws it could get.

Seth did something he hadn't done in years, something he wasn't even sure a man with his cursed affliction had a right to do. He prayed to God in heaven—not for himself, but for Mattie's safety, for the safety of the men buried in the stone jaws of hell.

For the first time ever, there was no hidden motivation that might save him from his bleak existence. He would gladly suffer all the torments of the damned forevermore if that one ray of purity, hope, and radiance that was Mattie Shaw might live.

And the miners, too, Seth tacked on quickly, because he knew Mattie's first thoughts would be for the men who might be, at this very moment, breathing their last breath in their rock coffins.

Another murmur of amazement spread through the crowd as Seth hoisted up a boulder the size of a tombstone and hurled it aside. He clawed broken rocks out of his way to unearth yet another jagged block of stone, then sent it flying the same direction as the one before.

The mountain rumbled and vibrations trembled beneath his feet as he labored and sweated and chanted prayers of deliverance. He worked like a madman, while grim visions of the mine shafts collapsing spiraled around him.

"Let her live," Seth whispered over and over again. "Please, God, I will gladly accept all the sins of mankind as my own if you will spare this woman who puts the needs of her friends above her own. Grant me the power to spare the lives of those hapless miners."

When the mountain groaned, and rocks tumbled from the ledge above, Seth had the despairing feeling that the prayer raised to heaven by a soulless revenant had been denied. The rescue workers drew a collective breath as dust floated away from the outlying ledge of stone. The rumbling mountain turned silent and hope died an anguishing death.

Then, from the ledge above, a feminine voice rang out, echoing down the face of the mountain. "Help us!"

The sound of Mattie's voice raised every sunken spirit. Men scrambled up the footholds of rocks, dragging ropes behind them. Seth scratched and clawed his way up the steep incline, pausing twice to thrust out a helping hand to Clem who followed in his footsteps but lacked the strength and agility to make the tedious climb up the vertical wall of rock.

Seth was the first to reach the outcropping of rock where Mattie was reported last seen. To his astonishment he saw a small tunnel—which had broken off into jagged fissures in the stone. This must be where she had crawled into the mountain in hopes of locating the trapped miners. Seth wedged himself between the crumbled rock, groping for footing in the dark abyss below.

"Here, Tremayne, you'll need a light to lead your way." A crusty miner rushed forward to offer him a torch, but Seth waved the man back.

"I'll need both hands free," Seth insisted.

"But—"

Seth slithered through the narrow opening. His exceptional night vision enabled him to survey the tunnel that wound into the mountain. "Mattie!" he called out.

"Seth? Is that you?"

Her voice rolled toward him, and he glanced to the right.

"I hoped you would come! I'm having a bit of trouble here. Some of the men are seriously injured."

She was all right—as all right as one could expect after a mountain caved in on her. Relief washed through Seth as he scurried off in the direction of her voice.

"Keep talking so I can find you, sweetheart," he called back.

"I don't have nearly enough bandages to tend the injured," she hollered. "Please ask some of the rescue workers to ride back to town for more supplies. Tell Mrs. Pruitt that I will pay for the supplies taken from the dry goods store."

"I'll pay the expenses," Seth insisted, then wheeled around to spread the word to the cluster of men waiting on the broken shelf of stone above him.

Seth wedged through the cramped passage, led by a dim glow of distant light. Mattie's candle, no doubt. The woman, it seemed, came prepared for anything.

Seth finally located the tiny niche where injured miners lay sprawled beneath a dome of solid rock. Mattie's candle sat like a miniature campfire in the open space. She was scrunched down, applying a poultice to a bleeding wound. Her royal blue gown was covered with dust, as was her unbound hair. Smudges of dirt streaked down her flushed face, but she smiled comfortingly at her patient as she reassured him that he would live to see the light of day, that he would soon have the use of his right arm so he could write home to his wife and children in Boston.

Mattie seemed to know the background of every prospector trapped inside the mountain. As she moved to her next patient, she commented on how much John

Meeker's young son must have grown since John last saw him.

This delicate female was truly an angel of mercy, Seth mused as he watched her in action. He could see the respect and admiration directed toward her. The men looked to her for inspiration and guidance. They realized what a rare jewel she was—worth more than the riches of gold buried in this unstable mountain. Mattie had defied personal danger to locate and tend to these men. She had squeezed her petite form through the crevice where the average-size man couldn't go—until another quake sent fissures spreading through the small opening.

Seth had never known how it felt to love, not in all his two-hundred-some-odd years, but he loved Mattie Shaw, even if he had to love her from a safe distance that would protect her from the beast within. She had his heart—his very soul if he had one—to claim as his own.

Seth cast aside the tender emotions that left him motionless. He glanced around to determine which injured man needed his immediate attention. He knelt to scoop up one of the men who, he recalled, had objected to his recuperating in Mattie's bed. Hurriedly, Seth carried the man toward the waiting rescue party.

"I take back every unkind word I said about you," Chester Darnell wheezed. "You came when we needed help, just as Mattie did. If you want to court her, then you have my approval, Tremayne."

Seth just kept on walking, saying nothing. He knew things about himself that this miner didn't, things that would prevent a future courtship.

"Don't know how Mattie found us," Chester said

raggedly. "Don't know how she found the strength to move us away from that collapsed shaft. All I know is that I roused to consciousness, and she had every man dragged under that solid dome of rock."

"Save your energy," Seth murmured. "You can sing Mattie's praises later."

Quietly, Seth offered Chester the kind of comfort and encouragement Mattie had, refusing to let the injured man spend too much time contemplating his bleeding wound. Over and over again, Seth assured the miner that he would live to tell of his harrowing experiences.

One by one, Seth carried the injured men to the rescue brigade. And each time, he was greeted with gratitude and appreciation. By the time he carried the last prospector to safety, he knew each man's name, knew the names of loved ones back in civilization who waited to receive a letter and news of gold discoveries.

When Seth strode back to fetch Mattie, he found her stuffing her bottles of home remedies and poultices in her dusty satchel. She looked up, exhausted, frail. Impulsively, Seth pulled her into his arms and held her protectively to him. With a sigh, Mattie snuggled against his chest, her head tucked under his chin.

For a split second, the ageless urge welled up inside him, but Seth tamped it down. It seemed nothing had changed, despite his selfless deeds, despite his fervent prayers. The beast still lurked, demanding to be fed. But Seth vowed that not one drop of this angel of mercy's blood would spill to appease him. He would feed solely on the pleasure of holding her, sharing a breathless kiss.

Seth bent his head, seeking Mattie's petal-soft mouth, finding welcome. And there, within the dark jaws of the mountain, Seth silently communicated the love he dared not speak in words. His kiss spoke of the tenderness he felt for Mattie, the protective gentleness that had become a part of him when he was with her. The lurking beast was no match for the all-consuming emotion roiling through him.

And for that long, satisfying moment, while he and Mattie were completely alone, Seth knew the true measure of pleasure and happiness. He didn't dwell on the futility of his affection for her, didn't give way to his despair. For this one bright, shining moment in the darkness, there was no past or future to torment him, only the glorious present. His greatest prayer had been answered. Mattie had survived.

"Tremayne?"

Reluctantly, Seth raised his head to stare toward the flickering torch at the end of the tunnel.

"Is Mattie all right?" the rescue workers chorused.

Seth smiled down into her upturned face. "She's alive and well. I'll have her back to you in just a few moments."

"Thank you for coming, Seth," she whispered.

Seth felt the impulsive urge to chastise her for crawling down between the opening in the rocks, but he wisely held his tongue. From what he had learned, her family chastised her often enough without him contributing to her aggravation.

"Thank God!" Clem chirped, as Seth lifted Mattie through the narrow opening. "My goodness, woman, you gave us a frightful scare. Why didn't you tell someone before you climbed down this hole!"

"I was in a hurry to find the men," Mattie explained, as Clem enveloped her in a hug that smashed her nose to his shoulder. "I wasn't in any danger," she added as she was passed to the next set of arms that waited to engulf her.

"Not in danger!" one of the men hooted. "The whole blessed mountain practically fell on top of you!"

Mattie listened to her friends voice their concerns, then waved them off, insisting that she was unharmed— more or less. All the while, her gaze strayed to Seth. Since she had last seen him, he looked much better. Though his complexion was pale, she knew he had regained his energy. She had felt his strength while he carried her in his arms.

Maybe, just maybe, he'd had a change of heart. Perhaps he was silently trying to tell her that he was interested in taking up where they had left off more than a week ago. Maybe it was the interaction of the various potions she had given him that made him standoffish and irritable. Perhaps he had spent the week alone, thinking the matter through and longing for her companionship.

Mattie set aside the thoughts that lingered long after Seth's sizzling kiss. She had patients to tend—many who needed stitches and splints. To her relief, Seth returned to her side, guiding her toward the wagon laden with injured miners. And to her great satisfaction, she heard dozens of men expressing their gratitude to Seth. Mattie hoped Seth would venture into town when loneliness crowded in on him and accept the companionship the miners offered.

The moment the caravan returned to town, Mattie hurried off to place pallets on the floors of her cottage. She wanted her patients close at hand so she could keep a continual eye on them. With Seth at her side, they set splints and stitched wounds, working late into the night to ensure each man was resting comfortably.

Although Mattie was near collapse from exhaustion, Seth was still prowling the rooms energetically, checking each patient. The man certainly had regained his strength. But then, Mattie reminded herself, he always seemed to function better at night.

"Take a load off your feet," Seth ordered sternly, then gestured toward the empty pallet in the corner of the kitchen. "Although I agreed to share a drink with the rescue brigade, I wanted to ensure that the injured were bedded down first. I'll be back in a half hour to make the rounds. In the meantime, you need to rest. You, love, look as if you could use it."

"I could at that," Mattie admitted.

Seth stared at her for a long, pensive moment. "I don't know how you managed to pull all those men to a safer location. That must have been a back-breaking task."

Mattie smiled tiredly. "I admit that it sapped all my energy. But I couldn't rest until I evacuated them from that crumbling shaft."

When Seth left, Mattie sprawled on her pallet beside the stove—the two men who were seriously injured were sleeping in her bed. Gracious, she felt tired. It had taken all the strength she could muster to assist in the rescue . . . .

That was the last thought to flit across her mind. Mattie slumped in motionless sleep and didn't rouse for hours.

* * *

Seth was greeted enthusiastically as he ambled into Wild Boar Saloon. The miners were burning midnight oil and passing around whiskey bottles in celebration. A leather-faced prospector pulled out a chair for Seth as he strode between the rows of tables.

"Sit yerself down, Tremayne. Did you get the injured tended to?"

"All present and accounted for, according to Mattie," Seth said, as he took his seat at the crowded table.

"Glad to hear it," Abe Lassiter mumbled, then chugged his drink. He wiped dribbles of whiskey off his whiskered chin with his shirtsleeve, then grinned, displaying the gap between his front teeth. "If you don't mind my asking, how'd you get so strong? Never saw anybody pick up boulders like they were blocks of wood before."

Seth shrugged nonchalantly. "I've had the gift as long as I can remember."

"Wish I had it," Billy Joe Garret spoke up. "After two years of mining for gold and digging shafts you'd think I'd have built up that kind of strength."

Seth sipped his drink, listening to the miners spin tales of their adventures and hardships in the Rockies. He glanced around the crowded saloon, expecting to see the Bakers pouring whiskey down their gullets— whiskey bought and paid for with gold dust from the tunnel of his cavern, no doubt.

The brawny scavengers were nowhere in sight.

"Have you seen the Baker boys around town?" Seth asked. He had a bone to pick with those rascals who had walloped him on the head.

"Nope, ain't seem them for a while," Abe replied. "Their tent is still staked outside of town, but I don't know where they wandered off to." He pivoted in his chair to address the crowd at large. "Any of you fellows seen the Bakers hereabout?"

No one seemed to know—or care—that the town bullies had made themselves scarce. It was just as well, Seth decided. Now that he had made peace with the prospectors in Slapout, he felt less vindictive. Giving the Bakers their due might damage the respect he had acquired among the miners.

Glancing at the aged timepiece in his pocket, Seth rose to leave. "Thank you for the good company, gentlemen, but I need to check on our patients while Mattie is sleeping."

"You're always welcome here, Tremayne," Billy Joe insisted. "Ain't that right, boys?"

The patrons of the bar nodded simultaneously, and Seth walked away, feeling accepted and appreciated. It was a good feeling. He would always be an outsider, but at least he could walk the rutted streets of Slapout without being looked upon as a threat and nuisance.

In high spirits, Seth strode off to dole out Mattie's home remedies for pain, just as the sun began its ascent into the sky.

Realizing that he was running short on time, Seth quickened his pace. A few hours spent in the glaring daylight and he would be as weak and helpless as the injured miners resting in Mattie's improvised infirmary.

Six

Groaning wearily, Mattie shifted on her pallet, feeling as if she had slept under a rock. She glanced around the kitchen, noting that her patients were wearing fresh bandages. Trays of bread crumbs sat on the cabinet, indicating the injured had been fed. Seth had worked tirelessly while she regathered her energy. She would have to remember to thank him first chance she got.

Rising, Mattie tiptoed outside to wash her face, then headed for the restaurant to prepare a hearty breakfast for her patients. Since there was no sign of Seth, she presumed he had returned to his cavern to rest.

Not once during the busy day of cooking and tending her patients did she see Seth, but he returned that evening to shuffle her off to bed and assume her duties with the wounded.

The following morning Mattie awoke to the sound of injured miners talking among themselves. To Mattie's amazement, they were discussing the gold nuggets that had been tucked in their shirt pockets. Each prospector had been given more than enough gold to tide him over until he was back on his feet.

Mattie smiled to herself. Seth had certainly raised the spirits of her patients with his generosity. She was so proud of him, so pleased that her patients now considered him their friend. Seth had become something of a hero in Slapout, putting an end to those rumors of a devil who guarded his bonanza with a vengeance.

More than anything, Mattie longed to hike up to Seth's cavern, to confess what was in her heart. She wanted Seth to know how she felt about him. It seemed only right that the man she loved should know the truth. Besides, after that passionate kiss they shared inside the crumbling mountain, her heart was nearly bursting with the need to speak the words to him.

She wouldn't expect to hear those three little words returned, she told herself, but maybe . . .

Spinning about, Mattie wiped her hands on the kitchen towel, then presented her wooden spatula to Clem, who was wandering around the kitchen at Wild Boar Saloon. "I have an errand to run this evening," she informed the waiter. "Would you mind stirring the stew and filling orders for meals?"

Clem nodded and smiled. "Sure thing, Mattie. The dining hall is full of hungry miners licking their lips in anticipation of your world-famous stew. Go tend your chores and I'll hold down the fort."

Nightfall settled over the majestic peaks of the mountains by the time Mattie made her rounds to tend her patients, then she scurried from town. She was going to bare her heart to Seth, to let him know how much she appreciated his efforts to rescue the hapless prospectors. Seth should be aware that he had become the local hero. When he had passed around his gifts of gold, he had proved his great potential for generosity, Mattie thought. The injured men were in the best of spirits now that they knew where their next meal would come from.

Seth Tremayne was turning out to be every bit the man she knew he could be. Now, if only he could find it in his heart to love her back . . . .

Squaring her shoulders, Mattie approached the cavern. A small cluster of bats, lagging behind the winged masses, swooped over her head, then wafted off into the night. Mentally rehearsing what she planned to say, Mattie stepped into the interior of the cave. Lanternlight glowed on the stone walls, flickering across the quilt on Seth's empty cot.

He stood with his back to her, rearranging test tubes on the shelves tucked in the far corner. The lizards scrambled back and forth across his booted feet.

Mattie smiled in amusement as she watched the reptiles encircle Seth's feet, but her smile vanished when Seth pivoted toward her. Her heart pounded like a sledgehammer and all her well-rehearsed words escaped her when she gazed into those glimmering silver-blue eyes.

"How are our patients feeling this evening?" Seth asked as he approached her.

"Fine," she squeaked, barely able to draw enough breath to eke out one word, much less begin a long-winded soliloquy that ended with: I love you.

"I'm relieved to hear that. John Meeker looked a mite peaked when I checked on him last night. You must have given him a double dose of your extra-special home remedy.''

''I did.'' My, wasn't she turning out to be a brilliant conversationalist!

Seth gestured toward the chair. ''After your long hike up the mountain you might like to sit down.''

''I love you.''

There, she had said what she had come to say. Her feelings were out in the open—to be accepted or rejected. No frills. Just the undeniable, unalterable truth that Seth Tremayne held her heart in his hands.

Seth's reaction left much to be desired. He looked pained, awkward, and Mattie felt the need to reassure and comfort him. ''You don't have to say anything, Seth.'' The words were coming easier now, spilling from her lips in a breathless rush. ''I only want you to know how I feel about you. I also want you to realize that the miners from Slapout hold you in the highest regard. I've heard your praises sung since we returned from the collapsed mine shaft. Your deeds of courage, generosity, and kindness are all the more reason why I care so deeply for you. You are everything I ever dreamed of finding in a man.''

''Mattie, please sit down,'' Seth requested. His voice held a hint of sadness that he couldn't conceal.

Her confession was both heaven and hell for him. He had hoped—and he knew it was a purely selfish whim— that his deeds of kindness and bravery would classify as the selfless acts that could cure his lifelong curse, but nothing seemed to have changed since the mining accident. His night vision was still exceptional, as was his acute hearing. His sensitivity to sunlight was as great as it had ever been. The urge to feed like the creatures of the night hadn't subsided. And damn it, there wasn't even one gray hair on his head to testify to his two-hundred-year existence!

Reluctantly, Mattie took a seat beside the table. She peered up at Seth with those luminous green eyes that touched him so deeply with their vibrant inner spirit and honesty. He couldn't send her away in the same manner as before. She had bared her heart to him, undeserving though he was of her affection. She had a right to know the truth—even if it pained him to see her reaction. He owed her an explanation.

Apprehensively, Seth wheeled around to pace the confines of the anteroom. He would have to work up a little more nerve before he met her curious stare, saw her love for him transform into disgust.

He drew a steadying breath and began to explain. It was the most difficult task he had ever undertaken. "Mattie, I suffer from a severe affliction that prevents me from sharing any kind of future with you."

"I am skilled at mixing potions to cure all sorts of afflictions," she assured him.

He smiled morosely and shook his head. "Not this particular kind of affliction, I'm afraid. I should know, because I myself have spent more years than you can imagine working on a reliable cure. At best, I manage to keep the condition under partial control so that I pose no harmful threat to society."

Mattie frowned, bemused. "To society?" she parroted.

Seth nodded. "That is why I have isolated myself. For years, my gravest concern has been the prevention of spreading my affliction to innocent . . . um . . . victims, shall we say."

Her eyes rounded. "You are contagious?"

"In a manner of speaking, yes, but only during a particular kind of contact."

Damn, thought Seth, breaking this to her gently was excruciating. He couldn't blurt out the truth the way she had spilled her confession of love. It was not at all the same. And furthermore, Mattie would be ready to retract her words of love when she realized what kind of man he really was. Or more to the point, what kind of *beast* he was.

Pensively, Mattie stared at him. "I see. I assume that this affliction of yours is spread by—" Her face blossomed with color as she stared at the air over his shoulder "—physical intimacy. Actually, I do have knowledge of a potion to treat the condition. But as you say, there is no known cure. However, I can—"

Seth flung up a hand, cutting her off in midsentence. He had to make her understand that his affliction was . . . not what she thought.

He tried a different approach. "Do you recall those newspaper clippings you found in my trunk?"

"Of course," she replied.

"Now that my memory has returned, I know why I saved those ancient clippings. I know how I came to have this ring and the pendant I'm wearing around my neck."

Mattie waited for him to continue, but Seth paused to formulate his thoughts, then began to speak.

"The clippings announced the deaths of my parents, my brothers . . . all six of them."

He paused from his nervous pacing to watch the look of astonishment spread across her delicate features.

"But those clippings are dated years before—"

"Yes, they are. And the certificates from Oxford belong to me," he broke in, anxious to have the truth completely out in the open, to endure her shock and disbelief, to end this conversation as quickly as possible so he could get on with the rest of his miserable life!

"King Louis the Fourteenth of France gave this ring to me personally," he hurried on. "Louis owed me a great favor, because I mixed just the right amount of poison for him to slip into the drink of his fiercest political enemy. He wanted it to look as if the man collapsed from a sudden stroke."

"Louis the Fourteenth? But he lived centuries ago."

Seth grimaced at the look of dismay on Mattie's face. The incident with Louis wasn't something he liked to remember. But those were different times, he reminded himself.

"This pendant—" He tapped the piece of jewelry that lay against the base of his throat, suspended by a gold chain—"was a gift from William the Third. I suppose you have heard of him, too."

Wide-eyed, Mattie nodded her head.

"By that time I had moved to England, because it became impossible for me to explain why acquaintances my age were dropping off like flies while I had yet to find one gray hair on my head or wrinkle on my face."

The impact of his words left Mattie speechless. Seth could see Mattie drawing her astounded conclusions. Any moment, she would put two and two together and realize she was sharing this cave with a creature that was not human, despite his appearance.

"My God . . ." she bleated.

Seth stepped closer, towering over her, allowing his gaze to take on just a hint of the blood-red stare that glazed his eyes when he was in a feeding frenzy. "Are you beginning to understand what I'm trying to tell you, Mattie?"

Dazed, spellbound, she nodded her head.

"For your sake, I have to keep my distance from you. No matter how cautious I try to be, no matter how many doses of potion I ingest in hopes of paralyzing the beast within, I cannot cure my ageless affliction. Now do you see why I share my existence with the bats that feed on their prey during the night? Do you understand why I function best when there is very little light? Do you understand why I had no difficulty navigating through the pitch-black corridors inside the crumbling mountain?"

"I can't believe it!" Mattie said.

"Believe it, love. I can give you the kind of kiss that carries the worst of all possible bites."

Seth waited, braced for the outpouring of horror he knew was about to fill her fascinating green eyes. But to his astonishment, she settled back in her chair and smiled, as if his terrible confession were of no great consequence to her. Next thing he knew, Mattie would unselfishly offer herself up to him, proving that her love for him was unconditional. He would not allow that to happen. She was not going to serve a sentence in hell with him!

"I want you to leave here and never come back," Seth growled for effect. "Promise me that, Mattie. Promise me that if I come for you that you will refuse me!"

"I'm sorry, Seth, but I can't do that. I care too much about you."

He braced his hands on her shoulders, giving her a firm shake. Snarling, he bared his teeth. "You can and you will avoid me forevermore!"

His ferocious command didn't even make her blink.

This woman was impossible to intimidate. Seth stared deeply into her eyes, planting the silent suggestion that she should rise and walk away without looking back, but Mattie didn't react.

He wondered if getting down on his knees and begging her to run for her life would have the slightest influence on her. He decided to find out, because he had few options left.

Kneeling in front of her, Seth clasped her hands in his. "Please leave me to my torment, to my shame, Mattie. I don't want to hurt you. That would make my hell more difficult to endure. I'm *begging* you to return to town and never, *ever*, set foot in this cavern so long as you live."

She wrested her hands from his to smooth away the tousled raven hair from his forehead. Then she traced her forefinger over his lips so trustingly, so adoringly, that tears clouded his vision.

"Do you care so much about me that you would spare me from your ageless affliction?"

"I care," he whispered achingly.

"Do you understand that I love you, in spite of what you have told me?"

He looked into her luminous eyes and knew it for the truth. "I understand."

She cupped his face in her hands and held his tormented stare. "Do you love me, Seth? Really love me? I need to know. I think I have a right to know the truth, all of it."

"Never in two hundred years have I fully understood what love is . . . until there was you," he admitted. "I do love you, Mattie. Never doubt that."

Seth knew he was probably consigning her to his

hellish brand of torment. She would probably offer herself to him, now that she had heard his confession of love. And lonely, tormented fool that he was, he would convince himself that a love this strong could somehow find a way to survive in his world of darkness and misery. But he had to remain steadfast, to refuse any offer of self-sacrifice that she whispered to him.

"But loving you won't change my dismal future," he continued, his voice wavering with emotion. "I cannot, will not, let you suffer endlessly. In time you would come to realize your mistake and wish for the normal span of life and the eternity you rightfully deserve."

She touched her lips to his, like a delicate butterfly alighting then gently drifting away. Seth savored the tenderness of her touch, the satisfying taste, the wispy scent . . . and then he did the unforgivable.

His eyes watered. He sneezed and ruined the moment.

"Bless you."

"That, Mattie, will never happen. Men like me have never been blessed, only scorned."

Mattie merely smiled at his bleak expression. "Now that I know what afflicts you, I can mix a potion that will control your allergic reaction to me."

Seth withdrew and came to his feet. "No potion will be necessary, because you are leaving."

"No, I'm not," she contradicted. She bounded to her feet, then gestured for Seth to take the chair she vacated. "Sit down, Seth."

Muttering, he plunked down in the chair and mustered his resolve. No matter what Mattie said in an effort to change his mind, he was not budging from his conviction.

Seven

"Now then," Mattie said as she stood over Seth. "If things were different, would this affection you claim to feel for me evolve into a permanent and lasting commitment, do you think?"

"Yes," he assured her. "But what is the point of asking? Things are not different and they never will be. I will not allow you to sacrifice your life to join the ranks of the undead. I am a vampire, damn it!" he blurted out, hating the word but determined to make a distinct impression on her. "A vampire, Mattie, don't you understand what that means?"

"Fine, you are a vampire and I am a witch," she flung back.

Seth slumped back in his chair. He didn't find her sarcastic rejoinder the least bit amusing. She was not going to cajole him into giving her the kind of kiss that left marks on her delicate throat. Nothing, absolutely nothing, she could say was going to change his mind!

"You, Mattie, are an angel of mercy. Everyone in these mountains knows that," he said sharply. "I refuse to let your generosity and compassion lead you into my kind of misery. You don't deserve that kind of life."

"Apparently, you aren't listening to me," she replied. "I said I was a witch."

Seth gave a caustic snort.

One perfectly-arched brow lifted in challenge. "You doubt me?"

"I think you are trying to persuade me to agree to this madness by making that ridiculous claim."

"Do you remember that night of the thunderstorm, when you thought I was preparing to leap to my death?"

Seth nodded.

"I wasn't trying to commit suicide. I was regenerating my powers in the storm," she informed him matter-of-factly. "And although I let you presume that I summoned the help of miners to tote you down the mountain to the bed in my cottage, I merely transported both of us into town with the flick of my wrist."

Seth couldn't help himself; he laughed aloud. This delightfully entertaining woman had a lively imagination, which she was using to plead her case. But Seth wasn't convinced, wasn't wavering from his stand. If he gave her that fateful kiss and later discovered that she had fed him a crock of malarkey, he would never forgive himself.

"The morning after you were knocked unconscious by that lightning-struck tree limb, you swore you heard several voices coming from my parlor," she reminded him. "That was my family, who dropped by to discourage me from housing a mortal man under my roof. As usual, the descending brood made me so nervous, while breathing down my neck and spouting ultimatums, that I tripped on the hem of my skirt and dropped the plate of food I had prepared for you.''

''Of course,'' Seth snickered. ''What other reasonable explanation could there be?''

''And as I recall, you were surprised the night you rode off on horseback, only to discover that I had arrived on the summit before you. I was having another one of those annoying conferences with my parents who have been popping up unexpectedly to offer guidance.

''And when I explained that horses and I don't get on well, it is true that I took a nasty fall as a child. But I don't ride simply because I am hesitant to climb back on the saddle. Fact is, horses have a natural aversion to witches, so I rely on alternate modes of transportation.''

Seth leaned back in his chair and crossed his arms over his chest. He did admit that Mattie had an interesting knack of taking facts and twisting them in a convincing manner to prove her point. Still, he wasn't backing down, no matter what.

''When I assured you that I took necessary actions to protect the gold in your cave while you were recuperating, I placed a boulder in front of the cavern so no one could trespass.''

Seth choked down a smirk.

''And did it occur to you that I was the one who dealt effectively with the Baker boys who came to steal your gold?'' Mattie quizzed him. ''I kept telling you that I was capable of defending myself, but you refused to believe it. You launched your attack on those three scalawags and received a bump on your head for your noble efforts. Truth is, I handled the Bakers in my own way." She called his attention to the lizards that were camped out under the shelving that held Seth's test tubes and chemicals. "As you can plainly see, I turned those scavengers into lizards."

Seth burst into uproarious laughter. He had always considered Mattie to be entertaining company, but she was in exceptionally rare form tonight.

"When I ventured off to replenish my supply of plants and herbs for my potions, I didn't just stroll down a nearby hill," she went on to say. "I made a hasty flight to China, then whizzed off to gather necessary mandrake, poligonia, alchone, and pisterion, which are plants indigenous to Europe and South America."

"Whizzed off on your broom?" Seth managed to ask with a straight face.

"No," she shouted, at the end of her patience. "I cast a spell on my broom so it would sweep up my cottage during my absence. And all the while, my parents were following me around, insisting that I was becoming entirely too attached to a mortal man, reminding me that nothing could come of it, because we Shaws are unique.

"And for your information, there is a specific reason why Abigail and Horace Shaw decided to have thirteen children. They wanted to form their own coven. You do know what a coven is, don't you?"

"Of course, the word was bandied around a lot during the Salem witch hunts," Seth responded. "So, how long have you dabbled in black magic, or is that a family secret?"

Mattie gnashed her teeth, exasperated that Seth refused to take her seriously. "I practice *white* magic. I am a healer, and I very seldom cast spells, unless situations dictate such actions. But your skepticism tempts me to turn you into a lizard so you can rub scales with yonder Baker boys. I made the Bakers an exception, because they deserved what they got, and you might, too, if you don't stop smirking at every explanation I offer!"

"You do have a talent for fiction," Seth said, and chuckled. Eventually, his smile melted away. "I think we should face the undeniable fact that we aren't meant for each other—"

Seth's voice dried up when the chair in which he was sitting floated off the floor—with him in it. He squawked when the chair wobbled, then tilted sideways. He clawed the air, then dropped like an anchor to sprawl, unceremoniously, at Mattie's feet. Thunderstruck, he gaped at Mattie.

"Sorry," she apologized. "I didn't mean to dump you on the floor. It's just that my powers need replenishing again. That mining mishap demanded more of my energy than you can possibly imagine. Holding up a crumbling mountain, while transporting so many injured miners to safe sanctuary was extremely exhausting."

Seth choked on his breath. He recalled what one of the injured miners had said about regaining consciousness to find himself, and his fellow prospectors, huddled beneath a solid, supportive dome of stone. Seth had assumed Mattie had dragged the men to safety by their boot heels. Apparently, she had *transported* them the same way she bodily moved him off the floor—chair and all!

Mattie smiled impishly when she saw the dawn of

revelation on Seth's handsome face. "I choose to use my magical powers for the benefit of mankind, because it gives my life satisfaction and purpose. But I can cast spells when I feel the need. If you are still unconvinced, you can spend the evening under the shelves with the Bakers in their lizard suits."

Seth chuckled as he clambered to his feet, then uprighted the chair. "We make an odd pair, don't we, Mattie?"

Mattie glided her arms over his chest, then levitated so she could stare him squarely in the eye. "A perfect pair, to my way of thinking," she whispered, before she pressed her lips to his. "I could have used sorcery to cast a love spell on you, but I wanted you to come freely, willingly. From this day forward, the only potions I will ever give you will be designed to control your urges, your keen sensitivity to someone like me—someone who is no more human than you are. My home remedies will provide substitute nourishment for your affliction. And together we will ease the trouble of humankind.

"When the time comes for us to move on, in order to avoid questions about our inability to age, we will travel together."

"We'll go anywhere you please," Seth murmured, as he slid his arm under her knees and pivoted toward the bed. "But tonight, all I want is to see my forbidden dreams come true—"

"Hold it right there, caveman," came a booming voice that left Seth's sensitive ears ringing.

With Mattie clutched protectively to his chest, Seth wheeled around to confront a tall, robust-looking man dressed in a swirling black cloak, top hat, and Hessian boots. The man's green eyes spewed fire and brimstone as he elevated his arms in a sweeping gesture.

"Papa, don't you dare!" Mattie shrieked. "If you harm one hair on Seth's head, I will never speak to you again, not even in the next eternity!"

Seth gaped at the man—who didn't look to be a day over thirty-five. This was Mattie's father?

Seth's astounded gaze skittered past the cloaked figure to see a dainty woman with spun-gold hair appear from the darkness. She slid her arm around Horace's elbow and glanced expectantly at Mattie. Behind the dashingly attractive couple, a dozen other figures that shared similar family traits materialized. Seth wasn't sure he should believe what he was seeing! Furthermore, the need to sneeze intensified as the scent of the intruders drifted toward him.

After several involuntary sneezes, Seth managed to draw a normal breath.

"I had hoped to spare you one of these family conferences," Mattie murmured. "But as I told you, my family has a disconcerting habit of popping up from nowhere."

Horace glared at Seth, then diverted his attention to the cot in the corner. "I warn you, caveman, that you are in imminent danger of experiencing the full extent of my temper. That happens to be my youngest daughter you're carting off, and I will not permit you to dally with her. She is a Shaw and no one tangles with a Shaw unless he has the hankering to wind up in the body of a turtle or snake!"

Seth turned his attention back to Mattie. She was staring up at him with all the love and devotion he could ever hope to share in life. He would not lose his greatest treasure. Mattie meant everything to him.

"Sir," he said, sparing Horace the briefest of glances. "I happen to love your daughter. I want her as my wife, from now until forever. And you—" Seth pinned Horace with a stare that glowed burning red in the dim light. "—are intruding. Next time you drop in, try knocking first."

The entire brood of Shaws gasped when Seth gave them the evil eye. Seth refused to be intimidated. If he was about to be put on trial—with a witch and warlock as judges, and a coven of witchcrafting practitioners as jury—he wanted it known that he was sincere in his feelings for Mattie.

"He's not human!" Horace realized, and said so.

"No, turns out he's not," Mattie replied, grinning happily.

"Well, blast it, why didn't you say so, girl?" A wry smile spread across Horace's face as he focused on Seth. "You did spring from good stock, I hope?"

"Good enough," Seth reported. "Seventeenth century French noblemen."

"Glad to hear it." Horace fluffed his frilly sleeve and struck a dignified pose. "We hail from England, sixteenth century. King Henry the Eighth did more than chop off a few heads. He also prohibited wizardry, so we decided it was time to begin our worldly travels. But the thing is, we don't want to see the Shaw name tainted, you understand. We do have our reputation to uphold. After all—"

"Papa," Mattie cut in impatiently. "Shut the door on your way out."

Horace glanced over his broad shoulder. "This cave doesn't have a door."

"Install one, then," Mattie requested.

To Seth's amazement, the coven of Shaws vanished in the blink of an eye. A planked door, complete with iron hinges, blocked the passageway.

"We could use a larger bed, witch," Seth pointed out, as he carried Mattie forward. "A bed for two would be nice, because I don't plan to sleep alone again."

The words were no sooner out of his mouth than Mattie flicked her dainty wrist. His narrow cot was instantly replaced by a spacious bed covered with silk sheets and spun-gold quilts. Although the bed was slightly lopsided—Mattie had already explained that her powers weren't functioning at peak capacity after the energy expended at the mining mishap—it still looked like heaven to Seth.

And when he eased down beside the very sunshine in his life—the *only* sunshine in his life—centuries of torment faded into oblivion. Mattie came to him with the gentleness of a breeze whispering over the age-old mountains. She matched touch for tender touch. And Seth knew the moment his lips glided over hers that the love they shared was no match for the beast imprisoned within him.

After midnight, while the moon glowed down on the rugged summits and plunging ravines, Seth cradled Mattie against his heart. He felt different, changed, complete. Could it be that he had earned a right to his soul . . . earned the right to a soul mate?

"I will always love you," Mattie whispered genuinely, sincerely. She reached up to glide her index finger over the mussed raven strands on his head. "And I grant your wish. Here, my love, is the one gray hair you wanted."

He grinned, then brushed his lips over hers. "At long last I have all I have ever wanted."

She peeked up at him from beneath a fringe of long, thick lashes. "All you ever wanted was one gray hair?"

"No, Mattie. All I really want is you, to have you with me always. That is all I need to keep me happy."

Mattie snuggled into Seth's possessive embrace, assured that her lifelong search for just the right man was worth the wait. Seth Tremayne was everything she dreamed her perfect mate would be. She had discovered love everlasting. And *that*, Mattie knew for certain, was the true gift of magic . . . .

HIGHLAND BLOOD

Colleen Faulkner

One

Isle of Lochalsh
The Coast of Scotland
1898

"Master, the mail steamer comes. Should I go doon tae the dock and fetch the bookman, or do ye wish tae go yerself?"

Gordon Fraser glanced up from beneath the brim of his Spanish leather hat, gardening shears poised in his gloved hand. "Early this month," he mused.

"Aye." Angus's broad shovel-face remained inanimate. His hands, as always, were tucked neatly behind his back. "By at least an hour, master."

Gordon snipped the rose he had chosen and placed it carefully in a basket at his feet. The Mary Jean, he called this hybrid, after his maternal grandmother. He glanced at Angus. "I should like to go." A frown creased his brow. "But I suppose it wouldn't appear seemly, would it? The Laird of Fraser Castle bounding down the hill as if in search of a new playmate."

Gordon parted the thorned bush in search of another exquisite flower. "Nay. Go with ye." He shooed his manservant with the shears. "Fetch him, and I'll stay my distance until nightfall. We'll dine in the great room. It's so long since last I had a visitor." He glanced up again quickly. "Since someone *visited* me, I mean. Not since I—" he gestured "—you know, *had* one."

Angus's mouth barely moved as he spoke drolly. "Nearly one hundred years, master. Tae both counts."

Gordon chuckled, unprovoked by his manservant's remark. Angus intended no offense. It was the truth. "Time does fly, does it not?"

"Aye. I suppose for ye." Angus took a step back. "I will bring the bookman from the dock. What room should ye like him—tae sleep in, I mean, my lord?"

"The green room. It has a very pleasant view of the bay and a small library of its own. I should think he would like it."

Angus bowed stiffly. "As ye wish, master."

Gordon returned his attention to the rosebush as Angus disappeared into the arched doorway of the castle's courtyard. A door hinge squeaked, and Gordon made a mental note to see to its repair. He sighed. The door was only three hundred odd years old. Craftsmanship just wasn't what it used to be, was it?

Thunder rumbled in the sky. Clipping one more Highland rose, Gordon picked up the basket. Each flower he'd chosen was prettier than the last. They would be perfect on the table at the evening meal.

Tugging on the brim of his hat to block out the

brightness of the stormy sky, he started for the house. He wanted to choose the perfect wine from his cellar to accompany the poached fish Angus would be preparing.

Thank goodness E. Bruce MacDougal had finally arrived. Gordon began making arrangements with a broker in London for Mr. MacDougal's services nearly a year ago. If the man hadn't come on this steamer, Gordon didn't know what he would have done. He had a Gutenberg Bible with a few water-stained pages in need of repair, and he wanted to be certain the work was complete prior to the *anniversary*.

Gordon frowned as he made his way into the rear of the castle and down a stone passageway. He had told himself he wouldn't think about the *anniversary*. There was no need to become melancholy over that which he could not change. Besides, the matter was settled. Mr. MacDougal could do the restoration and still serve his purpose when the time came.

As Gordon walked, he whistled an ancient tune. He didn't know what made him think of it, but it reminded him of his little sister. She had loved that song. He smiled, halting to close his eyes and luxuriate in the memory. She'd had the prettiest blue eyes.

Gordon continued on his way, still whistling. It would be so nice to have a visitor after all this time. Even though he kept busy with his books and other treasures, he missed human companionship. And MacDougal would be here for a month! Four weeks of conversation beyond Angus's limited contributions was indeed a pleasant thought. Gordon hoped he would like Mr. MacDougal. Well, perhaps not too much, else it would make it more difficult to kill him, when the time came.

* * *

Dark rain clouds swirled overhead as Emily MacDougal followed the huge, hunch-shouldered man in the black frock coat up the hill from the dock. One leather satchel in each hand, she glanced over her shoulder and mouthed, "Come on" to her companion, Ruth Greenfield.

Ruth, carrying three monstrous bags, made a hideous face and gestured toward the man who had been introduced by the steamer's captain as Angus, Gordon Fraser's manservant. Angus had yet to speak a word. Ruth lifted her satchels high and comically imitated his stiff, lurching walk.

Emily rolled her eyes and gestured with her chin for Ruth to hurry. The path wound around and up, gradually growing steeper. As she walked, her own cases grew heavier.

Ahead, perched on a cliff overlooking the bay, loomed a great gray stone castle complete with towers and turrets. Emily had expected Fraser Castle to be grand, but not so dark and . . . mysterious. And where had the dark clouds and ominous thunder come from? Hadn't it been sunny when they left the mainland only a mile away?

"The castle is built in the classic Scottish Z-shape," Emily said. Facts and figures always had a calming affect on her. "With two square towers at diagonal opposing corners, it's easier to defend." She glanced doubtfully at the churning gray water far below beyond the sheer rock. "Though how someone could sneak up on them, I couldn't say."

Ruth hurried to catch up. It was beginning to rain.

"We should have gone to Paris. I told you to take the job in Paris."

"It wasn't a Gutenberg."

"It was Paris, the city of romance," Ruth declared theatrically. She was now dragging one of her bags.

"And miss the chance to see the Scottish Highlands?" Emily grunted, thankful she needed only a few supplies. Another bag and she'd surely have not made it to the castle door. The path had become so steep that she had to concentrate to keep her footing on the loose stones.

The manservant remained only a few paces ahead, but made no offer to lend any assistance to either of the women.

"Miss the chance to see the Highlands?" At the crest of the hill, Ruth set down her bags with a groan. "I'd be willing to miss the chance to carry my own bags," she panted.

The manservant with his gangly arms and legs and stiff, awkward gait continued.

"Come on, Ruth, we're almost there."

Muttering under her breath, Ruth straightened the brim of her straw hat and grabbed up the large, over-stuffed satchel again. "Next time, we go to Paris."

The rain began to fall in earnest as the manservant swung open the great iron door guarded by a gun-loop in a turret. Emily ducked in behind him. Ruth gave a squeal and broke into a run.

Just inside the door, in a small entryway, the manservant turned. He made no eye-contact with Emily, but folded his hands neatly behind his back and stared somewhere over her head. The hall was dark, but for dim candlelight that came from a sconce on the wall. Two sets of full mail armor guarded the door.

"I am instructed tae escort ye tae the green room," the manservant said, his speech thickly accented with a Highland brogue.

So he can speak, Emily thought wryly.

"I will ask the master," Angus continued, "where the other will stay."

Ruth dropped her bags on the floor with a loud thud, and sat on top of them, giving Emily another of her wide-eyed looks.

"Together will be quite acceptable, sir," Emily said, all-business in manner. "Just lead the way."

The manservant started up a large stone staircase that turned sharply halfway up to the first floor. Emily stared in wonder as she climbed. The staircase was wide enough to drive two carriages up it, side by side. Its walls were covered with a dark walnut wainscoting that had to be five centuries old. The broker in London had said the Laird of Fraser Castle was wealthy, but Emily had never encountered this degree of *affluence*.

The two women followed Angus up the stairs, down a dark corridor, to a door on the left. He opened it and stepped back, still avoiding eye-contact. "The evening meal will be served at seven," he explained in a deep voice. "Have ye further needs, ye may ring the bell cord."

Emily and Ruth passed Angus, and he closed the door behind them.

Ruth dropped her bags where she stood. "Is that Igor human? Though I must say, he is rather handsome in a Simian, rough sort of way."

Emily laughed. "It's *Angus,* not Igor." She set down her bags and turned slowly to take in the magnificent room. It was some twenty by thirty feet in size, with ceilings at least fifteen feet high; the walls were hung with emerald green tapestries depicting various biblical scenes. There were three monstrous windows, hung with matching green brocade drapes.

Emily walked to the windows to stare out at the bay far below. "Come look at the view," she breathed in awe. "It's magnificent."

Ruth flung herself down on the four poster bed hung with the same green brocade as the windows. "View? I say we check out the view from the boat. This place gives me the creeps. It's so dark." She shuddered audibly. "Like one of Stoker's settings in *Dracula.*"

Emily ignored her friend's reference to the book she was reading. Ruth's taste in literature tended to run to the odd. "Too late." She watched as the mail steamer made its way through the rough water below. "The captain said the boat only comes once a month." She turned away from the window with a shrug. "So I suppose we'll just have to get used to it—or light a few more candles."

"Ha! You say that now." Ruth rolled onto her stomach on the bed, revealing far more stocking beneath her skirt than was appropriate. "Just wait until Igor serves us bugs for dinner."

"A woman!" Gordon exploded.

Angus didn't flinch. "In truth, two, master."

Gordon's dark eyes widened in disbelief. "Two women?"

"Aye. She brought ... a traveling companion, master."

"A traveling companion? A traveling companion?"

Gordon strode across the cluttered library. "How could this error have possibly occurred?" He stubbed his toe on a wooden crate he'd yet to unpack. Pain shot up his foot and he hopped on the other.

Angus continued to stare straight ahead. "I do not ken, master."

"By the wife of a drunken MacDonald, I say again, how did this happen?" He flung a hand in the air. "I was very careful. I hired an E. Bruce MacDougal without family. A good Scottish name—" He glanced at Angus. "Though I can say I never cared much for the MacDougals of Nairn. Big as oxen, but wee brains."

"Aye, master."

Gordon halted in mid-stride, brushing back the shoulder length of hair that fell over his eyes. "Aye *what*, for haggis sake? Aye, you don't know how this happened, or *aye*, the MacDougals are dumb as pruning sheers?"

Angus's gaze never strayed. "Aye tae both, master."

Gordon stared for a moment at his manservant. He didn't know why he put up with Angus, except that no one else but the fisherman had answered his bid for employment in the last one hundred and fifty years. It seemed no one needed a job badly enough to set foot on Fraser Island, which in truth, Gordon could nay blame them. No, Angus annoyed him, but it annoyed him even more to haul his own water from the well in the courtyard and to cook his own meals.

With an exasperated huff, Gordon went back to pacing. "Well, just . . . just send her back. *Them* back."

"I canna, master."

Gordon turned around sharply and caught his shoulder on another wooden crate, this one standing higher than he was tall. "Ouch!" He rubbed his shoulder beneath his new blue velvet frock coat.

Angus waited patiently for Gordon to cease cursing. "Will there be anything else, master?"

Gordon groaned. "This is a fine predicament we're in, Angus." He glanced up. "Well, see to dinner as we discussed, and set a plate for Miss MacDougal's companion."

"Aye, master."

Somehow Angus managed to back out of the library, through the maze of boxes and crates, leaving Gordon alone to his woes.

Ruth held tightly to Emily's hand as the two women wound their way through the castle toward the great hall. Emily held a candle high to light their way in the darkness.

"I think I'd rather take my meal in our room," Ruth whispered.

Emily squeezed her hand. She was a no-nonsense person and certainly was not afraid of the dark. "You'd best put your romance novel aside, Ruth. It's affecting your brain. Surely you didn't expect Edison's electricity in Scotland!"

"A handful of tallow candles would suffice."

The women's footsteps echoed hollowly on the stone floor and off the walls. Ahead, light spilled from an arched, flying-buttress doorway. Gargoyle faces grinned from above the door.

"They're watching us," Ruth whispered.

"Who?"

"Them." She pointed to the wall.

Emily lifted her candle higher to study the portraits that lined the walls on both sides of the corridor. Men in stiff ruff collars and women with headdresses and strings of jewels sat stiffly in pose. Emily thought they were as enchanting as the rest of the castle and wondered who they all were. The Laird of Fraser's ancestors, no doubt.

"Look, there's Igor."

"Angus," Emily whispered under her breath. "Really, Ruth, you're quite impossible."

The unearthly manservant stood in the lighted doorway, staring into the darkness, but not directly at the women. He stepped back, drawing his hand to usher them in.

Emily expected to find her employer waiting in the great hall and was disappointed to discover that he'd not yet arrived. She was looking forward to an evening of scholarly discussion.

The room was large and airy, and to Ruth's liking, no doubt, well lit, with candelabras everywhere. A long, polished wood table had been set for three place settings with exquisite antique china from the Orient.

Emily released her companion's hand, setting the candlestand on a small Persian table. "It's beautiful," she murmured, turning slowly in a circle. The walls stretched high to a painted plaster ceiling that domed nearly twenty-five feet overhead. The paintings depicted Greek and Roman mythology.

Unimpressed, Ruth walked to the table and lifted a plate to study the back. "He has good taste in dishes. These must be at least a hundred years old."

"Ruth," Emily reprimanded. "Put down the plate

before you break it. How will it look to the laird if he finds us authenticating his china?"

"Most likely he'll think I'm checking to be certain he can afford to pay you. Which I am. And I would guess he can. Your Scotsman is very rich."

Emily took the plate from Ruth's hand and returned it to its place. "I don't care how wealthy he is. I'm here to provide a service."

"He could be *the one,*" Ruth teased in a whisper. "I keep telling you, you work for enough frogs, surely one of these days one will make you his princess."

Emily ran her fingers along a Cyprus sea chest that looked Italian in design, and very, very old. "I told you. I'm not looking for a husband." She smoothed the bodice of her plain, but sensible, pale blue brocade evening gown. It was the only good dress she'd brought. The other two were plain and practical, like herself. "I've a career. Money of my own. I don't need a husband and certainly not one old enough to be my grand-daddy."

"But you need love, don't you?" Ruth turned in a circle, lifting her spotted voile skirt as she danced. Ruth had brought enough clothing to stay six months rather than one, and each gown was more frivolous than the last.

Emily crossed her arms over her chest. She and Ruth had had this discussion a million times. "For a modern woman who's taken off, leaving her prospective bride-groom practically at the altar, you certainly have old-fashioned ideas."

Ruth lifted her tiny shoulders in a shrug. She was a petite woman with dark hair, a round face, and intri-guing green eyes that caught the attention of many an

admirer. "I want to marry for love, not for security.
Aaron ought to marry Daddy if he wants a portion of
the Greenfield jewelry empire."

Emily laughed. She was glad Ruth had come along.
She guessed Gordon Fraser would be as formal and
stodgy as her employers always were. It would have been
a long month with such company without Ruth.

"I still didn't think you should have left on such short
notice," Emily reprimanded gently, but then she smiled.
"But I'm glad you came—"

"Ladies."

Surprised by the masculine voice, Emily turned in
mid-sentence. "Lord Fraser," she began. "I'm so—"
For a moment her voice was lost. The broker in London
said Lord Fraser had been a long time client, his father's
before his. Emily had expected an ancient, stoop-shoul-
dered, white-haired man, carrying a cane.

Emily had to tighten her jaw to keep it from dropping
to her knees.

Gordon Fraser was no older than thirty years, with a
slim build, roguish black shoulder-length hair . . . and
the most hauntingly handsome face Emily had ever laid
eyes upon.

Two

"M . . . Mr . . . Lord Fraser . . ." Emily fumbled, feeling like a complete fool to stare at a man so. "I'm Emily MacDougal and this is my traveling companion, Ruth Greenfield."

"My lord!" Ruth stalked over to the Laird of Fraser Castle, her hand thrust out, her hips swaying.

Gordon Fraser accepted Ruth's hand and shook it politely, but his dark-eyed gaze fixed on Emily. "Mr. Fraser will suffice," he said coolly. His gaze strayed to Ruth as she withdrew her hand, then back to Emily. "I'm indeed laird of the castle, but my family was never graced by title." He had a slight Scottish lilt, but it was nothing like Angus's heavy brogue.

Emily still stared, her mouth still agape. "I . . . I'm pleased to meet you, sir." She made no attempt to shake his hand. Surely this was a mistake. This was Gordon

Fraser's son or grandson. This man could not possibly have been served by the Boggs family for seventy years.

Gordon Fraser stood erect, his hands at his sides, but he had none of the stiffness of the manservant. "I do not mean to be inhospitable, but I believe a terrible error has occurred."

"I'll say there's been an error," Ruth murmured, amusement plain in her voice.

"An error . . . yes. I suppose." Emily felt like a complete imbecile. "I was hired by the Lord of Fraser Castle to repair a rare original Gutenberg Bible. He . . . my Mr. Fraser, well not mine, was elderly."

Gordon tore his gaze from hers. "How ironic," he said dryly, moving to the head of the table. "My E. Bruce MacDougal was male."

Emily felt her cheeks grow warm with embarrassment, and she averted her gaze.

Mr. Fraser pulled out a chair to his right, which Ruth immediately slipped into. He placed his hand on the back of the chair to his left, indicating for Emily to sit.

She took her seat. "I . . . I apologize for misleading you . . . if I did in some way."

He sat. "My guess would be that you misled me intentionally, *Miss* MacDougal, and I do not appreciate being misled. You should not have come here."

She lifted the linen napkin from the table and placed it on her lap. She had been repairing antique books and manuscripts for more than eight years. While studying art in Paris and Rome she'd discovered she had a touch for it. But in the last eight years she'd never had a position begin so awkwardly. Her employers were always surprised by the fact that she was female, but none had ever been so openly annoyed.

And what was the point of being angry now? She was here, whether he liked it or not, for the next thirty days. The mail steamer, the only way to and from the island, wouldn't return for a month, and she already knew the Scotsman had no vessel of his own. The captain of the steamer had said so himself, remarking how odd it was that a man should imprison himself on an island.

Emily wanted this job. She wanted the Gutenberg. And now that she was here, he was stuck with her.

"Mr. Fraser." She gazed directly into his angry eyes. "Would you have hired me, had you known I was female?"

He withdrew the cork from a bottle of wine. "Nay. Wine?"

She wondered how he could be so polite and hospitable as if he was glad for her company, and yet so obviously annoyed with her. She lifted her glass to him, intrigued. She had always thought of men as simple creatures, too elementary to bear more than one emotion, or even thought, at the same time. "Thank you."

He filled her glass with one smooth and elegant motion, his hand large but graceful. It was a fascinating hand, clean, with fingertips stained by ink. Like her own.

She watched the rich Merlot flow into the stemmed vessel. "That is why I do not indicate my gender when offering my services, though I certainly do not conceal it."

"It never occurred to me that a woman—" He corrected himself—"that E. Bruce was a man."

"Why would it not occur to you?" she challenged. "A woman could certainly repair your Gutenberg— should she be duly qualified—as adeptly as a man."

"I agree."

"Because I'm a woman," Emily continued her well-rehearsed version of a suffragette's speech, "that does not mean that my eye is not as well trained, my hands not as steady."

"Most certainly."

"I employ this minor deception—" Emily continued.

"Emily—" Ruth tried to interrupt.

"No, I am *forced* to use this minor deception because—"

"Emily," Ruth repeated from across the table. "He's agreeing with you. You'd better shut up while you're ahead."

Emily glanced up to see Ruth's eyes twinkling with amusement, her wine glass poised at her lips.

Emily's gaze naturally reverted to her employer. She wasn't prepared for a man who agreed with her. She had no speech for that. "If . . . if you concur, then why—"

"I hired a male rather than a female for my own reasons." He sipped the wine that was the deep red purple of blood. "Good reasons."

Her eyes widened. "What? A woman shouldn't pursue a career, even if she is talented?" That argument she had heard, from her own father.

"I dinna say that."

"That I would be better off at home, an apron tied round my waist, and my husband's children at my feet?"

"I dinna say that either." Mr. Fraser spoke louder, more agitated.

"Or is it merely that I should not be traveling without a male protector, for surely—"

"Miss MacDougal!" The Laird of Fraser Castle rose

from his chair, the heels of his hands pressing on the table. He leaned toward her, his masculinity frighteningly evident. "You speak of that which ye know nothing of."

She rose to lean across the table, not caring if it was an unlady-like gesture. She never was very lady-like to begin with. "Then tell me what I don't know. Why are you so angry?" Imitating his stance, she brought her face only inches from his. "Why don't you want me here?"

"Because it's not safe."

Emily laughed, but she was not amused. She was tired of the sexist manners and opinions of men. In two years the twentieth century would be upon them and she was determined to be a twentieth century woman, to lead the way for other women. She looked directly into his intelligent, but somehow haunted, eyes. "I assure I'm not afraid of you, nor your loping manservant."

Gordon Fraser drew back his sensual mouth. "It is not safe, Miss MacDougal, for you, nor your companion, because I am a vampire."

Ruth, who Emily had all but forgotten, burst into laughter.

Emily blinked, certain she had not heard what she thought she heard. "Pardon?"

He lifted his hands off the table and walked away. Emily remained standing.

"I don't want you here because I am a vampire, Miss MacDougal. I am one of the living dead." He turned to face her. "Surely a well-educated woman such as yourself knows what a vampire is."

"Count Dracula," Ruth whispered.

Emily flashed her friend a reprimanding glare to

silence her. She would handle this. Emily was accustomed to eccentric men. Most of the gentlemen who employed her were outlandish in some manner or another, by reason of wealth or age or both. One of her English employers had bathed only in wine vinegar thinking it a youth elixir. Another, in California, had owned a pack of spaniels whom he called his children and who all dined at the dinner table along with him, each possessing his own Louis XIV chair. But this was the first client she had served who thought himself a vampire.

Emily clamped her hand on her mouth to keep from giggling. There was no need to be rude—after all, she was to be this man's guest, like it or not, for the next month. "A vampire, sir?"

"A vampire." He began to pace. "Not because I want to be, but because I was a victim." He brushed back his hair in a most tantalizing way. "I'm cursed."

Ruth, too, had covered her mouth to suppress another fit of giggles. She nodded to encourage Emily.

Emily returned her nod and sipped her wine. "Cursed, you say?"

"Aye." He paced, making grand gestures. "I can't believe I'm telling ye this, but I don't get many visitors."

Ruth leaned on the table, propping her chin on her hand, watching as if she were at a performance. "I can see why . . . you being a vampire, I mean. Not because you're not rich and handsome."

Gordon Fraser sighed. "It's so difficult for a man to keep something like this inside," he explained.

Emily would have laughed again at such words coming from a man, but there was a sincerity in his voice that tempered her.

"I didn't want to be a vampire," he continued. "I was a farmer's son. We were forced to raise arms against the English. I was on the battlefield, minding my own business, killing Englishmen, when I saw one of my fellow Highlanders fall."

Emily couldn't believe she was listening to this nonsense, and yet she couldn't *not* listen.

"I laid down my broadsword to drag him off the battlefield. In the fog and confusion of the battle I became disoriented. I left him to go back for my sword when suddenly he appeared before me. I struggled, but his strength was inhuman. He bit me and drew blood." Gordon brushed back his silky black hair to bare his neck. "Here."

Emily saw no mark . . . not that she was expecting teeth punctures or anything as silly as that. "He bit you?" She wondered what had gotten into her. If she was going to spend the next month in this lunatic's home, she certainly shouldn't be encouraging him.

"Aye." Gordon turned to face her, as if he thought she was being taken in by his ridiculous story. "He drank my blood. I died, and then I came back to life as a vampire myself."

Ruth helped herself to another glass of wine. "Bet that made you angry."

"Aye. I was very angry, I have to confess, so angry that I killed him. I'm not proud of the fact, but it's true."

"Then what did you do?" Ruth said. "Drink the blood of everyone else on the battlefield—Englishmen only of course," she conceded with the show of her palms.

"No." He seemed quite insulted. "I did what I had to do. I came here to this island and made it my own.

I imprisoned myself here so that no other would come to harm because of me."

It was Emily's turn to chime in. She just couldn't resist. "So you're a vampire that does *not* drink blood."

"That's impossible," he stated flatly, almost painfully. "It's against our nature. And that is why you are in mortal danger, my dear Miss MacDougal."

Emily didn't believe in vampires. Not werewolves, nor mummies, or even witches with black cauldrons, but for the ones in the Shakespearean collection she had restored. But for a moment, one fleeting moment, she almost believed Gordon Fraser was a vampire. He appeared so sincere that she believed *he* believed he was a vampire.

Emily decided to play along, perhaps because she felt sorry for the self-imposed hermit, or perhaps because he was so damned attractive. "You fear you're going to bite me?" she asked. "That's why I'm in danger?"

"Aye," he exhaled. "Well, not immediate mortal danger." He began to pace again. "I have mostly been able to curtail my innate tendencies, but every century, on the eve of the anniversary of when I first became one of the undead, I must have human blood."

"Or what?" she whispered, feeling herself drawn in, against her will, to his delusion.

"Or I will die an agonizing death."

Emily felt herself shudder. Then she realized what he was saying . . . and how ridiculous it was. She smiled tenderly. "Mr. Fraser, I don't know who has filled your head with this nonsense, but you are not a vampire."

He strode toward her. "But I am. Ye must believe me. And ye must flee as soon as ye can."

She decided to play along, rather than argue. She

still wanted to lay her hands—her restorative touch—on the Gutenberg. "But the mail steamer won't be here for another month. Won't my companion and I be safe until then?"

He reached out his hand, as if he were going to touch her, then pulled away. "Aye." He went on with more confidence. "Aye, ye should be . . . ye *will* be. But you must go on the next steamer. My anniversary is but a month and a day from today." He returned to his seat at the head of the table, and Angus appeared toting covered plates.

Emily leaned back so that the manservant could serve her. Wondering if she should expect raw liver or worse, she was pleasantly surprised to see what he revealed beneath the cover. Apparently vampires not only drank the blood of humans, but also dined on poached fish, boiled new potatoes, and fresh green beans.

She returned her napkin to her lap. "Out of curiosity, Mr. Fraser, what had you intended to do with the man you thought you had hired?"

He passed her a wooden trencher of fresh bread. "To allow him to restore the Gutenberg, of course."

"And then?"

"Drink his blood."

Ruth picked up her fork with a shrug. "Of course."

"And when he did not return to the mainland?"

The Scottish laird took a bite of the fish. "A fishing boat accident." He shook his head. "Tragic."

Emily sampled the fish. The amazing thing was, Gordon Fraser didn't sound crazy, just what he said was crazy. "And how old are you . . . in vampire years?"

"The calendar is the same, I assure you," he said loftily. "Roughly six hundred."

Emily nearly dropped her fork. "Years?"

Ruth made a sound that distinctly resembled a snort of laughter.

"Aye." The Scotsman lifted the trencher. "Another bit of bread? Angus is a better baker than a fisherman."

Emily shook her head. "No, thank you." She grimaced. "So if every one hundred years you must take a life, the next one . . . in one month and one day will be your—"

"My sixth." He nodded. "Precisely."

Emily leaned toward her host, the vampire. "And what explanation did you offer for their deaths?"

"Fishing accident, of course."

"Of course," Ruth echoed.

"Because I am forced to partake only once every century," Gordon shrugged, "no mortals live to realize a man dies of a fishing accident off my island every one hundred years."

She smiled patronizingly, as fascinated by the man as by his delusion. "What of your manservant? Why have you not eaten him?"

Gordon grimaced. "Please, Miss MacDougal, we are dining." He took a swallow of water from a Venetian crystal goblet, as if to wash away the gruesome thought. "I am a vampire, not a cannibal. I do not *eat* my victims. I merely drink every drop of blood from their bodies."

"Phew." Ruth reached for the wine bottle again. "You had me frightened there for a minute, Gordy."

He flashed a handsome smile at Ruth. "You're very funny." He looked back at Emily. "Your friend is very funny."

"Thank you," Emily said, at a loss as how else to answer.

"You're welcome." He smiled again, but this time the smile was all for Emily. Then his expression changed to one of surprise. "As for your question, I could nay drink the blood of my manservant. Who would poach the fish?"

"Who indeed?" Emily cut a new potato in half and stabbed a piece into her mouth, still expecting to wake from this absurd dream at any moment. The potato was delicious and moist with a hint of the flavor of thyme.

"Well." Gordon wiped his mouth politely with his napkin and allowed Angus to remove his plate. "Since you're here, I suppose we should make the best of the situation."

Emily sat straighter in her chair, smiling. "You mean the Gutenberg?"

He pointed with one slender finger. "Wait until you see it, my dear."

If Emily hadn't known better, she would have thought the Scotsman was flirting with her. Not that she'd ever had much experience with that. She left all the cooing and eyelash batting to Ruth.

"Let me tell you how I obtained the masterpiece," he said.

She leaned forward, filled with excitement. She could tell by the sparkle in his dark eyes that he was as fascinated by the rare Bible as she was. At this moment she could have cared less if Gordon Fraser thought he was a vampire or President McKinley.

Three

"I think he likes you." Ruth giggled and snuggled deeper beneath the down bedcovers. The chamber was dark save for the light of the fire in the fireplace. The long case clock on the landing outside their door struck ten.

Emily slid closer to her friend in the big bed so that they might share body warmth. The wind howled outside and the fire crackled and spit as it was fed from the gusts blowing down the chimney. "Oh, he does not. He was merely being polite."

"Polite, my fangs." Ruth pushed up on one elbow to face Emily. "I saw the way his brown eyes twinkled. The way his hand *accidentally* touched yours when he poured you more wine. He'd have rattled on all night about those old dusty books if I'd not fallen asleep with my face in the pudding."

"You're being ridiculous." Emily rolled onto her side

to face Ruth. Despite the cold Highland air, she was toasty warm beneath the weight of the quilts. "He was only being polite. We share the same interests."

"Each other?" Ruth purred.

Emily flopped down on her back. Ruth knew her too well, better sometimes than she knew herself. She was captivated by Gordon Fraser, as much for his mind as his striking good looks. But she wasn't ready to admit that attraction, not to Ruth, not even to herself. "Ruth. I am a professional woman. I do not form *interests* in my employers." She cut her eyes at Ruth. "And certainly not my vampire employers."

Ruth burst into a fit of giggles and fell onto the mattress, kicking her legs wildly. "A vampire! Can you believe he actually said that with a straight face? I think he was hurt that we didn't believe him."

Emily elbowed her companion. "Ruth, hush. You're too loud. What if he hears you?"

Ruth popped up in the bed again. "You mean, what if Igor hears. Next thing you know," she said in a spooky voice, "he'll be crawling up the sides of the castle wall in haste to tell his master."

"Ruth!" Emily tried to sound appalled, but a moment later, she was laughing with her. "It really is quite funny," she whispered. "Gordon Fraser a vampire . . . a rather handsome vampire," she dared.

"A minor eccentricity," Ruth said. "Considering the man's obvious virility. I'd take him for myself, but he's not my type. I prefer a more . . . physical man."

Emily tugged the bedcovers to her chin and stared at the canopy overhead. The light and dark shadows thrown from the fireplace made eerie patterns on the rich fabric. Suddenly she was a little frightened, not of the eerie castle, or the hulking Angus, but by her own feelings.

"I'm telling you," Ruth whispered as her laughter subsided. "This one may be your prince."

Gordon sat in a chair beneath a reading lamp and attempted to concentrate on the copy of *The Canterbury Tales* he'd just acquired from Great Britain. He strove to hear the beauty of the cadence of Chaucer's middle English, but to no avail. Each time he tackled another stanza, Miss Emily MacDougal, the American, interfered. No matter how he tried to push her from his thoughts, she slipped in again, all bright-eyed, warm, despite her business-like attitude, and filled with the same love of books he possessed.

Finally, in exasperation, Gordon set aside the book and retrieved the snifter of brandy Angus had brought him.

"Ye would want another book, master?" Angus moved quietly about the tower bedchamber, tidying up. It was their usual routine, one they had carried on for the twenty years since the bright, young, seasick Angus had come to work for him at the age of twelve.

Gordon sipped the century old French brandy he'd bought just before the French revolution. It was as smooth as silk. "Nay. 'Twould make no difference. I'm not in a mood for reading tonight."

"The guests," Angus said simply, as he returned several books to the shelf beside Gordon's curtained four poster bed.

"Aye." Gordon leaned forward, resting his elbows on his knees. He'd dressed for bed in a Chinese silk robe and slippers with gold tassels at the heels. "She's so damned beautiful, Angus."

His manservant paused. "The companion, master?"

"Nay. Miss MacDougal. Emily. She's so damned beautiful, and her mind, her mind." He gestured with his hands. "She's so bright and articulate. Did you see the way she smiled politely when I told her I was one of the undead? That woman isn't afraid of anything, Angus. Sweet heather! I love a woman with a spine."

Angus went back to picking up books, papers, and assorted clothing from the floor, chairs, and tables. "She didna believe ye, master."

"Nay. She did not." He rose, casting a long shadow across the plastered wall. "For a short while I felt like the old Gordon Fraser I was, though a little older, a little wiser. It's been so long since someone showed interest in me, the man I am." He touched his left breast, then let his hand fall. "Not what I have become," he finished bitterly.

"Ye canna help what ye are, master."

Gordon glanced up, thankful for Angus's companionship. "No more than ye can help being born a fisherman with a weak stomach."

"Ye have told me many times." A path cleared to the bed, Angus pulled back his master's bedcovers. "We are what we are, my master."

"And thankful to have each other, aye, Angus?" Gordon patted his manservant on his back.

Angus took Gordon's drink from him. "Sleep, master; ye will nay feel so melancholy on the morrow. Ye have a full month of the lady's companionship to enjoy."

"And then what?"

"Ye will send her on her way, master . . . or keep her."

Gordon turned sharply and the round tower room seemed to spin with him. "Ye do not suggest I drink of her blood, Angus? Ye know I do not take women against their wills. Above all else, despite my curse, I am a Highlander and a gentleman."

Angus halted at the door and lifted his candle so that the light cast across his broad, plain Scot's face. "Mayhap it wouldna be against her will, master."

"I'd sooner die," Gordon said softly, "than take her life."

"I dinna say you must take her life. Ye could . . ." Angus hesitated. "Ye could make her one of your own, master, and then ye would share the joy of your books forever."

"A companion," Gordon said softly, turning away. "I yearn for a companion. A woman." He lowered his hands to his sides, tightening them into fists. "But I willna do it. I willna force my way of life upon her."

"Ye said yourself she had a mind of her own. There are many advantages to eternal life. Ye are a charming man. Perhaps she would choose to—"

"Nay, Angus." He took a swipe at the air with one hand. "I willna have it."

"As ye wish, master." Angus left the room and closed the door behind him.

Only once the door had shut and he was alone did Gordon realize the depth of his loneliness. Six hundred years was a long time to endure without a shared kiss, a caress, without a woman he cared for . . . loved. Emily MacDougal would be so easy to love. But would she be easy to kill?

* * *

Emily turned slowly in a circle as she stared at the shelves of books that lined all four walls, floor to ceiling, of Gordon Fraser's library. She was overwhelmed by the vast collection. She'd never thought there was another with a passion for old books to match her own, but she knew she'd found him. Gordon's interest didn't seem to be in the monetary worth of the tomes so much as the worth of what was inside them. That was as important to her as his love for the books.

"I've never seen so many books in one library," she breathed in awe.

Gordon leaned against the door jamb, his arms crossed over his chest. She hadn't been able to help but notice that his black frock coat was freshly pressed, his Irish lace cravat brand new. If she didn't know better, she'd have thought he dressed for her.

"I dare admit collecting and reading has become my major interest. It's a good way to pass many lonely days."

Emily ran a long, slender finger down the leather spines of his books. "Herodotus, Calderon, Machiavelli, Boccaccio," she said. "And American authors, too! Jefferson, Grant, Poe." She spun around to face him, secretly pleased she'd allowed Ruth to dress her this morning. She wore a blue brocade gown that Ruth said emphasized the color of her eyes and highlighted her red-blonde hair. "Where did you get all these books?"

He shrugged, seeming embarrassed by her attention. *Modest, too.* Emily admired a modest man.

"Acquired them over the years." He smiled almost bashfully. By the light of the day, he seemed younger, even more elegant than last night. "I've had many years to collect, ye know."

She smiled, realizing he was teasing her about his tale of being a vampire. By the light of day, the illusion was harmless enough, even charming. "Of course. You've been acquiring for what, about six hundred years now?" A book caught her eye and she pulled out the volume. "Is this really an original collection of Shakespeare's comedies?" She opened the cover and perused the first page.

"Aye to your first question and your last." He walked over to the bookshelf she stood before and pulled out a couple of volumes. "You'll want to see these, too."

She accepted the books, but weighed down by them, glanced around the crowded room for somewhere to sit.

"I'm sorry I've no chairs. I had my last manservant remove them so there'd be more room for the books. But you're welcome to take a crate." He scooped up a pile of books from the nearest chair-height shipping crate.

Emily didn't care where she sat, she just wanted to get a better look at the Shakespearean collection. Without bothering to dust off the box, she sat down. "Are all these boxes filled with books?" She glanced up from her perch.

There was a desk, piled with books, two tables, piled with books, and then at least a dozen slatted wooden crates, some as tall as she was, stacked in the room. To reach the shelves at the far side of the twelve-by-fourteen room, she would have to weave her way through the maze of boxes and draped objects.

"Aye, well, most of them. Also a few paintings. I buy

things, but then sometimes it takes me a while to get them unpacked and placed where I want them." He scowled, perplexed, as he gazed at the crowded room. "I've a DaVinci sketch I picked up from Rome some hundred, hundred and fifty years ago, and I've not been able to locate it." He pried back a slat in the nearest box, peered in, and coughed as dust rose from inside. "Nay, not here. This one's from Cairo."

She glanced up from the book, amazed by the man. None of her employers had ever amazed her before. No man, in fact. "Egypt?" She could have sworn she smelled hot, dry, sand. Of course he was teasing her again. One hundred and fifty years, indeed.

"Aye." He grinned at her boyishly. "A bit of sculpture from a tomb. I'd prefer to see the artifacts left where they lie, but alas, that's not always possible, is it?"

He seemed saddened by his words and she felt a softness for him. Then she felt silly for falling for his ruse. The box probably had no Egyptian artifacts from a tomb in it. It was probably just full of sand.

She lifted an eyebrow. "So you buy the artifacts to protect them?"

"Better I say that collectors such as myself should purchase them to keep them from being sawed in half and sold in pieces. Often I make an acquisition and then donate the artifact to a museum."

She lowered her gaze to the book on her lap. He was right of course. She'd recently had the same discussion with a would-be employer who had wanted her to remove illuminated pages from a fifteenth century book of prayer to sell as framed prints. Needless to say, she'd not taken the position.

"You're welcome to look at any of the books here. I

know you understand their worth, so you'll take care
with them." Gordon stepped over a small box and
tugged on a canvas dust cover. "Aha, there she is. I
wondered where she'd gotten to."

Emily stared in wonder as he uncovered a life-size
statue of a woman carved from stone. "Greek?" she
breathed, feeling again as if she were dreaming. It
looked authentic. Could it be?

"Most likely Macedonian. Found at the bottom of the
harbor in Athens about—"

She raised her palm. "Please don't tell me it was
found four hundred years ago."

"Actually about five hundred," he admitted sheep-
ishly. "I was just beginning to dabble in collecting then."

She closed the copy of Shakespeare in her lap, exasperated. She really liked Gordon Fraser. Why did he
have to be psychotic? "Mr. Fraser—"

"Please, call me Gordon." He began to recover the
statue of the woman, crowned with stone laurel leaves.

"If we're going to be together for the next month,
you might as well call me Emily."

There was that shy smile. Surely he wasn't flirting with
her again? "I should like that Miss . . . Emily."

She rose from the crate, setting the books down carefully. "Do you mind if I speak frankly then, Gordon?"

"Please do."

She rested her hand on her hips, suddenly feeling
silly in Ruth's blue dress, with her hair piled on her
head and little pin curls at her temples. Had she really
spent an hour readying herself for a day with a man
who thought himself a vampire? "Gordon, this vampire
. . . thing." She tucked one of the annoying little curls
behind her ear. "You don't really think you're a vam-

pire, do you? Last night's tale . . . it was just for entertainment. Like telling tales around the fire on cold nights."

"I was being honest with ye, Emily. I am a vampire."

The statue covered, he faced her. She had always been such an excellent judge of character. He looked so honorable and forthright. He looked like he believed what he said.

"You can't be a vampire," she said impatiently.

He leaned against the Egyptian crate. "Why not?"

"Well, because . . . because . . ." Uncomfortable, she glanced away. Sunlight shone through the room's only window. She looked back at him. "Because vampires can't stand the light."

He glanced at the arched window, amusement twitching on his sensual lips. "Everyone knows the sun nay really shines in the Highlands, lass," he said with a feigned Scottish brogue to match Angus's.

She had to admit even a sunny day did seem overcast here in the Highlands. She narrowed her eyes. "Do you sleep in a coffin?" she shot.

He crossed his arms over his chest and made a ghastly face. "Ods fish, no."

"See that." She pointed. "Ruth is reading Bram Stoker's *Dracula*. Have you read it? Just published last year. Dracula sleeps in a coffin."

"Stoker writes romantic fiction." He lifted a slender, masculine finger to point back at her. Their fingertips nearly touched. "Entertaining fiction, but fiction nonetheless."

Now she was really frustrated. She had been the best debater at her woman's college. Where were those skills now? "The vampire legend was created to frighten people." She folded her arms over her chest triumphantly.

"Everyone knows there's really no such thing as vampires."

"Everyone is wrong."

Emily threw up her arms. "We're really not making any progress here, Gordon."

"Emily, I canna change what I am, nor lie about what I am . . . not even for ye."

Emily froze as he freed the curl she'd tucked behind her ear. It was a simple gesture, innocent enough, but it made her palms damp, her knees weak, and her heart beat faster.

"I like the curls," he said softly. "They become your lovely face."

Emily moistened her dry lips. No one had ever called her lovely before. He had taken her completely off guard. These type of encounters were supposed to take place at night, in romantic gardens, shadowed hallways, not in mid-morning in a library stacked with books.

She swallowed. She didn't know what she would do if he tried to kiss her.

God help her, she might kiss him back.

Gordon held her gaze so long that she thought for sure he would kiss her. Then he glanced away and the spell was broken. "Would you like to see the Gutenberg?"

Suddenly she felt foolish. She must have imagined more than had actually occurred. Of course Gordon hadn't intended to kiss her. She was acting as flighty as Ruth. "Oh, yes, yes, I would. I'll get right to work on it."

He halted at the doorway to allow her to pass. "I didn't mean that ye must get straight to work. You have the entire month. I want ye to enjoy yourself at Fraser

Castle. I only meant that ye might like to see it. It truly is remarkable. It's above in a storage room." He shrugged. "More books than space."

She passed him, but then waited for him to join her at her side. The romantic moment had passed, and they were once again just colleagues. As they talked on their way down the corridor and up the grand stairs, Emily relaxed. This type of relationship she could handle. So what if Gordon thought himself a vampire? Was that really any stranger than the man with the dogs in the Louis XIV chairs?

"Fisherman, you say?" Ruth perched on the large oak worktable in the center of the cozy kitchen. She sat on her hands, swinging her legs as she chatted with Angus.

Ruth had originally come to the kitchen seeking Igor out of boredom. Emily and the vampire were so busy with the Gutenberg and each other that they'd barely acknowledged her presence in the dining room, where Emily had laid out the tools of her trade. Besides, the ink made Ruth sneeze. But now that she was here, she found she was actually enjoying the Scot's company. And he was a fine-looking man, in a hulking, au natural sort of way.

"Aye." Angus shook his head as he peeled an onion. He had removed his black coat and wore an apron over his linen shirt. "My whole family have been fishermen for as long as we've hated Englishmen. 'Tis what our men do."

"Then why did you come here? I mean that Gordon Fraser, he's nice enough, but you have to admit, he's a little strange, living in self-imposed exile on this island and telling everyone he's a vampire.''

Angus placed the onion on the table and split it in half with a small cleaver. "I had no choice," he said in his thick Scottish brogue. "My father wanted me tae be a fisherman like him and his father before him, but I couldna fish. I was an embarrassment tae my clan. A MacReed who couldna fish.''

Ruth watched as he cut the onion into tiny slivers, as fascinated by his voice as his tale. "Oh, I understand what it is to be a disappointment to your father. Mine wanted me to marry his partner, but he's just not the man for me." She snatched a cube of raw potato from one of the piles he'd made on the work table. "Why couldn't you fish, Ig . . . Angus?''

He sniffed and continued to dice the onion. "I am ashamed tae tell ye, lass, but I get deathly ill at sea.''

Ruth's eyes widened. "A fisherman's son who gets seasick?''

With the back of one meaty hand, he wiped at the tears that gathered in the corners of his eyes. "Aye. I tried. The sweet Virgin knows I tried, but I couldna. Whilst my father and brothers brought in the nets, I knelt with my head hung over the side." He sniffed again loudly.

Ruth dug into her sleeve and produced a fresh white hanky.

Angus set down his cleaver and accepted the lacy bit of fabric. "I had no choice but tae take the master's position as manservant." He dabbed at his eyes.

Ruth felt her throat tighten. "Oh, Angus, that's such a sad story.''

He hung his head, blotting his nose with her hanky.

"Aye. 'Tis, indeed. What kind of a man am I that I must find work in a kitchen?"

Ruth jumped off the table and ran her hand down Angus's muscular forearm. "I say that makes you more a man. You stood up to your father."

"I should have been a fisherman."

"Do you like being a manservant?" She let her hand rest on his arm.

"Aye."

"Do you like cooking and cleaning?"

"Aye."

"Then you are a man among men. You sought the life you wanted, not the one that was forced upon you by bloodlines or a manipulating father."

Angus glanced up, his eyes red from his tears. "Do ye think so?" He sniffed.

"I do. Now blow that nose of yours." She patted him. "How about you show me how to make that Highlander stew? I bet my matzo balls would be great in it."

Four

Gordon walked the lee side of the island's shore, gazing at the dark, churning water. Seagulls soared and sang overhead, and the waves crashed against the rocks as the last of the sun's rays sparkled off the surface. But his mind was not on the beauty of the ocean or the setting sun.

Two precious weeks with Emily lost, he thought.

Where had the days gone? Spent talking, laughing, walking in the rose garden. Gordon watched her work at the dining table in the great hall by the hour. He was fascinated by the way her nimble hands moved as she brushed the gilt paint onto the damaged pages of his Gutenberg, bringing the illuminations alive again. He was entranced by the way her blue eyes sparkled as they discussed and sometimes argued over literature they had read. At some point, Gordon had fallen in love with those hands, with that laughter, with those

blue eyes, bluer than the skies over his beloved Highlands.

And now in two weeks his Emily would be gone, gone
from him forever, and he would be alone again.

Gordon felt a lump rise in his throat and he swallowed
against his sadness. He picked up a piece of driftwood
and tossed it carelessly into the water. The foaming
white surf picked it up and carried it away . . . just as it
would soon carry Emily away. The cold water splashed
at his ankles, wetting his shoes and trousers, ruining
the fine wool, but he waded deeper.

The last few days he'd been thinking long and hard
about his plight. In a fortnight and one day he would
require human blood. If he did not take it, he would
die. In the past, on each anniversary, he had taken a
life not because he wanted to, but because he had not
wanted to die. Now, he wasn't so sure he wanted to live.
Before Emily, he'd been content with his books and
paintings. He'd been satisfied with his rose garden, and
with Angus, and with the manservants that had come
before the fisherman. But now, since he had come to
know Emily and the life that bubbled from her, he knew
he hadn't really been living. Life was not an isolated
island, a castle filled with magnificent treasures. Life was
someone to love. Life for Gordon had become Emily.

Angus's suggestion crept into his mind as it had many
times in the last fortnight. *Take her as your own; make her
one of your own,* the manservant had suggested. Gordon's
dark side was tempted. The thought of living eternally
with Emily was wickedly enticing. They could share in
collecting together; they could read, discuss, dine,
dance, make love . . . forever.

Gordon clenched his fists at his sides, fighting the

temptation. If he made Emily a vampire, she would live at his side forever. He would taste her hot, sweet blood, and they would share an ecstasy no human could comprehend—

"No!" Gordon shook his fist at the gulls and the sea. "I canna. I won't. But I want to," he finished softly.

He kicked at a rock that jutted from the shore and savored the pain that shot up his leg.

He was sickened by his own thoughts, desires. It was an element of the vampire's curse that as he neared his anniversary wicked thoughts began to seep into his mind.

Of course he could not make Emily a vampire. Not even—his heart gave trip—even if she would be willing. He would not have it. Gordon knew she cared for him, perhaps even shared the love he felt for her, though they had never spoken of it. But he could not take Emily as his own because that would mean that every one hundred years, she too, would have to drink of human blood. She, too, would be tortured by the overwhelming desire to kill. He would not wish that curse upon anyone, not even his greatest enemy.

So what was he going to do? The anniversary grew closer, even now, minute by minute, creeping up on him like the shadows that sometimes disturbed his sleep.

What would he do? Gordon opened his eyes wide to see the majesty of the great blue ocean. He already knew the answer before he asked himself the question.

He would live his life to the fullest for the next two weeks and then ... He summoned his courage.

Then when Emily and her friend Ruth were safely on the steamer, he would send Angus away with his fishermen brothers who often passed their shore, and Gordon would die alone in his castle.

A sound made Gordon look up and to his surprise he saw Emily. He halted in the surf, mesmerized.

Her back was to him; she was unaware of his presence. She had discarded her woolen stockings and button boots on the shore and waded into the shallow water. She lifted her skirt and laughed, looking down.

He wondered what she saw. What made her laugh? Small fish nibbling at her ankles, perhaps?

As she turned, still not seeing him, her red-gold hair reflected in the setting sun. She was beautiful, so innocent.

Her blood would be so warm, so sweet . . . .

Gordon suddenly felt a painful tightening in his chest. Without warning, his breath caught in his throat and he was dizzy. Black spots appeared before his eyes. Her innocence, her innate goodness, was making his own black heart sick.

"Gordon?"

He heard Emily's voice, but she sounded as if she were at a greater distance than she was.

"Gordon, what is it? Are you all right?"

He heard her splashing toward him. The darkening sky spun overhead and the seagulls seemed to cry his name. She appeared beside him. Her warm touch on his hand . . . her soft, urgent voice. His desire for her blood faded. All he craved now was her gentle touch.

"Gordon, what is it? What's wrong?"

The pain in his chest gripped like a vise. The twilight sky spun faster overhead. The sea roared in his ears. Gordon felt his knees buckle and Emily's strong grip on his arm as he went down. Then there was nothing but blackness . . . and relief from his tortured soul.

Emily turned the page of her book and glanced up at Gordon, who still slept. It was past midnight. Twice, Angus had come up to the tower bedchamber to suggest she turn in for the night. He promised he would sit with his master, but she wanted to stay. She needed to stay.

Emily stared at the pages of Irish poetry but didn't see the words. She was sick with worry over Gordon.

She didn't know what had happened down on the beach, but she feared his heart was infirm. He'd been standing there on the shore smiling at her when she'd turned around, and then his face had gone pale. Suddenly he appeared to be in agony. He had lifted his right hand to his chest as if it were his heart that pained him. By the time that she reached his side, his knees were already buckling.

Emily had broken his fall and dragged him out of the surf. Then she'd run all the way up the cliff, around the winding path to Fraser Castle, to fetch Angus. By the time she, Angus, and Ruth had reached Gordon, his face had relaxed, he seemed no longer in pain, but in a deep sleep.

The hulking Angus had carried his unconscious master on one shoulder, up the steep cliff, up three flights of winding stairs to the tower bedchamber. Here Gordon had slept, without waking, for more than six hours.

Angus insisted his master had no history of heart trouble and suggested it might have something to do with his coming anniversary. Emily had gotten so angry, she'd wanted to scream at the manservant and pummel him with her fists. Despite all her reasoning, both men still doggedly insisted Gordon Fraser was a vampire. Even with his master ill, Angus refused to change his story.

Gordon moved in the massive four poster bed hung with ivory and blue brocade bedcurtains, and she glanced up from her book expectantly. He still slept.

"Please let him be all right," she whispered softly. Then she smiled. "Even if he does think he's a vampire."

In the past days Emily had come to know Gordon Fraser better than she knew anyone—even Ruth. She and the Scotsman had so much in common. He was easy to talk to, so fascinating. He was unlike any man she had known. Despite his opulent wealth, he was generous. One of her satchels was already full of books he had insisted she accept as gifts. And despite his education, he was completely unpretentious. He swore he had not attended any of the fine colleges in Edinburgh or London, but was self-educated.

Emily gazed at Gordon. His dark, silky hair fell over one cheek and splashed onto his pillow. Her hand ached to reach out and brush the hair from his face. She'd come to crave his touch. A brush of fingertips here, a tug of her hand there. It was completely innocent, of course. She was a respectable woman who knew how she must behave if she expected to continue to work in a man's world. But secretly, she wondered just how respectable she would be if Gordon made an advance toward her. What would it be like to share a kiss?

"No," she said aloud, her own echo startling her. "I won't take that path."

When she had decided to support herself restoring books, she had abandoned the possibility of having a husband and a family. Even with her father deceased three years, his bitter words still rang in her head. *A working woman who goes from house to house, strange man to strange man. No decent, God-fearing man will have you as a wife. The best you'll be able to do for yourself is become some rich man's mistress,* he'd scoffed.

It had been a difficult decision for Emily to choose between family and a career. But her father had forced her to choose when she'd been invited to France to study art. She wondered now if she had chosen the career just out of spite. That, and because her own mother had been so unhappy in marriage.

Emily's mother, Abigail, had been an actress when she and Emily's father had met. They'd fallen in love, married, and William MacDougal had put an end to the stage career his wife loved. Abigail had given birth to Emily, but even a child had not filled that void left in her life. She'd died when Emily was six, some said of a broken heart.

None of this had mattered to Emily until she met Gordon. She was getting as bad as Ruth with all these silly romantic ideas. What made her think Gordon Fraser was interested in a bookworm like her?

He stirred again. Emily set the oil lamp on the table at his bedside. "Gordon," she said softly. "Can you hear me?"

His eyes fluttered open and she was rewarded with a smile. "Must be a dream," he said, his voice weak. "Miss E. Bruce MacDougal in my bedchamber."

He reached out with his hand and it seemed only natural that she take it.

"What happened?" he asked.

She scooted on the edge of the chair so that he wouldn't have to wear himself out talking louder. His hand, joined with hers, was warm and strong. "You don't remember?"

He closed his eyes and massaged the bridge of his nose with his free hand. "I remember walking on the beach . . . seeing ye . . . then this pain . . . in my chest." He brushed the coverlet where it touched his heart.

"Has this ever happened before?"

He opened his eyes. "It's nay my heart, if that's what you're thinking. I'm as strong as a Highland bull."

"Then what happened?"

He shook his head. "You wouldn't understand." There was a sadness in his tone.

"Try me."

His gaze met hers.

For a moment there was no one in the world but the two of them. Then she moaned and rolled her eyes. "Oh, please. Not the vampire stuff again, Gordon." She withdrew her hand from his to fold her arms over her chest. "You know, I have to tell you, I'm growing a little impatient with that nonsense."

"We don't have to talk about this."

"We do have to talk about it. You and I have been so honest with each other in a world that's not always honest. That's what's been so special about our friendship." She heard her voice quaver. "Gordon, the vampire story is getting old."

He laughed wryly, looking up at the bed canopy overhead. "Old for ye in a fortnight. Think how old it is for me—six centuries."

She pushed back in her chair, trying hard to be understanding rather than just exasperated. "You really think you're a vampire, don't you?" It sounded so ludicrous to her, just saying it.

"Emily . . ." Gordon sat up in the bed.

It was of course completely inappropriate that she should be in his bedchamber now that he was conscious again, but propriety seemed of little consequence right now. She wanted to understand Gordon and this delusion of his. She needed to understand. "Yes?" she said simply.

"In a fortnight you'll have to go." He reached out and took her hand again. "I hope I'm not too forward in saying that I've come to . . . care for you a great deal. And I think you feel the same way about me."

She felt her heart flutter beneath her breast.

"Let's just enjoy what time we have left together."

Her gaze locked with his and she saw that his eyes were moist.

He did care for her.

The word *love* floated in her head.

"I could stay longer," she heard herself say, before she had time to consider her words. "I've no further engagement. I could repair the Shakespearean book of sonnets, if you like." She didn't know what made her so bold except that the thought of leaving Fraser Castle suddenly seemed an impossibility. She didn't want to leave. Not ever. "Without charge, of course," she added, feeling foolish.

He held her hand with one of his and smoothed it with the other. "I wish that you could stay, but you canna. Ye mustn't."

"That's right," she conceded, hiding her hurt with sarcasm. "Your anniversary. I wouldn't want you to drink my blood or chew the bones from my flesh with your canines."

The pain that she saw flash in his dark eyes made her wish she'd not said that. The truth was that it didn't matter what she believed. *He* believed he was a vampire, and more importantly, he believed she would be in danger if she stayed. He thought he was protecting her by sending her away.

"I told ye, I do not eat human flesh," he said, his voice barely a whisper.

She wanted to argue the point, but she couldn't bring herself to do it. Maybe Ruth was right. Maybe believing one was a vampire *was* a minor transgression in such a fine man. If only his belief was not so strong that it threatened to keep them apart. But perhaps there was still time to change that. "All right. You're right," she said, listening to her heart instead of her head for once. "So I have to go in two weeks. We can enjoy each other's company until then."

"A fortnight," he said huskily, lifting her hand to his lips.

She watched, mesmerized. He didn't kiss her hand, just drew his warm lips over the back of it. A tremor of what could only be sexual desire ran through her. She wished that he would kiss her hand . . . her mouth.

Emily pulled her hand away, suddenly unsure of herself. Of Gordon. What *was* that strange light in his eyes?

Gordon lay back on the feather bolster and pressed his hand to his forehead. "Ye should return to your chamber; it's late."

She rose from the chair, feeling a little unsteady on her feet. A chill overtook her that she couldn't shake.

She grabbed her book. For the first time since she came to Fraser Castle she wondered if she should be afraid.

"Angus said that if you need anything, just ring." She pointed to the bell that rested beside his bed as she made her retreat.

"Good night."

She had just reached the open door when he called her name. She turned slowly. He sat on the edge of the bed in his nightshirt, casting a strange shadow against the wall that didn't seem to quite match his position.

"Emily, you needna fear me."

She gripped the book to her chest, her heart pounding in her ears. "I don't."

But he must have heard the tremor in her voice.

"I wouldna harm ye, or Ruth, or even Angus. I will see myself dead first."

Emily retired to her bedchamber and the bed that she shared with Ruth, but she couldn't sleep. For more than an hour she tossed and turned; she couldn't get the image of Gordon's face out of her mind. She couldn't stop thinking of his inference that there could have been something more to their relationship than their friendship. She couldn't stop thinking of the way he'd held her hand and the strange light that illuminated his eyes.

Finally Emily surrendered to her restlessness and climbed out of bed. She put on Ruth's frilly white night robe and a pair of woolen stockings and took an oil lamp to light her way. There was only one place to go when she was restless, only one haven: the library.

Emily was not frightened by the dark cold castle, or

the shadows cast from her lamp, as she descended the staircase. Inside the library with its stacks of books and crates piled everywhere, she lit several more lamps and began to peruse the shelves. Perhaps one of Gordon's books would take her mind from her troubled thoughts.

She ran her finger along the leather bindings, studying the titles and authors. In the last few days she had become as familiar with Gordon's collection as she was with her own back in Philadelphia.

Nothing caught her eye immediately, so she pulled out a stair-step on wheels and, after lifting her night-clothes, climbed the steps. Perhaps she'd overlooked a book that would interest her.

On the higher shelves, Gordon placed books he read infrequently. There were Russian poets, Greek myths, essays by American patriots. Always fascinated by American literature, she retrieved a stack of original pamphlets featuring the writings of Thomas Jefferson. When she pulled them from the shelf, she was surprised to find a palm-size book behind them.

Curious, she retrieved the book and replaced Tom Jefferson on the shelf. She ran her hand over the crude brown leather binding in fascination. This book was old, very old. It smelled of disintegrating leather and paper and time.

Emily sat down on the top step of the rolling ladder and drew the book closer to the lamplight. The cover was embossed with faded gilt lettering across its front.

The book was written in what could only be ancient Pictish.

She flipped open the cover. Bits of paper dust filtered through her fingers. The book's pages were so thin they were transparent. It had not been type-set, but handwritten in scrolls. Much of the ink was faded beyond recognition. Pages were stuck together.

Though Emily couldn't read Pictish, she recognized the book's form. It seemed to be some sort of instruction book.

Instructions? Instructions on what? she wondered excitedly. She always loved a challenge. Perhaps the book couldn't be saved, but maybe the information inside could be. She wondered if Gordon read Pictish.

Filled with a sense of excitement, Emily carefully turned the pages. As careful as she was, some of the pages splintered when she touched them.

"No, no," she whispered. "Why did he keep you hidden? Why did he let you die like this?"

In the center were hand-sketched ink illustrations. A castle on a cliff. Fraser Castle? A circle of standing stones.

She turned the page.

What Emily saw made her blood run cold.

The last sketch was of a dark-haired man in a cloak. He was a handsome man with dark eyes and an aquiline face.

A man with bloody red fangs.

Five

Emily slapped the book shut and let it fall from her hands, as if merely touching it could somehow harm her. She leaped off the ladder and dashed for the hallway. She ran out of the library and into the cold darkness. She didn't stop until she reached the front door.

What am I doing? she thought, gripping the doorknob with both hands. All around her the darkness was oppressing, yet as her panic subsided, so did her fear. *What am I doing?* she asked herself again. *I've never run from anything in my life.* She released the knob and turned to rest her back against the door. She was breathing hard, her heart pounding. *I can't run from this either.*

Why? she argued with herself.

Because I love him.

The thought was startling. Yet it felt right.

"*I love him,*" she whispered.

Still shaky, Emily walked back to the candlelight of

the library. Inside, she slowly approached the book, lying harmlessly on its back. She stared at it for a long moment before she had the courage to pick it up.

How can it be true? she wondered, as she flipped the pages to the center of the book. But as she stared at the sketch of the dark-haired, fanged man, she knew it was true. She knew it in her heart of hearts. Gordon Fraser was a vampire.

"No," she whispered as she sank onto the bottom step of the ladder. Tears filled her eyes. It was true. Everything he had told her was true. And it all made sense. His vast knowledge. His collection of books and artifacts. All true. All real.

Her heart ached for Gordon. How could such a good man deserve such evil?

She wiped at her eyes with the sleeve of her nightgown. So was what Gordon told her that first night at Fraser Castle true? Was there no escape from his damnation?

Emily knew she should be afraid. She knew that she should fear for her life and that of Ruth's, but right now all she could think of was Gordon's life. How horrible it must have been for him to have become what was in this sketch. A man with fangs. A man who must suck the life's blood of others to sustain his own life.

But surely there had to be a cure . . . an antidote. Wasn't there always a way to reverse a spell or a curse? Just thinking such thoughts made her heart spin. Emily had spent her entire life thinking analytically, rationally. There was no room in her world for fanciful tales or belief in myths.

"There has to be a way," she said, rising. She began

to pace, the book open in her palm. "There has to be an answer, Gordon. And it just might be here."

She flipped through several pages. *But Pictish,* she thought. Even if the answer was here, how could she read it? If the answer had been here, wouldn't Gordon have found it centuries ago?

The moment her head began to fill with negative thoughts, she caught herself. She knew from experience that nothing could be solved with pessimism. She had to believe in herself. She had to believe that good conquered evil.

She closed the book and brought it to her chest. She had to believe that the answer was here and that she could find it. She had to believe her love for Gordon could save his soul.

Ruth was the first to appear in the morning to break the fast. When she entered the great hall, Emily was sipping coffee she'd made for herself in the kitchen, and poring over the pages of the vampire book. She'd been up all night.

"Morning," Ruth called cheerily.

It had not escaped Emily that Ruth had been all smiles for more than a week. Nor did it escape her that her companion's cheer had something to do with the fisherman-turned-manservant.

"Good morning," Emily said.

Ruth plopped herself down in a chair across from Emily and poured herself a mug of coffee. "And where were you all last night? Tending to Gordon, I suppose?" She winked. "Keeping him warm and comfortable?"

Emily closed the book. "Ruth, I have to talk to you. About something serious. I found a book last night."

"A book in this place?" She made a face. "Imagine that."

"Ruth. It's a book written in Pictish." She raised it as proof. "It's about vampires."

"Certainly would make for a nice bedtime story, if I read Pictish, of course."

"Ruth, listen to me." Emily took a deep breath. "He really is a vampire."

Ruth burst into laughter, spewing coffee. "He . . . he . . ." She couldn't speak for choking.

"It's not funny."

Ruth wiped her mouth then the table with a linen napkin. "Is this something you two lovebirds cooked up last night? Pretty strange bed games if you ask me."

"I'm utterly serious. Look at me." She gestured. "Look at my face. I'm not laughing."

Ruth peered at Emily's face, then laughed again. "You do look serious." A frown creased her brow. "Tell me you're not ill, too."

Emily rose, leaving the book on the dining table. "I'm not ill, but I'm scared."

"Think he'll bite us?" She pulled the necklace she always wore from beneath the collar of her dress. "I don't have a crucifix. Do you think my Star of David will fend him off?"

Emily was suddenly so frustrated she could have screamed. "Just look at the book. Look at it!" She gestured. "The pictures in the center."

Obviously to mollify her, Ruth reached across the table and retrieved the small book. She sipped her coffee as she flipped through the pages. "Pictish, hm? Refresh my memory. What is Pictish?"

"An ancient dead language. The Picts were here before the Celts."

Ruth found the center of the book. "Hey, looks like Fraser Castle."

"Exactly."

"So?" Ruth turned to the last picture and studied the vampire for a moment. "Handsome hound." She tilted her head one way and then the other. "Looks a little like Gordon, don't you think?"

"No. Yes. I suppose so. I don't know, but I don't think he wrote it or drew the sketches." Emily threw up her hands. "All I know is that that's a picture of a vampire and Gordon is one of them."

Ruth set down the book. "That would be a reasonable deduction, dear friend, except for one thing."

Emily rested one hand on her hip. "Being?"

Ruth leaned over, pressing both hands on the table, and spoke slowly. "There are no such things as vampires."

Emily turned away just as she heard a footfall in the hallway. It was Gordon.

"Good morning to you, ladies," he said brightly, as he entered the great hall.

Emily kept her back to him, trying to gather her wits about her. "Ruth, could you please excuse us?"

"Certainly. I'm to the kitchen to see what my fisherman has in store for today. He thought we might actually go fishing, from the shore, of course."

Emily heard Ruth leave.

Gordon approached Emily from behind. To her surprise, he lowered his hands to her shoulders. "How are you this morning, my—"

She spun around. "I found it."

He drew back. "Found what?"

"The book."

He stared at her with those dark eyes that seemed so familiar to her now, as if she'd known them her entire life instead of just a fortnight. "Which book?"

Emily circumnavigated him and snatched the book off the table. "This one."

Gordon looked startled for a moment. Then a darkness clouded his face. "Give that to me. It's not meant for you."

He reached for the book, but she pulled back.

"It's true, isn't it?" she said softly. "You're a vampire."

"Yes, it's true," he snapped. "What do ye think I've been telling ye for days?"

"Don't you shout at me!" She shook the book at him, taking a step closer to him. "What makes you think you can just walk up to me and declare you're a vampire and have me believe it? This is the nineteenth century! People don't believe in vampires in the nineteenth century, Gordon."

He lowered his gaze. "I'm sorry."

Her heart was breaking. It was true. She could see it in his eyes. She could hear it in his voice. "It's all right," she finally said softly. As she spoke, she reached out and touched his arm. She found no coldness as she feared she might discover. He was still the same Gordon she had come to care for, to love.

He glanced up. "You're not afraid of me?"

"A little. But . . ."

"But?"

She was lost in his gaze. "But . . . but I think I love you, Gordon. No." She drew back her hand. "No, I know I love you and even if you don't feel the same—"

"I do," he interrupted. "I have. I have since the first time I saw you here in the room." He glanced at the floor in front of her. "I've said nothing because I felt I had no right. I have nothing to offer. There is no future for us . . . for me."

Emily could feel her heart fluttering. She wanted to throw her arms around him and hold him tight. Let him hold her tight. But that wasn't how it was to be, was it? They were both too logical. "There could be a future," she said.

He shook his head. "Haven't you heard anything I've said?"

"I want to help you. I want to save you from this curse. I want to make a future possible."

Slowly he lifted his head until his gaze locked with hers. "There is no way to save me."

"The book. It could be in the book." She shook it. "Have you read it?"

"I don't read Pictish. You should put it back. It's not for . . . mortals. It's mine. Inherited with this house, this damned immortality," he finished bitterly.

"You give up too easily. Come sit down. We'll have something to eat." She walked to the table and he followed. "We'll do this together, Gordon."

He caught her hand and stopped her. "Wouldn't it be better if we spent our last days together doing something else? Something fun. Something we'll . . . you'll remember the rest of your days."

"Like what?" She sat back in her chair, set down the book, and poured them both coffee. "Books are what we do, Gordon. It is what we enjoy. Sit down." She indicated his chair.

"Yes, madame." He saluted, his mouth twitching with amusement. "Had I known you were going to get militant with me, I'd have dug up that coat of Napoleon's for you."

She glanced over the coffee pot. *"The* Napoleon? You have one of Napoleon's military coats?"

"Aye." He sipped his coffee, frowning. "I think it's in the same box with a pair of your George Washington's pistols. I can't remember just where. It's in one of those crates somewhere in the house."

Emily laughed. She couldn't help herself. Gordon just looked so utterly perplexed. It tickled her to hear him speaking of misplacing Napoleon's coat as others would speak of misplacing a shoe horn. It made him sound so human. It gave her hope.

"Emily, we've less than a week." Gordon paced behind her as she sat hunkered over the *Vampire Book of Rules and Regulations* at the dining table. "Let's go out to the rose garden, or walk along the shore."

She held up one finger. "In a minute." She was trying to separate two pages of the book with a razor blade and was not having much success.

"Not in a minute. Now." He grabbed her hand and tugged.

"Gordon, don't. I'll cut myself."

"Then put down the blade. I've resigned myself to my inevitable fate. Why can't you?"

"Don't talk like that." She removed the glasses she wore when doing intricate work. She rubbed the bridge of her nose. She was tired. Weary. Afraid. The sands of their hour glass were falling and she was still no closer to finding an antidote. She was sure the answer lay in this book. She just couldn't find it. "I told you, I won't have it."

"I've resigned myself to my death. You need to do the same."

She raised her palm, rising from the chair. "I don't want to hear it, Gordon. I don't want to cloud my thinking with any of your vampire wisdom."

He walked to one of the windows to peer out. "Ye be a stubborn woman, E. Bruce."

She came up behind him and wrapped her arms around his waist. Somehow in the last week they'd fallen into a very comfortable relationship with each other . . . almost as man and wife.

He sighed and leaned back. "Look at them."

"Ruth and Angus?"

"Aye." He indicated the window with a nod of his chin. "Outside walking hand in hand. I think they've fallen in love."

Emily smiled, glancing out the window. She rested her cheek on his back. He folded his hand over hers. He felt so warm, so steady. "She's making noises about taking him home to Philadelphia to meet her parents."

"How does she propose to get him there?" he teased. "Hot air balloon? You know Angus will not take a steamer all the way to America. I can't get him to take the steamer to the mainland."

"I don't know. Ruth hasn't said how. She just said Angus would be quite a sight at her father's dining table. I think he's asked her to marry him," she finished wistfully.

"Ah, Emily." Gordon turned to her, wrapping her in his arms. "I wish that I could . . . that we could—"

"We can."

He kissed the top of her head. "All right. I surrender for the moment. If you say there's an answer in the book and that you can find it, I'll believe you."

She looked up, into his eyes. "You better."

"But . . ."

"But?"

"But ye must promise me that if, if ye do not find an answer, that ye will take Ruth and leave on the mail steamer that arrives Saturday."

"Gordon—"

"Emily," he said firmly. "Ye must promise me you'll go. Angus can join you. I have a feeling he'd swim across this bay to be with Ruth."

She smiled tenderly. "You're such a romantic."

He brushed a lock of hair behind her ear. "Emily, I haven't kissed ye because I thought it wouldn't be seemly. But—"

"I wish you would."

He lifted one eyebrow. "Kiss ye?"

She smiled. "Aye. Else I'm going to have to be an independent American woman and kiss you first."

"I'll make a bargain with ye. Meet me half way?"

Emily let her eyes drift shut. She had never been kissed by a man. Never wanted to kiss or be kissed until Gordon.

His mouth met hers with warm, gentle pleasure and she sighed, parting her lips. Their breath mingled. She felt lightheaded, ecstatically happy, dismally sad.

"I love you," he whispered.

The kiss was so innocent. So perfect. But she wanted

more. She knew by the way he held her, he wanted more.

"Emily . . ."

She opened her eyes. "I can't," she whispered. "I want to. But I can't."

He guided her head to his shoulder and smoothed her hair with his hand. "How did you know what I was going to say?"

"I knew because I was thinking the same thing. I want to make love to you." Her voice was shaky. She could hear his heart beating to the same rhythm as her own. "But I can't. Not without marriage, Gordon."

"I understand."

She lifted her cheek from his chest to gaze into his eyes. "Do you?"

"I admire your ability to resist my charms."

She laughed, but she felt like crying.

"It's one of the things I love about you." He ran the back of his hand across her cheek. "You're so worldly and yet there is such an innocence . . . no, goodness, about you. You make me see goodness in myself."

"I'll find the answer. I know it's in the book."

"Promise me just the same. Promise me because I know you'll keep the promise."

She felt tears sting the backs of her eyelids. What if she didn't find the answer? There was that doubt, creeping in like a dark shadow. She pushed it aside. She would not consider the possibility. She would find the answer.

"Promise me," Gordon pressed.

"I promise."

He kissed her again, but then, before the kiss became too intense, he pulled away. "Come on. Let's go out and play. A skipping stone contest. I know I can beat you this time.''

She laughed. "You sound like a child."

"It's been a long time since I've had someone to play with. Come on." He bumped into one of the crates Angus had hauled from the castle's bowels for Gordon to inventory. When Gordon struck the box, the corner popped open and something tumbled out.

"What is that?"

"Aha! My word. There they are."

"What?" She walked around to the front of the box. To her astonishment there was a diamond tiara, necklaces of gold and silver, and puddles of loose emeralds and rubies. "What are they?"

He crouched and scooped up the jewels, pushing them back into the crate. "I wondered where they'd gotten to."

Emily stared. "What jewels are those, Gordon? Where did you get them?"

He dusted his hands, making sounds of exasperation as he rose. "I told Angus they had to be here somewhere."

"Whose are they?"

"Mine." He smiled.

"Before that, Gordon!"

He grabbed her arm, leading her away. "Oh, some Spanish queen. That one that sent Chris Columbus on his merry way."

"Queen Isabella?" Emily tried to look over her shoulder at the crate again, but Gordon dragged her away.

"Come on, before it gets dark. Race you to the shore."

She returned her attention to the man she loved.

"That's not fair. I've a cumbersome skirt to contend with."

"So have I." He tugged at the handsome kilt he wore.

"I think mine is a little longer."

"I'll give you a head start then."

Emily glanced back at the vampire book left open on the table. "I really should work another hour."

"Ready . . . set . . ."

She grasped her black cotton damask skirt and pulled it above her knees. "Go!" she shouted and took off.

Their laughter echoed off the walls of the great hall as they dashed for the door.

Six

"I don't want to go."

"Ye promised me, E. Bruce."

Emily sat on the bottom step of the grand staircase, her hand in Gordon's. Their time was up. She had failed. Her bags were packed and waiting on the dock. Angus had carried them down an hour ago. The two lovebirds had gone to wait for the mail steamer to give Gordon and Emily a few minutes alone.

"We have to go to the dock," Gordon said, entirely composed. "The steamer will be here any minute and it won't wait." He spoke as calmly as if they were discussing a book restoration, or dusting the library. He did not sound like a man who was about to die an agonizing death. "Now Angus will go with you. I've insisted. He'll just have to hang his head over the rail. He's to return alone in a week and dispose of my body."

A choking lump rose in her throat. "Gordon—"

He squeezed her hand. "Let me finish. We really haven't much time. I can already feel . . ." He let his voice fade.

"Feel what? Tell me." She gripped his hand, gazing into the face that she loved so dearly.

"Please don't ask me. I want to protect you from this evil."

"You are *not* evil."

He took a deep breath.

She hung her head. "Go on," she said softly.

"Now when it's safe—" He returned to his business-like tone. "You can return to Fraser Castle or send someone, if you prefer. You're welcome to anything I have. Give the rest to museums." He smoothed her hand in his, his brow creasing. "I just wish I'd gotten to opening some of those other crates. I know there are some of those fancy Russian eggs here somewhere. What do you call them?" He clicked his fingers together.

Tears filled Emily's eyes. "Don't make me go. Let me stay here with you. Let me hold you."

He smiled bittersweetly and kissed her palm. "Nay. I canna. I've told you, I canna control the urge. You would be in mortal danger."

"I don't think I care. Please, just—"

"Emily," he said firmly. "If you love me, if you truly love me as you say you do, you'll go. I'll be the happiest vampire alive, knowing you're safe."

She couldn't resist a smile. She brought her lips to his. "I do love you," she whispered.

"And I love you, E. Bruce MacDougal, even if you did get your hand on my Gutenberg on the sly." He rose, pulling her up with him. "Now ye must go."

In the brighter light of the hall she noticed the shade

of his eyes was changing. Where the pupils had once been dark brown, they were now streaked with green. His face was beginning to appear gaunt. Had he not been eating well lately and she'd just not noticed, or was some physical transformation taking place?

"Will you at least walk me down?"

He shook his head. His hand trembled as he freed one of her springy red curls from behind her ear. "Nay. Go, whilst I still have the power to let ye."

Emily could feel her heart ripping in half, its jagged edges oozing blood, pain. She wished now that she had made love with him. She wished she had more of him to take with her than a few books, a few pieces of Egyptian jewelry, and the precious Gutenberg, still in need of repair.

"You do have more," Gordon said.

She stared at him. How had he known what she was thinking? "I do?"

"You have my love." He brushed his fingertips over her left breast. "Here with you, always."

Emily didn't say goodbye because she couldn't bear it. She turned away, lifted her heavy black skirt, and ran from the hall. She ran out the door and down the same winding path she'd climbed up a month ago. Only now it seemed as if centuries had passed.

By the time she reached the dock, Emily's tears were spent. She walked the last one hundred feet and composed herself. Gordon wanted her to be brave. She needed to be brave for him, for herself.

She found Angus and Ruth on the floating dock, perched on the baggage, hand in hand. Angus was already looking a little pale, a little green.

"Storm's coming in," Ruth said. She pointed overhead. "Angus says we have to take the steamer but I think he'd be better to wait for calmer seas. I wouldn't mind staying another month." She rolled her eyes. "But you know he's protesting. I seem to be the only one who's not gone daft around here. You're willing to leave a man you're clearly in love with for fear he'll bite your neck, and this one here—" She hooked her thumb in Angus's direction. "He's willing to risk eternal sea-sickness just to get off the island."

Emily gazed up into the sky as she pushed back the hair that blew in her face. Where had the wind come from? It hadn't been windy this morning when she and Gordon had walked. The ocean had been calm.

Before her eyes, the sun disappeared behind dark, swirling clouds that seemed to circle the castle. It was the oddest weather phenomenon she had ever seen.

"Does this happen often here?" She lifted the hood of her cloak. Suddenly she was cold, cold to her bones.

"Nay." He rose, lifting the tiny Ruth to her feet with one meaty hand. "But I was nay here when last the anniversary came."

Suddenly the sky seemed to open up and rain pelted them. Ruth gave a squeal and drew up her bonnet. Angus shrugged off his black frock coat and held it over her so she'd not get wet.

"There lies the steamer." He pointed, swaying with the shifting dock.

Emily lifted on her toes and stared at the horizon. The sea was churning and the waves rising. White caps speckled the sea. Water splashed up over the dock.

"We'd best move to higher ground." Angus grabbed half the bags. Ruth hurried after him, fussing in the rain.

Emily scooped up her two bags from the wet dock. Another wave splashed over, wetting her shoes and stockings. "What about the steamer?" she shouted above the wind. She glanced over her shoulder. The mail boat was less than a quarter of a mile from them, being thrown in the rough sea.

On solid ground, all three lowered their bags and stared at the churning ocean. They watched in eerie silence as the steamer slowly turned and began to chug its way back toward the mainland.

"Too rough to dock?" Emily whispered, unable to believe her eyes. What were they going to do? Gordon had made it clear that no human could be near him at the hour of his bewitching.

"Guess that's that," Ruth declared, and started up the rocky path toward the castle.

Emily was touched by how matter-of-fact Ruth was. She didn't believe so she didn't realize what danger she was in. Perhaps it was better that way.

Ruth's bustle swayed as she climbed the muddy slope. "Igor, love," she called over her shoulder. "Cart those bags back up to the castle, will you? Emily and I will have to make a run for it."

Emily's gaze met Angus's.

"We canna return," he said simply.

Of course Angus understood the danger. He lived with Gordon Fraser. "We've no choice," Emily whispered. "The boat's not coming back for us. Not tonight at least."

Angus's wide, ruddy face went even paler. "We must do something. My master will be very angry with me." A message passed without words between them. He feared not so much for himself but for her and Ruth. The fact that Ruth did not believe Gordon was a vampire would not protect her.

"It's not your fault, Angus. We'll think of something. We still have a few hours." She gripped his arm. "Now let's get Ruth out of this rain before she catches her death." She forced a smile. "And look on the bright side. This will give me a few more hours with the vampire book. Maybe I'll find the antidote."

"Why have ye returned?" Gordon met them in the front hall. It was him and yet it was not. His voice was deeper, laced with fingers of . . . malevolence.

Emily felt a trickle of fear. But she stood her ground in the hallway, dripping water on the ancient tiled floor. "The steamer didn't come for us, Gordon. We had to come back."

Ruth tiptoed by them, with Angus trailing her. They disappeared down the corridor lit by flickering candle-light.

"You shouldna have come back," Gordon said.

Emily felt the eyes of the portraits on her as she met Gordon eye to eye. "We had no choice. What did you want us to do? Stand on the dock in the rain?"

"I wanted you to go!" He swung his fist at the standing suit of armor in the entryway and hit it so hard that it crashed to the ground.

Emily jumped in her skin. This was not her Gordon, not her man of laughter, of lost Fabergé eggs. This man was dark and brooding. This man was frightening.

"Go," he said through gritted teeth, pointing a long, tapered finger.

She stared at his face. Had his incisors grown? Were

they longer, overlapping his lower teeth slightly, or was she just imagining it?

"Go!" he shouted again, taking a step closer.

It was all she could do not to cower. But she didn't. She wouldn't. This was her second chance to save him, perhaps even divine intervention. She would not fail this time. "No," she said softly. "There is no place to go."

"The hour approaches!" His bass voice reverberated off the high ceiling and echoed ominously. "You canna stay!"

She strode past him, whipping off her wet cloak. "We'll have to think of a way to protect ourselves. We'll lock ourselves up. Lock you up."

He shook his head violently. "No . . . they . . . I am very clever. If I smell human blood—"

She threw up her hand. She'd not let the gruesome detail distract her. "We don't have time for this, Gordon. Now where's the book?" She let her cloak fall to the floor. They were running out of time. She could hear it in Gordon's voice. She could smell it in the air.

"What book?" He followed her. He had changed out of his kilt into black trousers and a black frock coat. His cravat was red . . . blood red splashed against a lily white linen shirt.

"You know what book," she said patiently. She refused to be intimidated. This man was not Gordon Fraser. He was not the Gordon she loved. He was an impostor, an evil impostor created by the spell all those hundreds of years ago. "The vampire book. Get it for me."

"Nay, I willna," he sneered.

She pushed him lightly on the chest with her hand.

"Dammit, Gordon. Listen to me. I'm trying to save your life. One of our lives. Because if what you say is true, if we don't come up with a solution in the next six hours or so, you may kill one of us."

A light passed through Gordon's dark brown eyes that had turned a brilliant green. A light of understanding.

"Get it," she repeated firmly. "Now, Gordon."

To her relief, he turned on his heels and headed for the library.

An hour later Emily sat at the dining table poring over the vampire book. It was in such poor repair; so many pages were either missing or damaged beyond recognition that she was beginning to think this was a hopeless cause.

"Ye called for me, madame?" Angus appeared behind her.

"Yes. Gordon's becoming very agitated. He says you may be able to get a rowboat. He wants you to row him to that little island off the leeward shore of this island." Emily didn't want to let Gordon go, but she knew in her heart that this back-up plan was logical. If nothing else, if it could be arranged, perhaps it would calm Gordon.

Emily massaged her temples as she continued. Her head was pounding. "He says we'll be safe because he could never swim it, not even in an empowered state." She glanced up. "So can you get the boat, Angus? I wouldn't ask if I saw an alternative, and I feel as if I need to protect Ruth. I brought her here."

"Aye, for my Ruthie." Angus hung his head, his face turning green before her eyes. "I'll do it. I didn't think the master knew, but I can set a signal with the lantern. One of me brothers will leave a rowboat on the shore of the far side. They never liked the thought of a MacReed keeping house for a vampire.''

She returned her attention to the book. She was using her razor blade to try and separate pages. Something seemed to be stuck between two, but so far she'd not been able to pry them apart. She glanced up at him again, feeling badly about sending Angus into the rough seas in a rowboat. "Perhaps I could row him to the island. I'm strong for a woman.''

"Nay.'' Angus swallowed. "He wouldn't allow it. I must do this for my master myself.''

Emily didn't argue because she understood. Because of his relationship with Ruth and Gordon, Angus seemed like a brother to her. She knew he felt the same pain she felt. The same fear. "See it done, Angus.''

"See what done?'' Emily heard Gordon's agitated voice behind her.

She turned in her chair. "Angus is going to get the boat.''

"Hurry, man,'' Gordon ordered as his manservant took his leave. "There's little time left. If I'm not gone from here I don't know what you'll do . . . I'll do.'' There was a tremor in his voice. It seemed to Emily that he was battling now, Gordon the man against Gordon the vampire.

"We've plenty of time, Gordon,'' she assured him. Then she returned to the book and the knife.

"I don't know why you don't give up with that.'' He paced behind her. "There is no answer, I tell you. Let me die.''

"I won't give up on you.''

He halted behind her and she felt his hand brush her shoulder. She felt a tremor of desire . . . laced with fear.

"No. I doona suppose you will, my sweetness." He lifted the hair from her back and placed a kiss on the nape of her neck. She closed her eyes; her heart raced. His kiss made every fiber of her being tingle. It made her warm in the pit of her stomach. It made her burn with desire for him.

I could surrender, she thought, light-headed. Give myself to him . . . save him.

Then she realized what he was doing . . . drawing her into the spell. It was the evil inside him overcoming the good. "No, Gordon." Though it took every ounce of her resolve, she pulled away from him. "Don't touch me. Go back to the library. I have work to do."

He let her hair fall to cover her neck. "You do not ken what you're missing," he said huskily in her ear.

She held perfectly still, fighting her desire for him, knowing that if she gave in, she would be giving up her soul. "Go."

His footsteps echoed hollowly in the great hall as he retreated. Emily drew an oil lamp closer and hunkered down over the vampire book. She had to find the answer . . . .

More than two hours later, Gordon appeared behind her. This time she never heard a sound until he was there. "It is time."

She started. "Not yet. Not so early." She turned in her chair to look up. "Not—"

Who she saw, what she saw, so astounded her that

she couldn't finish her thought. It was Gordon, yet it was not. Even in the last two hours he had transformed more profoundly. His face was gaunt, his eyes ringed with black shadows. Those were definitely fangs she saw now.

She rose from her chair but stepped away from him, rather than toward him.

"Close your eyes, Emily," he whispered. "Let me leave with the memory of days past. Not now, not this way."

She closed her eyes, a sob rising in her throat.

Gordon put out one finger and touched her lips. She kissed his finger.

Emily opened her eyes to see Gordon stride toward the door, his black cape fluttering behind him.

Ruth appeared in the doorway and handed Angus his cloak. "You're really going to go through with this, aren't you, Angus? You're going to row out into the middle of this. With any luck at all, you'll both drown." She crossed her arms over her chest, obviously perturbed, but also concerned for his welfare.

How could she still not believe, even seeing Gordon like this? Then Emily wondered if everyone could see this transformation or just some people.

Ruth stepped out of the way to let the men pass. "Men and their ridiculous little games. And what are you going to say in the morning when you have to haul him back, alive and wanting breakfast? Hm?"

Angus put himself between Ruth and his master and leaned over her, dwarfing her tiny frame. He kissed her soundly on the lips.

Emily watched as Gordon disappeared through the door. As he disappeared, she felt the blood drain from her face . . . her heart. Perhaps it would have been better that she give her soul so that he might live . . . .

Emily stood there feeling sorry for herself for a full minute before she got a grip on her herself. "Sit down," she said aloud. "You're so clever. You think the answer is here. Find it."

Seven

It was close to eleven when Angus returned, wet and seasick.

Emily didn't glance up from the vampire book. It wasn't that she didn't care, only that she knew each second counted. Her heart raced. She nearly had the stubborn pages peeled apart. "Are you all right, Angus?"

She heard him gulp. "Aye."

She glanced up quickly to see the giant man swaying precariously. He appeared as if he were going to be ill at any moment. "Get yourself warm, dry clothes. Something hot to drink, maybe eat."

He shuddered, his massive shoulders hunched. "Nay, I willna eat. Ever."

"Ruth." Emily woke her friend, who sat in a chair asleep at the table.

She lifted her head off the table and blinked sleepy-eyed and confused.

"He's back. Take him down to the kitchen and warm him up."

Ruth went to Angus's side and looped her arm through his to lead him away. "Got the vampire settled for the night, have we, my mighty sailor?" She pressed her cheek to his wet sleeve. "Let's see if we can get you warm."

Emily drew back the razor. Just one more slit and the two pages would be free. She didn't know what she would find between them, but she knew instinctively it was important.

"Aha," she breathed. "There we go." She set down the blade and pushed her reading glasses further up on the bridge of her nose. Cautiously, she peeled the pages apart to reveal what was inside. "Oh, God," she whispered, not in blasphemy, but in praise.

It was a translation, written in old English. She could read old English. But a translation to what?

She studied the faded ink, glanced at the two pages that were stuck together, then back at the translation again. "This is it. This is it." Tears clouded her eyes, and she dabbed at them beneath her lenses.

Her heart pounding, she read the two paragraphs of scrolled, faded writing.

"It's so simple . . ."

Emily slapped the book closed, tossed her glasses on the table, and leaped up. She had the answer! She laughed aloud as she raced across the room, nearly hysterical with happiness. Fear. She was the answer.

Now if only she could get to the island in time.

* * *

Emily kept her head bowed as she rowed, her back into the wind as waves crashed over the side. She was soaking wet, with water in the boat over her ankles. Her arms felt like lead weights from the exertion. She was so cold that her fingers were numb. But she clutched the oars tightly and rowed. Rowed. It had to be nearly midnight. The bewitching hour of Gordon's anniversary was upon him.

Emily had sneaked out of the castle, not telling Angus and Ruth where she was going. If she'd told them, they wouldn't have wanted her to go. Perhaps Gordon might have even given Angus instructions to physically restrain her if she attempted to reach him.

Emily glanced over her shoulder in the direction she rowed. The wind and rain stung her face. She could see the island. She turned back and rowed harder. The island was small, but not that small. What if she couldn't find him in time?

Only minutes later, as she rowed furiously, she heard a scraping sound and felt the rowboat ride up in the sand.

"I have waited for ye, my sweetness."

She knew it was Gordon, of course, even before she turned around. She'd been foolish to wonder how she would find him.

"I knew you would come. Even this clever plot to sequester me would not work."

She felt his hand unclenching hers from the oar, and he raised her from the plank seat. The sky was dark and yet there was a light that came from somewhere. Him?

Emily trembled from head to foot, her teeth chattering as he led her up onto the shore. She was so afraid, and yet she knew this was what she had to do. She knew it was the only chance to save him . . . save herself now.

"Why did it take you so long, my sweetness?" His husky voice curled around her nerves, relaxing her, calming her. "I've waited for ye for an eternity." He chuckled deep in his throat, a laughter that seemed not his own, but someone else's.

Emily could not respond, but it seemed of little consequence to him.

"This way, out of the wind. Ye are so cold, Emily. Let me warm ye." Gordon slipped his arms around her, drawing her into his cloak. It was so warm with her body next to his. Heat emanated from his body as if he were a flame.

"There, there, are ye warmer now?" He turned her in his arms so that she faced him, wrapped inside his wool cloak. Behind the piling of rocks the size of the boat, there was no wind. Either the rain had stopped or the rocks were shielding them from it. All around Emily and Gordon there was still that strange glowing light that came from nowhere.

For an instant, just an instant, Emily rested her head on Gordon's chest. He was so warm and he smelled so good.

"I have waited for us to be alone like this," he whispered in her ear.

She shuddered as he pressed his lips to her cheek. She felt weak in the knees as his warmth spread to her limbs . . . to her loins.

"Make love with me, Emily." He caressed her hip, her thigh, molding his own hard, muscular body to hers. "Love me. Love me."

Her eyes drifted shut of their own accord. The storm

around them subsided. There was nothing but the two of them now, the two of them and eternity . . . .

"I do love you," she breathed, trembling, aching. "I do love you."

He cupped her breast and through the wet fabric of her blouse and underclothing, she could feel the heat of his hand, the heat of his desire for her. Burning. Burning as it was in her.

Emily moaned softly. She was warm now, as warm as if she were sunbathing on the beach on a summer day. The glorious light surrounded them, washing away her fears.

Why had she been afraid of Gordon? He only wanted to love her . . . to make love to her.

Gordon lifted her off the ground and Emily looped her arms around his neck. "Aye?" he whispered huskily. He was kissing her. Her cheek, the bridge of her nose, her lips . . . the pulse of her throat.

"Aye, you will love me? Love me forever, Emily?"

It was not Gordon's husky, sensual voice she heard this time, but someone else's. Someone evil. Her eyes flickered open in sudden fear.

Gordon stared into her eyes, his face gaunt, his lips drawn back. The fangs were clearly visible.

"There will be no pain." His voice was so mesmerizing that she believed him.

"No pain, only . . . pleasure."

Emily's eyes felt heavy. Against her will, she could feel herself relaxing in his arms, lowering her head, exposing the soft white flesh of her neck.

"Emily . . ."

She felt the warm brush of his mouth on the pulse of her throat, then a sudden coldness.

"No!" she screamed, startling them both. Her eyes flew open.

This was it. This was the moment.

Her gaze met Gordon's and she was filled with icy fear. This was not the Gordon she loved . . . this was Satan. Satan had captured her love and taken him. . .

Emily wanted him back.

She grasped his cold face between her shaking hands and brought her mouth to his. She kissed his cold lips, her lips brushing the ivory fangs.

Gordon cried out in pain, as if her mouth had burned his, and sank to his knees taking her with him. Emily screamed as she fell in the wet sand. As she hit the ground, she rolled away from Gordon, terrified.

She sat up on her knees, dragging the wet hair from her face so that she could see him. The eerie light was fading as Gordon faded. She watched in horrified awe as he curled into a fetal position, his cloak covering him entirely.

"Gordon! Gordon!" she cried. But she didn't dare approach him. Not yet.

He made groaning, whimpering sounds as he seemed to grow small under the cloak. He was disappearing. There no longer seemed to be anyone beneath the cloak.

Hot tears ran down her cheeks. She was shivering again. "What have I done? What have I done?" she moaned.

Emily squeezed her eyes shut, clutched her cold hands, and prayed fervently. "Let him be all right. Let him live."

She made herself open her eyes.

It was dark now. The light was gone. But so was the

wind, the rain. Behind her, the seas had calmed. In confusion she stared up at the sky that had been dark and swirling only moments before.

Before her eyes, bright pinpricks of stars appeared in the dark canopy of the night sky. Pale moonlight was just beginning to seep from behind the clouds. The moonlight fell . . . on Gordon's cloak.

She rose. "Gordon? Gordon, can you hear me?"

Once again there was someone beneath the cloak. She fell to her knees beside it. But who? What if she had not saved Gordon, but saved the demon?

"Gordon?" It took every fiber of nerve she possessed to pull back the cloak.

"E. Bruce MacDougal, is that ye?" It was Gordon's voice. Gordon's humor.

"Oh, you're all right!" She threw her arms around him, not caring what he looked like or whose body he possessed. What mattered was that it was him. "Oh, you're all right!" She clasped his face between her sandy, wet hands and covered it with kisses.

Gordon grasped her by the waist and pulled her down beside him. "This is rather pleasing attention." He kissed her on the lips. "But could you tell a confused Scotsman what's happened?" He glanced around. "And where are we?"

"You don't remember?"

"I remember breakfast. Fish, biscuits with a little jam."

She laughed. This was Gordon. Her Gordon.

She quickly recounted the tale to the point of her arrival on the island. Gordon held her hands tightly in his.

"Ye shouldna have come, my sweetness. You shouldna

risked your life for me. Do ye know what would have happened if ye failed? Do ye understand what I would have done to ye? At best killed ye. At worst . . . taken your soul?"

She grinned. "But I didn't fail. And now you're a mortal just like me. You'll grow old and wrinkled. We'll grow old together."

He lifted his hand to his lips and kissed it. "So what was the answer?" His green eyes had turned dark brown again. The fangs were gone. He was his handsome self again. "Tell me."

She knew her cheeks colored. She could feel the warmth of embarrassment spreading. But she did not look away. She held his gaze in hers: "The voluntary kiss of a virgin at the moment of her death."

He stared in amazement. "You saved me with your kiss?"

"My virginal kiss." A smile twitched on her lips. "See that. I told Ruth I was saving myself for something special."

Epilogue

Fraser Castle
Two Years Later

"Gordon?"

"In the library," he called.

Emily followed the corridor, her high-button shoes clip-clapping on the slate-tiled floor. She checked the pocket watch that dangled on a chain and rested inside her skirt pocket. "Gordon, the book has arrived on the mail steamer." She entered the cluttered room to find her husband perched on the library ladder, his back to her. He was replacing books on one of the high shelves. "I thought I'd get right to work on the repairs. So could you look after Isabella when she wakes from her nap?"

"Aye." Gordon turned.

Emily gasped and brought her hands to her face, her heart tripping. "Gordon," she breathed.

He smiled handsomely, baring long white fangs. "Aye, love?"

"Gordon, are you all right?"

He climbed down the ladder, seemingly unaware of his transformation. "Aye, why do ye ask?"

She touched her lips with two fingers. Her heart was pounding, but she knew she had to remain calm. Surely there was an explanation for the fangs. Gordon was now entirely mortal. He was no longer a vampire, she was certain of it. "Your teeth. Gordon, you . . . you've grown fangs."

He touched his own teeth and then gasped so dramatically that Emily was immediately suspicious. Was he playing some sort of prank on her?

"Ods fish! I *have* grown fangs." He wiggled his eyebrows, feigning a sinister laugh. "Come here then, my pretty, and let me sample your sweet, hot blood."

She thrust out her arms and struck him hard in the chest. "That's not funny!" She tried hard not to laugh. Her heart was still pounding. "You scared me half to death. I thought you were turning into a vampire again."

"Aye, 'twould be a great problem, wouldn't it, as there's no longer any virgins on hand."

She lowered her hands to her hips, attempting to appear unamused. "Ha, ha. Very funny." It really was funny, but she didn't want to encourage him too much, else this would lead to an entire string of vampire practical jokes.

He pointed a finger. "Had ye for a minute, didn't I, E. Bruce?"

She playfully bit the offending finger. "Didna."

"Did, too."

She squinted, getting a closer look at his fake fangs. "How did you do that?"

He walked to the desk and picked up a candle. "Some melted wax."

She peered over his shoulder. "You just softened it, formed them with your fingers, and attached them to your own teeth?"

"Aye." He rolled a ball of wax between his fingers, his dark eyes twinkling with amusement. "Want to try a set of your own?"

There wasn't a day in Gordon's life since his "rescue" from damnation that he didn't make the most of that day. He had to be the happiest mortal man on earth, and Emily knew she was the happiest woman on earth to have Gordon to love, and be loved by.

Emily chuckled. "I really should get to work on those repairs."

"Come, lass. It will be fun."

A few minutes later, Ruth called Emily's name from down the hall.

"In here!" Emily hollered, laughing with her husband. "We're in the library."

"Look who I found wide awake in—" Ruth halted in the doorway, little red-haired Isabella perched on her hip. "What do you think you're doing?" Ruth stared. "What is that on your teeth?"

Emily circled Ruth, her new fangs bared. "Turn over the child," she said in her best vampire's voice. "And perhaps I'll not drain every drop of blood from your wee body."

Ruth grimaced, turning in a circle, clutching the baby to her.

Isabella laughed at her mother and clapped her hands merrily, enjoying the game.

"You two are really sick, you know that?" Ruth scolded. "I told Angus after we married that we should have seriously considered that move to Paris. If I could get him off this island, I think I'd go now."

Emily opened and closed her hands. "Hand over the child."

"Hand over the child," Gordon echoed, joining Emily in the game, circling Ruth.

Eleven-month-old Isabella put out her chubby hands to her father and Gordon swept her into his arms. The baby immediately reached out to explore his fangs.

Emily caught Gordon's hand and together they spun their daughter around in play.

Ruth watched in good-natured exasperation. "You know Emily, I never understood this whole vampire nonsense with Gordon and Angus, and now you're fixated on it, too." She walked out of the library. "I think all three of you need to seriously consider psychiatric care," she called, as she disappeared down the hall.

As Emily's and Gordon's gazes met, they both beared their fangs.

"She's never going to understand," Emily said with amusement. "She'll never believe the truth."

"Nay, never." Gordon brushed his lips against her neck. "But we know," he whispered. "And I'll love ye forever for what ye did for me. The risk ye took with your life for mine."

Emily brushed her hand over her daughter's golden-red hair, her heart so filled with love for her and Gordon that it ached. "For our lives."

"For *our* lives." Gordon sealed their words with a kiss

and nuzzled her nose with his, the baby between them. "I think our fangs are locked."

"I think so." She laughed as she brushed her lips against his again. "Guess you're stuck with me for the next fifty years now."

He grinned wickedly. "The pleasure is all mine, E. Bruce."

A DANCE IN THE DARK

Karen Ranney

One

"Hello?"

There is no one here, Louisa. But it didn't seem that way. Somehow, incredibly, she didn't feel alone, but as if she were being watched. As if someone was there, waiting in the shadows. A feeling of alarm skittered over her skin and then was silenced by a thought. *There is nothing here, Louisa.* It's simply that you have always disliked dark places. They make you feel unnerved. That is all it is. She discounted the fact that she'd not been afraid of the dark since she was a child.

Ever since she was eight and had come to live at Bainbridge Hall, she'd explored Hodge's Hill and the surrounding countryside. But this afternoon, the sun gleamed just right on the outcropping of rock, illuminating the shadows behind it and the stone entrance that opened up to become this large, very dark, and previously unknown cave. As a child she would have willingly explored it, she thought, then stopped herself as truth washed over her again. As a child, she had been timid and shy. She would have run from the spot and not asked a soul about it. Even now, so many years later, the echo of that child's voice resounded in her mind as she stood in front of it. *It's dark and dirty and bats live there. Not to mention spiders. Maybe even worse. You'll soil your dress and muss your hair and people will know you've been somewhere you shouldn't have been.*

She waved her hand in the air in front of her as if to banish so many admonitions. She was no longer a child and dark places didn't really scare her anymore, and it was so odd to see something nearly hidden from view and then to magically come upon it. Almost like a plain rock that turns out somehow to be a diamond. The cave lured her to investigate, to take one step and then one more into the solitary silence of a place she'd never known existed.

Perhaps she should not have explored this place on her own. It was not as if she had meant to, after all. She had left Bainbridge Hall with her drawing materials under her arm, intent upon a little solitude and promising her maid, Abigail, her grandfather's secretary, and all the other assorted persons she'd met that she would be quite fine, that she was only going as far as Hodge's Hill. They had reluctantly refrained from accompanying her, granting her a precious gift of time.

"I know you're there. Why aren't you answering?" Another step. She stood there in the silence, absorbing all the sounds she heard. Somewhere, water dripped, the wind soughed loudly as if it rushed through a chimney hole. Another sound, unexpected and yet not totally so.

"I can hear you breathe."

Silence again, and then the voice came.

"Are you always so intrusive?" The tone of it was decidedly annoyed.

She could not blame him, of course; she herself had sought privacy often only to have it interrupted by yet another well meaning soul. No one in the world was more cared for, cosseted, confined, and concerned about than Louisa Patterson. Very rich young ladies normally are, she was told.

"No," she answered honestly. "I do not believe I am. But I'm very good at hiding from others, which is probably why I knew you were here. If you truly wish me to leave, I shall."

There was no response to that statement.

"If you're trying to be unmannerly, you're succeeding quite well." The darkness of the cave was pervasive. All she could see was blackness, the color of night at its loneliest.

Why on earth had she come in here? Curiosity, it seemed, had gotten her into a dilemma, one from which she could not politely extricate herself. After all, she could not simply turn and walk away. Could she?

"You are not going away, are you?"

"I was just thinking how I could accomplish that with more manners than you've evinced so far." She frowned into the darkness.

"Is it entirely mannerly to lecture me on deportment, then?" The voice held a distinct note of amusement now. Louisa felt her cheeks flush.

"I am sorry. My grandfather says I tend to think first and use reason only later."

"A lamentable habit."

"I did not say that I agreed with him." She touched her lips with her fingers, more than a little surprised that such a thought had actually been said. Despite her grandfather's claims, there were few times in which she actually transgressed socially. She was Arthur Patterson's granddaughter, a position about which she was reminded daily, if not hourly. She owed a duty to her grandfather, one of love and affection and strict attention to propriety.

"Ah, a woman with an opinion. How utterly rare."

"Did you know that sarcasm is the pediment of fools?"

"Are you quoting, or is that, perhaps, a sentiment you've learned from someone?"

"By that remark, am I to infer that it is your belief that women cannot maintain a thought of their own?"

"Did you come in here to argue with me, then? Is there no one at Bainbridge Hall to perform the chore with you?"

Surprise held her rigid for a moment. It was too good to be true, then, this anonymity.

"Then you know who I am?"

"There is not much that goes on around here that I'm unaware of, Miss Patterson."

"And, I suppose, you shall mention to my grandfather how dreadfully unmannered I've been."

"You really must not sound so disconsolate. I have never exchanged a word with your grandfather. Nor am I likely to. I simply am aware of a place not too far removed from my own, much humbler, abode."

"You cannot mean you live here?"

It was not silence between them then, the air carried too many sounds, a soft shifting noise that might have been a footfall, a breath, a brush of fabric. All these things seemed magnified and compressed in the darkness.

"You disapprove, I take it?"

She clasped her drawing pad closer to her chest.

"Come, you must have a thousand or more questions. I can almost hear them popping from beneath your bonnet. Does your grandfather know of my existence, or even this place? How can a man live among rock and stone? Why, above all, would I choose such a place in which to make my home? Are you not suffused with curiosity?"

It might be advisable to simply turn and leave after all. But the alternative was to return to Bainbridge Hall and it was so lonely there lately.

"Yes," she sighed, trapped in honesty. "For the answer to each and every one of them."

"A truly honest woman, then. Why did you come in here?"

"I have never seen the cave before. I wanted to see it."

"And you discovered a hermit in residence, and a surly one at that."

"Is that what you are?"

"Surely not a reason to sound so absurdly gleeful."

"Well, it is because I have never met one. My own life is too filled with people."

"You are young and unmarried. Such a circumstance is normal. As this meeting between us is not."

"Oh, but this cave is part of Hodge's Hill and therefore part of my dowry."

"So, you claim ownership to my home. Does that fact demand an invitation? Even outside the bonds of propriety, then?"

"No," she said slowly. "You are correct of course." *It is just that my entire life is comprised of being ever mindful of what other people say and what people think of me. It had been refreshing to spend a few moments simply not caring.*

"Sit down," he said, and his voice was so close to her that she jumped, startled. The impenetrable blackness was like a murky fog, shielding everything. "Did I frighten you?"

"Yes," she said, too discomfited for politeness.

Something brushed her hand, and she jerked it back, startled. It had been like touching a spider's web, something felt but not seen.

"Sit down, then, and I shall endeavor to be a host."

"I cannot stay." She fumbled with her drawing materials, grateful for something to place between her and the deep shadows in front of her.

"Then go." The voice was annoyed again, and did she imagine it, or was there a tinge of disappointment there? *Don't be a silly goose, Louisa.*

She really should not have said the next words; they were hideously improper. "May I come again?"

"Perhaps I shall not be here."

"If you are, may I visit you?"

There was no answer to her question, and long moments later, in the silence, she turned and left the cave.

Two

"Hello?" The sound seemed to career around the cave.

Douglas sighed inwardly, stood, and walked to the cave entrance. His footfalls made no sound except to his ears.

"I did not expect you to come." No, that was not quite true. He'd hoped she would not be so improvident as to return. But it appeared that Miss Louisa Patterson was a more courageous creature than she'd first appeared. Or she was as lonely as he.

"No, only my grandfather's bailiff with orders to escort you from his land."

He could not forestall his soft laughter. "You judged my skepticism well, then."

"Did you really expect me to betray you?" She walked into the darkness of the cave, as if daring herself to fight her fear. He could feel her emotions, the pounding of her heart. A mouse, exploring the cat's basket. How foolishly brave she was.

He did not consider that she might reach out her hand, a night-blinded creature fumbling in the dark. Was it wonder that kept him rooted to the spot? Or merely surprise?

"Yes," he said, coming forward and taking the basket from her hands. He knew that even then as close as he was, she could not see him. She shrugged off her cape and folded it in front of her. "It has been my experience that people do not feel comfortable with someone who chooses to be different."

"So you calmly awaited your banishment?"

He bowed, then remembered she could not see him. He could easily make himself visible to her, but for various reasons he did not. The darkness had the added advantage of slowly removing the layers of her fear.

"Can I coax you outside? It is a glorious day, with a nearly cloudless sky. I've brought cheese and roast beef and some of cook's most wonderful pastries."

"You must not think me one of your charities," he said, placing the basket on the large outcropping of stone that served as his table.

"I do not." Her chin lifted, and although he was immersed in darkness, she gave him a look meant to scorch and burn.

" 'My dear young maiden clingeth / Unbending, fast and firm / To all the long-held teaching / Of a mother ever true,' " he murmured, thinking that someone should be here to warn her of such incautious behavior. Or, better yet, to ensure that she did not repeat it.

"What was that you quoted?"

"An apt little verse from Heinrich August Ossenfelder, my dear, that urges caution in the face of too much curiosity.''

"You do not think it proper that I have come.'' She looked so absurdly disappointed that he wanted to scold her as one might discipline a child. Yet, she was no child. She was an heiress, sought after for her money, if for no other reason.

"I do not think it proper that you have come,'' he agreed, wishing in an odd way to spare her the hurt so easily read on her face. "But since you have, we might as well partake of your generosity.''

"If you will not leave the cave, I've brought candles,'' she offered. "But no wine. I've a container of tea, sweetened too much for your taste probably, but a solitary picnic was the only way I could escape, and Cook knows how I like my tea.''

"Are you given to solitary musing?'' He stepped away from her. Her scent was warm woman and an expensive perfume. Something light and flowery and crafted for maidens. It lured him to forget what he was, the easy danger he posed for her. Such a moment was filled with peril of its own.

"My grandfather wants me married, and therefore I must give much thought to the man I would choose as a husband.''

"So you spend it sitting upon the hill and considering all your prospects?''

Her laughter surprised him. So, too, did the brittle underlayer of it.

"More like I escape their companionship.'' Again, her honesty startled him.

"Give me your hand, Miss Patterson, and I'll escort you to my dining hall, where you can sip your warm tea and entertain the hermit with tales of an heiress planning her wedding.''

She stretched out her hand and he took it without thinking. His fingers were warm, but hers were warmer, and for a second, just a fleeting second, it seemed as if he could melt into her skin. He could feel his pulse and hers, the booming beat of both hearts. As if their blood fused together, their skin became one, the light of her soul poured into his.

When he dropped her hand it was as if a link had been severed.

''Aren't you going to light the candles?'' Her voice sounded tremulous, a maiden becoming aware of the danger? Perhaps.

''No.''

''No?''

''The light hurts my eyes,'' he explained, ''which is why I decline your invitation to partake of the outdoors.''

''How horrible for you.''

He paused in the act of uncorking the flask. A smile lit his lips, but she would not be able to see it. ''Perhaps. But I have occupations that suffice and I do not feel the lack.''

He poured her a measure of the tea, unerringly and with competence. The stygian darkness that confused other people did not disturb him much. He could see what others could not, could hear what they could not. And knew what they wished to keep hidden. Their minds were almost as transparent as the darkness to him.

A curse, Douglas, worse than any other.

If not for that, if not for being able to feel her thoughts and know her mind, he would have banished her upon their first meeting. But she had touched a chord long thought forgotten, or perhaps he'd never known of its existence: *". . . My entire life is comprised of being ever mindful of what other people say and what people think of me. It had been refreshing to spend a few moments simply not caring."* He had pitied her, both for her despair and for the hopeless yearning he'd felt in her heart.

Pity. What an absurd notion. She was Louisa Patterson, rumored to be the richest heiress of this season or any other. Pampered and cared for, living in a home whose accoutrements rivaled that of the Crown. Anything she wanted was hers for the asking. Except for acceptance. She so wanted to be loved.

A kindred soul then. Almost.

He mitigated the ebony depths of the darkness by lighting a candle in the entrance to the cave. She turned, focused on the soft glow of a candle, blinked, then smiled as if reassured. He wanted to warn her that darkness held no terror and light did not promise sanctuary, but those lessons were ones she should have been taught in the nursery, not eighteen years later.

The light did not illuminate the cave entirely, leaving the area in which she sat in deep darkness. It framed the area, however, gave it dimension. Exposed some of his secrets.

"It is quite large, isn't it?" she asked, her eyes growing wide as she looked around her. There were bookcases built into the nooks and crannies of the cave, each shelf filled with well worn, well read volumes. A fire was laid but would not be used until nearly midnight, warming the cave and all his possessions, carefully collected throughout the years. A comfortable chair, a scattering of pillows, a few objects crafted in gold, a particularly appealing statue in marble. Little things, all bringing about a memory, some not quite as appealing as the object that induced it.

It was not an unexpected move she made, as she left the cocoon of darkness and entered his living area. Her thoughts did not require the degree of his skill to read. She was alight in wonder, a maiden trapped in a mystery and delighting in it.

"You read French," she said, her fingers scanning the treatise of Dom Agustin Calmet. Douglas damned his generosity. He should have immersed her in darkness. She would not then be able to catalog his library. Soon she would see Burgher Lonore and the tales of Elizabeth Bathory. Or, perhaps it was something he'd meant to happen, an act crafted by his mind against his will.

He smiled at the thought of such duality, plucked an apple from the basket, leaned back against the wall and bit into it. The taste was almost blissful after months of living on dried fruits and nuts. He must soon venture out into the world and equip his hermitage again. A necessity he avoided until need drew him out among others. He thrust aside the thought of the agony to come and concentrated upon the taste of the apple and the wonder of her thoughts. They came to him with the same sweetness as the fruit.

A sense of fatality gripped him again. She was not a stupid woman. She would discover him. Is that what he had wanted?

"You have a wonderful collection of books," was all she said, however, when she turned and looked at him as if she could see him through the shifting shadows. She said nothing more as she returned to her chair,

sat, and stared at the cave floor as if it were utterly
fascinating.

"Tell me of the candidates for your hand in marriage,
Louisa."

He could feel her sudden tremor. She was trembling,
fine tremors that made her clasp her hands together in
front of her. She would not look at him, but the racing
of her heart was audible, as was the confusion of her
mind. *Speak to me, Louisa*. It was a gentle command, one
that forced her chin up and made her look at him.

"I am quite ugly, you know," she said then, shocking
him. "I am the inherited sum of all my distinguished
relatives. I have the pointed chin of my grandmother,
the hawked nose of my maternal grandfather. My father
granted me his protruding teeth, and my mother a high
forehead. I am, regrettably, as close to a horse face as
anyone could possibly be. I have known how truly ugly
I was since the moment I first peered into a mirror and
noted the difference in my reflection from the faces of
other people."

"You are quite severe with yourself." He could not,
in all honesty, cozen her. She was not attractive, but
he had learned in his years that beauty was an easy
commodity to attain. What was more difficult to earn
was a sweetness of the soul, an acceptance of life and
all its myriad possibilities and restraints. He did not
know her; to learn her intimately would be to bare her
soul to danger, her mind to his explorations. But he
suspected she was as innocent in her soul as she was in
her flesh. He did not, on the whole, choose maidens
to feed upon. Their excitement was too heady, almost
addictive, their lust for life a rush that he felt only too
keenly.

"I do not expect you to mollify me," she said, addressing the floor with her comments.

It angered him, this self-imposed cruelty, this candor. *It is only because she does not allow you to cloak yourself in lies, Douglas. It is only because she has set a precedent for the truth and you resent her for doing so. You cannot comply, and she has rendered you helpless in the face of it.*

"Therefore," she continued, as if this were a normal conversation between two bosom friends, conducted in a drawing room amidst all the trappings of her not inconsiderable wealth, "it is a manner of temperament more than love that leads me to choose my husband. I do not, you see, expect him to love me."

"Love is not merely based upon appearance, Miss Patterson."

She raised her head and looked at the shadow that embraced him as if she could peer beneath the shroud of darkness. Was her look truly as pitying as it appeared?

"That is a sentiment much espoused by poets, sir. Or my grandfather. But he does not have to ignore the shocked looks of those who have heard of my wealth but not of my appearance. It is an exceedingly fond hope, and a thought that is quite nice, but it is not, unfortunately, shared by any of the young men who have courted me.

"It is not just that I am plain, you see. Plainness is a condition I could accept. I could spice my wardrobe with bright colors, or take to wearing face paint. But I am not plain, I am ugly. Taken from any angle, my face is rather hideous. Separately, perhaps, each feature is unfortunate, but being rendered together creates a combination that would have terrified even the most fond and doting parent. I have often wondered if my mother succumbed to the sweating sickness with a sort of delicate relief.''

He had nothing to say to her, could offer not one word of comfort. It irritated him, not that he was rendered silent, but that she did not seem to expect anything. Where was her need?

"Do you know, I realized I do not know your name."

"And here you are, my landlord."

Her smile seemed oddly forced. "Not until I'm wed, and even then, I shall not be an onerous one. I would replace those bushes in front of the cave, however, lest some of the neighbor children have a yen to explore."

"Or a poacher looks to store his purloined game?" He smiled, another lost gesture. "In truth, my home is more than difficult to find, but I grew tired yesterday, and did not remember." Perhaps it was more than that. Perhaps he had sensed her coming, had welcomed it, encouraged it. Perhaps he had even summoned her with some long dormant need to speak and listen and hear another's voice and thoughts. He banished that idea. It would be a form of self-destruction, and as much as he decried the life he led, he loved life itself.

"My name is Douglas Traherne."

"Have you lived here long?"

"Not that long."

"I shall not divulge your secret, you know." She looked so damnably earnest and young sitting there.

"I have begun to think you would not."

"For a hermit, you are quite amiable."

"Ah, but then you've admitted your acquaintance of hermits is rather limited."

She fingered the material of her skirt. "And why do you hide there?"

He smiled, thinking that she was too young after all. She envisioned some romantic tale, no doubt. A quick visit to her thoughts proved that true.

"Would you be a more sympathetic landlord if I confessed to pining for a lost love?"

"No, I do not think so. I would probably judge you quite harshly, declare that you owed me a tax. You see, I imagine you left a young woman with fond thoughts of you, her heart in pieces, and crying buckets of tears." Until she smiled, he had not known she was teasing him. It was such a novel experience that he studied her in the silence for a long moment, intent upon burrowing beneath the trappings of Louisa Patterson to the young woman beneath. Oh, if he could only do it without hurting her. The temptation was almost too great.

"I am sorry," she said. "I did not mean to be forward." There was regret and embarrassment in her tone. Perhaps she teased as little as he was the recipient of it.

"You have not been. I was merely planning my defense, wishing to tell you of her perfidy, of the fact that she quite broke my heart."

"Did she really?" There was remorse and even more embarrassment on her face. He damned his long unused skills. Evidently communication was something not easily put aside and then taken back.

"No, not really. I am a hermit because I choose it, not because someone forced me to seek seclusion. I nurse no broken heart or battered pride, Louisa."

She smiled, a relieved gesture, one that was not mirrored in her eyes. There was curiosity in her gaze, newly mined, and bright as gold. It would need to be deflected.

"Are there truly no suitors you prefer, Louisa?" he

asked, returning to their original topic. She did not demur at his familiarity, said nothing as her name rolled twice from his lips. It seemed so right that it do so, as if it had spirit and force of its own. Louisa. Curiously, it suited her.

She looked down at her folded hands as if never having seen them before. "There are scores of men seeking my fortune, Douglas," she said, startling him with the ease with which she spoke his name. There, the answer. Without a thought they were on a first name basis, all conventions of their day to be swept aside. Friends, perhaps? How utterly absurd. "If you line them all up single file, they would stretch to London, I am sure."

"And are none of them acceptable?"

She smiled again. He wondered if she felt safe in the darkness, secure in the mistaken notion that he could not see her.

"They are all eminently acceptable. And yet they are all eminently poor. There is not one among them who has more than two farthings to rub together. I have a penurious Duke's son, two poverty-stricken earls, four barons, and more than a few second and third sons to count among my suitors."

"More than most, I would wager."

She shook her head. "Much more than anyone, I would counter, Douglas. I am quite sure that I have cornered the entire matrimonial pot, so to speak. There are simply too many of them."

"And not one you would consider?"

For a moment, she seemed to consider. "There is one, perhaps, who is less fawning than most."

"So, you would have an admirer who is suitably attentive but not so much so."

It was as if she could see him, so blistering a look she gave the shadows.

"I am quite blessed, in that I do not lack for money. But because my family is wealthy does not mean that I lack sense. Each and every one of these suitors has claimed himself ravished for love, swept to the shore of devastation lest I consider his suit. I have been exclaimed the fair Louisa, the beauteous one, the one of golden curls."

"And?"

"I am not a total ninny, Douglas. My hair is quite unremarkably brown, and anyone who would claim me as the fair Louisa is almost certainly blind!"

He really shouldn't have laughed, but the look of disgust on her face was too refreshing.

"It is very lowering," she said, "to have someone believe you so utterly lacking in intelligence."

"I can imagine."

"I am quite sure you cannot."

"Because I am a hermit?"

"No."

"Then why would I be so disposed to not understand?"

"I am not certain I can explain it."

Was she embarrassed again? One moment she used the truth as a whip, the next she was cowering behind her thoughts. How utterly fascinating she was.

"What do you look like, Douglas?"

Should he show her? It was foolish, but the afternoon seemed littered with broken barriers. He had no right to be with her, to call her by her first name, to laugh with her as if they were friends of long standing. Still, he knew her appearance well, to hide in the darkness seemed almost cowardly now.

But his appearance would only make her hesitant again, trap her behind a rigid politeness. He was coming to like the Louisa Patterson who sat in the light-limned darkness and talked to shadows.

"I am unremarkable, Louisa," he said, hoping it would be answer enough.

"I suspect you are not, Douglas, just as I think you would not understand."

She turned away. Douglas wondered what capabilities she possessed that she could irritate, charm, and embarrass him within moments.

"You are a singularly confusing young woman."

"You have a note in your voice, Douglas, that all attractive people have. Perhaps it's confidence. A certain arrogance that states to the world that they are accustomed to getting what they want. It is a sad but undeniable fact, Douglas, that the world caters to those who are beautiful."

"Arrogant?" He had been called dangerous, soul-thief, even likened to Lamia, a creation of the Greeks, a monster with a serpent's head who sucked the blood of children. But he'd never been labeled confident, and no one had the courage to name him arrogant.

He smiled.

"I think you are too concerned about appearances, Louisa. There are quite a few of the demimonde who are not legendary beauties, but who manage to tempt a great many men."

Her eyes widened, then she burst into laughter, startling him even further. "How utterly wonderful a hermit you are, Douglas, that you should know such things. And how shocking that you should say them."

He stiffened. "I beg your pardon. I forgot myself."

She stood and walked to the cave entrance. "Thank you for forgetting yourself, then, and for being honest. It's the first delightful afternoon I've had for a very long time."

"I am grateful to have been amusing."

"Oh, Douglas, you've been so much more than amusing. You've been a friend."

And with that surprising, and totally unwelcome remark, she left his home.

Three

"And I tell you, Charles, that I'd sooner bed a nag than that girl."

"I'd heard rumors of your proclivities, Harold, but I had no idea." There was more than a touch of humor in that voice; it dripped sardonic amusement.

Louisa stepped even further back into the curtained alcove, wishing she had not the acute hearing of her great Aunt Winifred.

"Afraid your little mare will neigh at an inopportune moment, Harold?"

"Damn your sense of humor, Charles. I haven't two farthings to scratch together, but it's almost worth debtor's prison to avoid looking at that face for the rest of my life."

"Cheer up, man. You aren't the first man who's married for fortune and found amusement on the side."

"Yes, but I doubt any other man was saddled with such a bride. There can't be two of them in England."

"Keep the blinds drawn, Harold. Forbid her candles, and keep her awake all night so that she sleeps in the light of day."

"Better yet, grit my teeth, blindfold myself, render her with child and ship her off forever to one of her family's homes in Scotland."

"That's the spirit. And live the high life on her fortune."

Finally, they moved away. A moment passed and then another, during which there was only silence, the echo of a far off quartet playing a minuet. In the hall a clock ticked, and someone laughed.

A tear fell and washed her hand.

She released the curtain she'd scrunched up, smoothed out the wrinkles in its crimson folds, and used the backs of both hands to brush away the orphaned tears on her cheeks. She should grow more hardened to times like these. It was not the first time some young man had commented about her appearance. Nor, she was certain, would it be the last. Even her family, a most loving and noble gathering once so large but now so sadly diminished, had not dulled their dismay at the way nature had taken all of its assorted unacceptable traits and joined them together in her person.

Half of England had been invited to Bainbridge Hall this weekend, an opportunity not for the young bucks in the country to get an eyeful of her, but, as her grandfather had announced, for her to choose which one of them would be her stud. Louisa had said nothing to this pronouncement. She was long past being shocked by anything her grandfather did or said. Nor was she brave enough to argue with him; therefore she'd been ready and on time when the first of the innumerable carriages had rolled up to the front door.

The young man with the cutting sense of humor and so obvious a horror for her had been a favored suitor. With him, she'd forgotten the hideousness of her face, the reflection that stared back at her in the mirror. She'd forgotten deportment enough to have even laughed with him. She had been charmed by his sunny blond hair and the beautiful blue eyes and the smile that seemed to come from the depths of his soul.

More likely the cavernous interior of his empty coffers.

Her grandfather would call him out if he knew. Despite the fact that he was in his seventies, he would have demanded satisfaction on the field of honor. But her grandfather was nearly blind, both in truth and with affection. He never seemed to see the looks directed her way, or the sudden shocked gasps of guests who had never before viewed the Patterson heiress. Even those familiar with her looks seemed not to be able to refrain from staring, like the young maids who'd been assigned duty on the floor of her suite. When she chanced upon them, they would stop their dusting, and turn to stare at her.

She could not blame them; she would have done the same thing.

She had no brother or sister, which was a blessing she supposed. Fate might have put as her sibling someone remarkably fair, and then she would have been doubly cursed. As it was, she was the only one in succession for the Patterson millions. A fact that had brought a horde

of young men to Bainbridge Hall for this weekend, all
with empty purses and willingly averted eyes.

Dreams die hard. This one crashed to earth with such
a thud that it was as if the world shook for just a moment.
Harold Minter, Viscount Lacorn, was not interested in
her because of her sparkling wit. He did not think her
charming or insightful or intelligent. She had been willing to accept that, and even to recognize that it was
only her money he desired, not her person. She was,
after all, Arthur Patterson's granddaughter and he
counted himself fool for no one. But to be ridiculed so
publicly seemed an even more insensitive cruelty. She
could, after all, not help the way she looked. If there
was anything she could have done to alter her ugliness,
she would have long since done it.

Did people actually think she *liked* being this way?

The drawing room was empty; most of the guests were
sunning and strolling on the front lawn, being treated
to crystal flutes of champagne and enough food to feed
a small army. On the north side of the lawn, a huge
maze had been transplanted for the amusement of the
guests, a feat that had required the importation of fifteen dozen six foot tall hedges, their roots balled in
burlap. It was a pity, really, since the creation would last
no longer than the week.

Huge parasols had been erected to protect the ladies'
complexions, and there were two separate quartets of
musicians, both playing the same tune so that wherever
a guest strolled, the echo of music followed him. The
weather had cooperated and brought a sunny day with
just a dot of clouds.

All of this Louisa noted with the detached air of a
born hostess, a position her grandfather's love of postur-

ing had made necessary. She loved him, but she wasn't under any delusions as to his character. He wielded power with an ingrained and habitual love of it. He was one of the country's most able statesmen, a man of peace who also maintained his influence over the military because he'd distinguished himself in King George's War. In addition to his stirring oratory, he had transformed a meager inheritance into a fortune coveted by many. The Patterson fortune had been mined in Canada and bartered in the Americas.

It was perhaps a sign of how desperate he was that he would barter Louisa's hand in marriage, submerging his own disdain for men who would rather marry for money than earn it.

Or a sign of how truly unacceptable she was.

She left the house by the great terrace, taking the steps quickly. Her slippers had not been constructed for granite steps or for the lush grass that flanked the terrace. It seemed as if she could feel each small pebble, the coolness of the grass beneath her feet. If she hadn't been wearing stockings, she would have pulled off the slippers completely, tucking them into the pockets of her demurely styled dress. She would have been labeled a hoyden then, instead of just ugly. An heiress, talked about in delicate whispers that whirled around her like smoke.

She truly wished she could be a hoyden sometimes and bathe in the stream that bordered Bainbridge Hall and laugh loudly and sing at the top of her voice and wear clothes that weren't modest or demure or pastel. She craved reds that were daring and emerald greens that mimicked the yews and blues that echoed the color of sapphires. And maybe yellow, like the sun's rays. But that was a wish never to be fulfilled. Her modiste had recommended subdued colors, pastels so delicate and barely colored that it seemed to Louisa they were only a shade of white. The better to blend into the walls, my dear.

She glanced behind her at the crowd of people. They were laughing in groups, glasses held high, glinting in the sun. Footmen carried silver salvers from one group to another, another a tray of tidbits, morsels to tempt the appetite before the afternoon tea. No one turned their head, not one person missed her.

Should she not have felt some hurt at their easy dismissal of her? In truth, she did not. Nor did she hate them. The fact was, she was possessed of a lamentable habit of fairness. They envied her the wealth that was hers, the love of a family gone, but strong in tradition and affection. Too, she had the Patterson name, a heritage to be proud of for all that it had been awarded because of trade, good fortune, and bravery.

No, she did not hate her guests, most of whom tittered about her behind her back. She was, for all her ugliness, more fortunate than they. She would be able to choose her own husband, would be free to control her own money. If she did not wish to live in London, she could maintain her suite at Bainbridge Hall, or Powerscourt, or Damsen House, or at least twenty other places her grandfather had purchased over the years. It was a heady sort of freedom, and one she did not discount.

But sometimes, she would have gladly exchanged it all to be pretty, to be like the other young girls who congregated at Bainbridge Hall. What would it be like to discuss materials that flattered the complexion and the face-enhancing shape of one's bonnet? To giggle about blushing, or whisper about drops to make the eyes sparkle, or even to wield a fan with delicate and rapier precision, knowing that the object of such determined scrutiny could not avoid the invitation for long.

It was simply easier for Louisa to ignore herself for long stretches of time. And infinitely less painful. She had perfected the technique of going for hours without being conscious of herself. Her maid would help her dress, would arrange her hair in the morning. There was no need to study herself in the looking glass to know that the night before had not changed her appearance. Sometimes nearly a whole day would pass until she caught a glimpse of herself, a reflection in one of the display cases in her grandfather's library, or the polished sheen of mahogany. Until that moment, she could pretend that she was different. For a few hours, in her heart, she had willed herself to forget.

The group of people from whom she escaped now was like a large mirror, seeing only the outside of herself, in all her hideousness. They did not peer beneath the surface to see the dreams and hopes and essence of Louisa. They only reflected what was horribly obvious and hideously ugly.

For a moment, a fleeting moment, she wanted to be far away from this place, from the home she'd called hers for most of her life. It was here her grandfather had brought her when she was barely eight, a young and shocked orphan. She'd been suddenly deprived of both parents and terrified of the booming-voiced man she'd seen rarely in her life. It had only taken weeks for her to understand that beneath that glowering exterior was a man who was capable of the greatest tenderness. Later she looked back on that time and marveled at his kindness. He suffered too, in the loss of his only child, yet he always had time for her. And the home that had seemed so terrifyingly large had become a magical castle in which she dreamed and played and pretended.

She wished she could go to the stables and have her favorite mare saddled. But someone would tell her grandfather and he would come looking for her, perhaps summon her to his library for a lecture on courage. Right at this moment she didn't want to see anyone. In fact, she wanted so fervently to burrow into the woods surrounding Bainbridge Hall that it would be weeks until anyone could find her. Not exactly a brave deed, but a fervently held wish.

She could no longer hear the music, and the cacophony of speech seemed no more intrusive than the sound a flock of geese might make. The absence of noise seemed a blessed benediction. But no, there were sounds, she simply had to stand still to hear them. The chittering of a forest creature, the call of a bird, the flutter of wings. Overhead, a gentle melody of leaves as they brushed against each other, the rasp of branch against branch.

A breeze lifted the hem of her skirt, played with it, flirted with a tendril of hair at her cheek. She spread out her fingers as if to catch it in her palms, and she smiled when she realized what she had done. As if she could capture the wind.

She gathered her skirts in her hand and climbed a gentle hill. She'd once come here as a child, lonely and afraid. There, on that spot, she had thrown herself down and wept out her grief. Not for her face then, but for a mother's hug long absent from her world, a father's smile she'd never see again. She stood on the hill and felt the bite of shame. She rarely thought of them anymore. Was that what death truly was, then? To be forgotten by those who must love us? She bowed her head and stared at her folded hands, then wrapped her arms around herself. Ten years. That's how long it had been, and in the interim, she'd known love, the gruff affection of a man who'd tried his best and managed better than he knew.

Oh, if she could only be a credit to him, instead of someone so needful of kind words and bracing talks. "Courage," he would have said had he been standing there. "They do not deserve the time you take to think of them. Young pups," he would have snorted, the derision on his face plain to see. "Won't countenance your marrying a fool, girl."

She turned and walked down the crest of the hill, turning right to follow a path almost obscured by weeds and brambles. She knew it was not proper, but somehow that did not seem to matter at this moment. She had known ever since she left Bainbridge Hall that she was going to visit him. To sit in the darkness with him and listen to his sardonic voice tell her she was too fixed upon appearances seemed the only possible alternative to a day grown cloudy with introspection and made tearful by the truth.

Four

He closed his eyes, concentrated on the people around him, forced himself from Dorset and into London's crowded streets. All he need do was stand there and let it bathe him, all this mass of humanity, walking, running, pushing past, rolling carts in the streets, riding in carriages, wagons. Life; it pulsed around him like a giant heart. He leaned back against the brick of a building, feeling the sharp edges gouge into his skin even through his coat. Such was the experience of it, this life he wished for with such urgency that it frightened him.

And it was his. All he had to do was hold out his hands and absorb it like a giant sponge, and no one who passed him would know why they were more fatigued today than the day before, why they felt in need of rest or a bracing toddy. They would never know, because he did not wish them to know, unlike some of his kind who terrorized those they fed upon, making them believe it was their blood they sucked dry. No, only the life force, the essence of the soul, the gleam in bright eyes, what made a smile real and unfeigned. Worse than blood, this. More important than simple blood.

It had been told to him that those of his kind are born, not made. But no one knew why, of all the people birthed on a certain day, in a certain country, under a certain star, only Douglas Traherne was born this way. A question of heritage? Of timing? Of a vengeful god who punished the Traherne dynasty for a sin too long ago to be remembered? Or because of nothing at all? Simply because it was time for another being to walk the earth, to live in loneliness and despair, and to die in myth?

It was normal for those like him to band together, to live in groups set aside from others. They lived in towns created by their ancestors, places like Venice and Paris and Rome, cities known for their beauty and their darkness and their attraction. It was the supreme irony. They each desperately wished to be part of those who feared them, and mankind feared them because they wished it so. If they were shunned, then, let it be for fear, not because they were born different and alone and apart.

Yet from the beginning, Douglas knew he could not be part of that fear, could not promulgate the myth, would not circulate the rumors they willingly told about themselves. Nor could he be one of those who allowed the loneliness to descend into depravity. To trap the wary, to fool the wise, to enchant the disillusioned. It was better simply to be alone.

But were there others like himself? Was there a place

somewhere in the middle, between hermitage and depravity?

Was that why he sympathized with Louisa Patterson? Why his heart had been touched and his mind had been charmed and his soul had been caught unawares? Because they were different, they had each been cast adrift in life.

He allowed himself to listen to the thoughts of those who passed him, the better to ignore his own. He did not wish to feel anything for Louisa Patterson. To do so added layers of complexity to a life that was already difficult enough.

She stood in the darkness, hands fisted against her skirt. She'd left her shawl behind and the cave was chilled. She whirled and he was there, a giant shadow blocking the faint light from the cave opening.

He brushed past her and she heard sounds in the darkness, then saw the glow of a fire being set. The flue was a natural chimney hole, the fireplace an out-cropping of rock, the mantel a sheared bit of shale. He stood looking down at the fire, his back to her.

"You'll freeze in that ridiculous garment."

"It's new," she said, looking down at the soft ivory confection. "Designed to bring a suitor's attention to my more laudable attributes."

"You're nearly falling out of it."

It was true, there was quite a large amount of skin showing. But she would rather have a gentleman's eyes upon that portion of her anatomy than fixed upon the mismatched features of her face.

Douglas turned and walked into the shadows. How

odd that he'd never allowed her a view of his face. Was he scarred or otherwise unpresentable? She felt a surge of gratitude that it should be so, then felt the bite of shame for such a thought. If she were a better person, she would coax him from his hermitage, lead him to believe that people judged not on the surface, but the worth of a person. And all of it would be lies.

People, on the whole, did not like those who were different. Knowledge she'd learned as a child touring her grandfather's chinaware factory. The cups that came from the kiln were sorted and judged. If the paint was smudged and the handle cracked, the cups were put into a box and set out upon a bench to be offered for nearly nothing to thrifty housewives. The pretty ones were sent to fill orders throughout England, to adorn shop windows and the homes of nobles. People were like that, setting a person aside because his nose was too long or his ears too wide, or her smile was too filled with teeth, or because she was too thin or too fat. She would have been placed in a box, too, save for the fact that her cracked handle was made of gold and her paint was silver.

"Are you going to stand there all day?" His voice interrupted her reverie. She shook herself and followed Douglas into the shadows. Once seated, she folded her hands in her lap and leaned her head back to stare at the ceiling. Even with the faint light from the fire, it was impossible to see, as if a big black cloud had settled over them.

He threw his hands up in the air and stalked away, returning in only a moment with a soft garment that he placed around her shoulders.

"At least you will not freeze this way, Louisa."

"Thank you," she said, burrowing her nose into the soft wool. It smelled of spices and was as soft as a kitten's fur to the touch.

"We cannot all be finches, Louisa," Douglas softly said. "Some of us must be sparrows."

The statement was so in tune with her thoughts that she turned her head and surveyed the shadow that shrouded him. "I find I do not much like being a sparrow, Douglas. I have forever wished to be a robin, or something with more color and more adventure."

"Then you must learn your place in the world."

"I know," she sighed. "I do not rebel, Douglas. Except sometimes in my heart."

"And dream of being an opera singer or an actress?"

The thought was so outrageous that she smiled. "No, of course not. But perhaps a traveler, someone who would see the world."

"And where would you go if given the chance?"

"To Egypt, to Spain. To France and to China." She fingered the material of her skirt and smiled into the blackness.

Why did it seem easier to talk to him than anyone? Because she could not see him? Because the darkness that enshrouded them also protected her? She had lied; she was a rebel. At least at this moment. She was defying all the conventions of her life by sitting in the darkness with a man she did not know, who had certainly never been introduced to her, who held his own quota of secrets about him. She could imagine what people would think to see her here. Poor ugly Louisa, riddled by madness. Poor thing, she sat in the darkness and conversed with a shadow, thinking to find herself a friend.

"Hermits do not have friends, Louisa."

"You have a disconcerting ability to do that, Douglas. To guess at my thoughts."

"Is that what I was doing?" A shifting of sound, then his voice closer.

"Your thoughts are not that difficult to gauge, Louisa. Why are you here?"

"Perhaps I only wished to hear a kind voice, Douglas."

His laughter was unexpected. Not so, the bite of embarrassment. Louisa had had too many years of becoming acquainted with that emotion.

"You ascribe to me a virtue few others would, Louisa. Indeed, I never thought myself kind."

"But you do not call me names, nor do you ridicule me for what I cannot help." There, the truth was out. Without conscious thought, she recalled every painful moment of that overheard conversation.

"Why do you care so much what someone said to you?"

"Because he did not smell of spirits, and was capable of holding a conversation. Because I thought him capable of ignoring how I looked." Should she have been that honest?

"It does not seem as if he is as much a paragon as you first imagined."

"No," she softly said. And until he'd ridiculed her, she'd not known he had thought of her with such contempt. How easily she was fooled. Or wanted to be.

"And you opine too much upon appearances, Louisa."

"You do not judge me, however, Douglas." *You do not hold my ugliness against me, do not counsel me on protecting myself not because of who I am, but of what I represent.*

I am the Bainbridge heiress. How long has it been since anyone noted that I am also Louisa Patterson?

"You would make a saint of me, Louisa, and I am not." In a second, he was so close she could feel the brush of his hand upon her neck. A sweet and intoxicating and forbidden touch. "I am as far removed from piety as a man can be."

She closed her eyes tight, willed herself not to feel the trembling of her limbs. It was not fear, but more awareness. A sense of knowing she'd never experienced before. It was as if she could feel him touch her in his mind, calling out in some odd way that alerted each part of her that he was there. It was as if she existed in that timeless moment only to be what he wanted her to be, as if she could tell where he was, what he saw, how he felt, a true intrusion of thought and empathy. She blinked and the feeling was abruptly gone. She blinked once more and he was there standing so close that she could feel his breath upon her cheek.

His hand reached out and tipped up her chin. Did he smile at her, or was his look solemn? Did he ridicule her or only pity her for her silliness? She could not tell, he was surfeited by shadow. But the touch of his fingers upon her skin made her achingly aware that this was embarrassingly real. This was no dream.

"I can do that, Louisa," he softly said. "I can banish all knowledge of me from your mind again if that is what you wish. I can make this seem only a dream, one from which you awaken refreshed and eased."

Another moment, a mindless silence.

"Who are you?" she asked, and placed her hand over his. The warmth of him seemed oddly reassuring.

"You do not truly wish to know, Louisa," he said, in the softest and most gentle of tones.

This impossible afternoon, these implausible hours taken out of her life were about to culminate in knowledge she most desperately wanted and that she was certain she would never forget. Did she truly wish to know? Did she honestly, and most fervently, want to hear the words he was about to utter?

"I do," she said, and she did not know if it was a lie or the truth.

He hesitated for a moment, then spoke the words in a soft and tender tone. "I am vampir, Louisa."

Five

"I shall not swoon, you know," she said, long minutes later.

"I did not expect it of you."

"If I could read your mind, I believe I would find that to be a falsehood. Not unkindly done, I might add. But I'm most assuredly certain you were prepared to catch me."

"You are a slender woman; it would not have been a burden."

"How utterly polite we are being. Is this normal?"

"I do not know, never having told anyone before." He stood beside her, a presence in the dark. "You are trembling, like a sapling in a storm wind."

His collection of books, his voice, the allure of it, the sensation she felt when hearing him speak. As if a warm ribbon of words curled around her, pulling her toward him, cascading through the air only to wrap themselves around him. Too impossible by half. Ridiculous.

"This is almost as adventurous as traveling to China, Douglas." She cleared her throat. "I have never met one of the undead before."

His laughter echoed through the cave and beyond, out into the sunlight, the groves of trees, the green and rolling meadows of his homeland.

"Wherever did you get that idea?"

"My nurse was Russian," she said. It was a very distressing experience, really, standing in the dark, the sound of warm laughter her only real connection to him.

"And your Russian nurse put you to sleep with stories of the undead, did she? If I am, am I, like most Russians believe, the child of a witch and a werewolf? My mother would be distressed to hear herself called such. Or perhaps I am the seventh son of the seventh son. Or do your beliefs run a bit further afield and are versed in dogma? Rome has declared corporeal incorruptibility a reward for a good life, if one lives in the principles of the church. Perhaps I am only a sinner, then." He moved; she could feel it by the eddies of air stirring around her.

"I am no more undead than you, Louisa. My mortal body will seek its own end in time. For the nonce, I am what I am and no nursery tales will alter it or expose me."

"Then what are you?"

"Have I not already told you?" he asked, his voice touched by a strange note of kindness. "And did you not already suspect? My library, this cave, my reticence, your own wish for an event steeped in romance and legend. You added a sum, and although it was enough to frighten most people, you still returned.''

A touch upon her cheek. It was both warmth and tenderness.

"You count yourself ugly and would shun the world. I count myself solitary and wish it banished for different reasons. Who is the undead between us?"

She could feel herself flushing.

"Why, then, do you hate the light?"

"I do not hate it. You misunderstood. My eyes are sensitive to sunlight. To candlelight. It does not mean that I hate what I cannot tolerate. Unlike those insubstantial suitors of yours."

"You tell me what you are not, but have not yet divulged what you are." She felt oddly weary, with a deep and sudden craving for sleep.

A few moments of silence, a brush of wind against this secure shelter. Louisa wondered why she felt he lured her from stepping too close to the truth.

"What do you wish to know, Louisa?"

"What kind of powers do you have, Douglas? And how did you obtain them?" *You hear my thoughts, don't you?*

How odd that she could feel him study her.

"What powers I have were obtained through my birth, not misadventure. I have never been excommunicated, and I quite like dogs. I was not born on the winter solstice, or between Christmas and Epiphany, and I have not murdered anyone, either angel or sinner. No, Louisa, I am not one of the undead." *But, yes, I can hear your thoughts.* His voice sounded so utterly kind and filled with warmth.

When she dipped her head and stared, sightlessly, at her hands, he drew closer.

"You drink blood."

"I prefer fresh fruits and vegetables to meat or blood of any kind. My craving for blood is yet another myth. The world is fashioned of falsehoods about my kind, Louisa. I see nothing hideous in a cross, I do not dislike garlic unless it is used in excess. I am as easily killed as any man." A touch on her hand, that was all, but it felt as if a spark had burned her.

"And yet you hear my thoughts, see in the dark, and slip easily around this cave with great agility and even more disconcerting speed."

"I wondered if you would realize that," he said, withdrawing his hand.

"What is real, then, and what is myth?"

"And why would you want to know?"

"Can you not read my mind?"

"Your thoughts are too confused, Louisa. And above all of them is a terror that you hide quite well. Are you that afraid?"

"Yes," she softly said.

"Your honesty will be your undoing one day."

"At your hand?"

"Is that what you're afraid of, that I'll grow fangs or a hole in the back of my neck and drain you of blood? In Bulgaria, those like me are called Obour and are rumored to have one nostril and a pointed tongue. In China, the Ch'lang Shih are never human at all, while in your nurse's Russia, the Viesczy are supposed to gnaw their own feet and hands while resting in a daytime grave. Which of these shall I be, Louisa, since you are determined to see the horror that has never existed, while ignoring that which does?"

She turned as if to view him, wishing for the first time that the darkness was gone, that the light would make it possible for her to see him.

"What color are your eyes?" It seemed necessary to know. What did he look like, this hermit who eschewed the light? And why did she feel so compelled to be here today, banishing rational thought, breeding, endless lectures on propriety, and her own niggling sense of something unsaid and unspoken, yet blatantly aware? Vampire? Had she guessed it before? And had he been right? Had she wished for something steeped in romance and legend?

"It is more correctly vampir, Louisa. From the Magyar. And my eyes are green," he said. "My mother's heritage."

"Does she know?"

He smiled, a quite lovely smile. "Of course she does. My parents were not bound by superstition as so many of our countrymen. They realized early on that I was a strange child, incapable of taking my place at the head of the family. Even so, my banishment was not at their hands but at my own."

"But, if you are not like the myth, if there is no truth to all of those horrible tales, then why do you hide? It is easy enough to explain away a certain knowledge of people. A great many seem to be possessed of intuition. And your agility could be dampened for polite society, could it not? And if you dislike the light, then could you not simply sleep during the day?"

"I warned you about taking me on as one of your charities, Louisa. And you have totally ignored something I've said. Is it, I wonder, that you do not wish to hear what you do not wish to learn?''

"You are going to tell me, aren't you? About the horror that does exist.''

He nodded. She wished he would not speak.

"I can kill, Louisa. Quickly and without much thought. It is for that reason I seclude myself from others. I feed, dear Louisa, not on blood, but on the life essence. Each time I've touched you, I've taken from you, which is why you're so exhausted now. And the reason I can be seen is because of it, because of that life force you've unwittingly surrendered.''

He came close, but did not touch her.

"It is as if you're giving up part of yourself each time, without knowing it. Should you be my constant companion, our friendship could only exist in your death. Until you had nothing to give at all.

"Do you know where I was when you came, Louisa? I was feeding.'' A gentle stroke upon her cheek, a flash of fire, as it seemed to follow the meandering path of his finger down to her chin. "My solitude had become so burdensome that I could not tolerate it any longer, so I found myself in London, Louisa, amidst those who did not care of my mission, being so concerned with their own lives. I walked among the nobles and the commoners and drank of their energy, until I felt as strong and as mighty as an English oak.''

She wiped her palms on her skirts, wishing that she could face him, but being too cowardly to do so.

"I will not fault your behavior, Louisa,'' he said, again in that soft voice. "You've shown more courage than any person I've known in all my life.''

She looked at him then, wishing she could peer through the darkness.

She did not want to leave, but she could hear the words as if he spoke them plainly in his soul. There were too many questions she wanted to ask, too many things she wanted to know. Answers she would probably never learn. Still, he had not said she could not return.

She blinked again, feeling incredibly foolish. Still, she reached out her hand and cupped his cheek, feeling provocative and beyond courageous. He stepped back away from her touch and she followed him, intent upon experiencing that emotion that had swamped her before, as if she was part of him, could echo his breathing with her own breaths. It was as if her skin was part of his, or shockingly, that he could reside just beneath her heart, become Louisa Anna Patterson for that period of time he chose to be hers.

"What are you doing?" His tone was brusque, but not dangerous enough. It lacked the edge of terror he'd held up to her to frighten her away.

His cheek was absurdly soft, delineated by a line where whiskers grew. Afternoon's bristle, they scratched her palm. His hair was as soft as a child's, black and straight and thick, inviting her fingers. And through it all, the silent moments were marked by his stunned acceptance and her bravery. It was utterly shocking, of course, and something for which she should be chastised, but it was a soothing gesture she made, something so necessary and needful that she did not stop to count the cost. A child in pain, a tortured animal, a woman in childbirth, a man wounded in battle. Who could turn away from these? Or from Douglas, with his despair written in such large letters that it was impossible not to feel it?

Finally, he gripped her wrist and pulled her hand away.

"Do not," he said, and it was the tone of those words that separated them. He stepped away finally and huffed out a breath. "You challenge fate, Louisa."

"Do I?"

"I can hurt you, you little fool, don't you understand that?"

She stepped away, obeying the command he issued with a soundless voice. Louisa hesitated at the entrance to the cave, bent down, and snuffed out the branch of candles resting upon a slab of shale. She turned and smiled at him.

"I will come back, you know."

"It is better that you don't. Or should I simply remove myself?"

"Then I will think of you, here. Are thoughts acceptable?"

"Accepted and appreciated. You may even say a prayer or two, if you're so inclined." At her look, he smiled. "I am not devoid of religion, Louisa, simply removed from it."

Unspoken were the rest of the words. *And from all mankind.*

Six

"I knew you would not leave."

He glanced up at her. He'd heard her progress through the cave, to the chair in which he'd sat. Could see her quite clearly by the candle he'd lit to augment the fire. He could see in the darkness, but he had a difficulty reading without some light. Or perhaps it was a function of age. The thought was almost amusing. He merged into the shadows, hiding himself.

"You complain of being too adequately guarded, Louisa, yet you have no difficulty arranging your schedule in order to visit me. And why did you think I would be here?"

"It's an immodest thought, Douglas; can you not read it?" She placed the basket she'd brought on the cave floor. He hoped she remembered this one when she left. The other had become a talisman of sorts, something to rifle through when he was feeling particularly lonely.

During the last week, he'd taken out its contents one by one, as if to assure himself that her incursion into his solitary life had been real and not simply his own type of dream. The stoneware jug, the embroidered napkins, the plate on which a delectable assortment of pastries had once rested—they were all icons of memory. Absurdities.

"Why should I, Louisa, when you are bursting to tell me?"

"Very well," she said, planting her fists on her hips and smiling at the shadow that hid him. Another dichotomy of Louisa Patterson. Giving him a scowl and a smile at the same time.

"I believe that you are not particularly averse to my presence, Douglas."

"Else what, Louisa, I would have tried to drink your blood before now?"

"Do you truly not?"

He held up his hand and crossed his palm with the fingers of the other hand. How idiotic. She could not see him. "I will swear a double oath that I never have. The idea is particularly appalling."

"Yet, your reading matter would lead one to believe differently."

He glanced over at the bookshelves. "Vlad Tepes and Elizabeth Bathory? He was a madman and she a lunatic."

"Then why do you study them?"

"Why do you lance me with your curiosity, Louisa? Does no one wish to answer your questions at Bainbridge Hall?"

"And who should I ask about vampirs, Douglas? My

nurse would run screaming into the night. And besides, if I did not bedevil you, you would be sitting here alone.''

"Such is the meaning of hermit, Louisa."

She seemed to draw back, pull into herself in such a way that he knew he'd wounded her with his words. Little innocent. She had not the way of teasing. As ill prepared for social discourse as he.

He decided to give her a part of himself as penance. A slice of truth and history, one not easily divulged.

"When I was a young man, Louisa, I wanted to know everything I could about those who reputed to be like me. They were but a few of those I studied. There was Peter Pogojowitz and works by Calmet, Gilles de Rais, and a score more rumored to be vampir.''

"And they were not?"

How quickly she punctured his privacy. With what ease she leveled his consequence.

"What else did your Russian nurse tell you, Louisa?"

"Only what we've spoken about. You cannot die, you feast on blood, it is possible for you to change your appearance, and night is the time you awaken."

"The latter two abilities are also shared by most nobles," he said, surprised at the humor he felt. But then, he'd never discussed this with anyone outside his family, and even then, he'd mitigated his own sick horror at what he was to spare his parents. "The truth, Louisa, is somehow more complex than fairy tales. Do you truly wish to hear?"

"Very much, Douglas. But only if you wish to tell me."

He smiled. He did not, but perhaps it would act as purge of a sort. And then again, it might banish her from his presence forever. *A not unwanted event, is it,*

Douglas? Or have you begun to anticipate her singing hello, her smile?

He should have terrified her with his knowledge, could have easily hurt her if necessary. Others like him would have stolen her life's essence without a qualm or a spark of internal despair. Instead, he'd heard her, felt the excitement barely escaping from that hidden place deep in her soul.

"I was born the way children are, and nourished by a wet nurse and my mother's love. The Trahernes are not as wealthy as your family, but well enough endowed to hold their own. My childhood was spent as most are in such circumstances, being lectured on duty and tutored by a selection of well meaning but penurious young men." He leaned his head back, focused on the ceiling. There were smoke stains there from years of fires.

"It was not until I was in my thirteenth year that I began to realize something was wrong. Up until that time, I had been sheltered, I suppose, being my parents' only child."

"What happened? Did someone hurt you?"

He closed his eyes.

"The life I live, Louisa, is as a result of ignorance. I am not hurt by it, I am altered by it." He could not hide the bitterness from his voice. Would she hear it?

She sat on the footstool, her chin propped on her hand, seemingly intent upon the fire. "I would alter your circumstances if I could, Douglas. I know what it is like to be shunned because of what you are, or even be sought after because of what you have. People have a way of ignoring the truth about a person, of not wanting to know what lies inside."

"I wish it were that simple. All my childhood, I had heard voices inside my head, heard my parents' thoughts, the wishes of my nurses. I thought it normal, an ability shared by others. I never realized it was not so until I was sent away to school." He smiled. "Everyone remarked how bright I was, how I seemed to score so well on all my exams. It never occurred to them that the answers were as easy to read as my don's mind."

Her eyes were shining now. Admiration? Envy? He closed his eyes again. She believed him touched by magic. Hell more likely. Was it fair to destroy her innocence that easily? A conundrum. Leave her steeped in her ignorance or take advantage of an audience willing and eager to hear him speak of things he'd never said. Who would triumph in this exchange? There was no doubt, was there? He would burden her with the truth and see if it grew lighter in the sharing.

"I began to experience an almost constant fatigue. My parents attributed it to my rapid growth. I towered over my father and other male relatives. I knew, somehow, that I was different." Even now, if he did not take care, he felt it again, that unnerving sensation of being trapped beneath glass, all the world as it was but his actions slower, more cumbersome. It was as if each movement was performed in a viscous liquid, clear and thick. Was that how normal people felt?

He opened his eyes, stood, walked into the darkness, selected a bottle of wine from the cache aligned there, and poured himself a full glass. He did not offer any to Louisa. The very last thing he wanted was to have her return to Bainbridge Hall muddled in her wits and babbling of knowing a vampir.

He returned, stood gazing into the fire. Soon, the

weather would cut off his cave from the curious and the unwary. He glanced at Louisa, one of the few who'd ventured past the opening of his home. Courage? Or simple curiosity? He didn't know. She stared back at him, not at all modest in her scrutiny, but then, they'd come beyond that, had they not? Secrets swirled between them. Her hatred of artifice and his identity.

"What happened then, Douglas?" Her voice was kind, coaxing, gentle. His mother had been the same. Always, even after that day.

"I met another one like me. Someone who delighted in being as he was, who used his birth as an excuse for depravity." *As most of his kind did.*

"He taught me to feed, the power of it. Showed me that I was as different from others as they are similar to themselves." *Taught me that I was unique and rare and better than those I fed upon, as if they were prey and I was a vulture. I began to delight in my eccentricities, in my differences.* How stupid he had been in his youth.

"What happened to your friend?"

His laughter was short and mirthless. "Adrian was not a friend, Louisa. An opportunist, perhaps. A hedonist, of a certainty. Perhaps even a fiend. But not a being to trust, or even hold affection for. As to his whereabouts, he is probably in Venice, or a thousand other places that seem to welcome people such as us."

"And yet, you do not join them."

"I am considered a rebel, even among my own, Louisa. I espouse restraint."

"And hide yourself away in a cave so that you are not tempted."

He turned to look at her again. How had she known that?

"Penance, Louisa. I could not live with myself if I killed again."

She seemed to stiffen, as if just now becoming aware of the danger his presence posed.

"I killed my father," he calmly said in the silence. "Is that not reason enough to be punished for a lifetime?"

"How?" How tiny her voice sounded.

"I had not learned," he said, staring into the fire once again, "to control my feeding. All I felt was this voracious hunger, an almost soul deep need to quench it." He sought out his chair, sat down heavily, and drank the rest of the wine. "Of all the men I've ever admired, he was the finest, the best. And one moment, his arm was around me, and we were laughing about a new colt that had just been born, congratulating ourselves in our wisdom in purchasing its sire. The next, he was on the floor nearly dead, as pale as if I'd sucked the blood from him in truth."

"It could have been his heart, or a brainstorm, or a thousand other things. It was not necessarily your actions."

"You think I have not excused myself on one hand and condemned myself on the other? So my mother reassured me, but I knew better. Even when he died, a month later, I knew better. It was me."

"You cannot know that."

The words burst out of his soul, seemed to light the room with fire of their own. "I killed him, Louisa. Do you think I have not tested such a damnable skill in the intervening years? Shall I feed on you in order to prove it?"

The silence seemed heavy, as if it still contained all

his rage, the bitterness he'd lived with for years, the longing to be something other than what he was.

"If you wish," a small and tinny voice said. It swirled around him, the invitation. The longing for her expanded in his mind, in that dormant part of him that he kept chained and barred and carefully restricted. It had been a week since he last fed, and he could go for much longer than that. As long as there was sustenance he had no craving for the life energy of others. To feed on Louisa would be the most damnable sort of thievery.

He looked down at her.

"You do not know what you are saying, Louisa. Even youth is no excuse for such foolishness."

"I do not doubt your power, Douglas," she said, looking up at him with an expression he could not decipher. "I only doubt your guilt."

"It is not true, you know," he said almost absently. He reached out and captured a lock of her hair. It curled around a finger as if it had a life of its own. So like Louisa, intrepid, incautious, so desirous of affection that she would gamble with her life. "I do not require an invitation to take what I wish from others."

Do it, Douglas. She near begs for it.

She doesn't know what she's doing.

"And you do not sleep until night, because I've brought you lunch and you were awake."

"Was that a test, then?" He could not prevent his smile. How guileless she was.

She shook her head, smiling also.

"And what other myths surround me, dear Louisa? That I can make you vampir simply by nibbling upon your flesh? Or that I cast no reflection? Do you know that people suspected of being vampir are buried with their decapitated heads stuffed beneath their thighs, so that they cannot see to raise the coffin's lid?''

She didn't speak, just pulled away, stood until she was too close to him for his comfort's sake.

"None of them are true, are they?"

He smiled down at her. How certain she sounded, while there was a time in which he'd believed all the stories about his kind.

"What is the truth, Douglas? You can hear my thoughts and control my memory. You see so well in the dark and move so quickly. Why, then, can you not live among other people? Why do you hide in this cave castigating yourself for something that was not your fault?"

She'd asked him that before. He'd warned her then. The temptation to prove himself to her was too alluring.

He reached out and pulled her to him, so close that her breasts were pressed against his chest. She had beautiful breasts, full with plump little nipples. He could feel them swell even now. She said nothing, not even when he pulled her closer, inserted his leg between hers, feeling the heat of her through all the layers of her clothing. Her eyes widened, her lips opened just a little. A gasp restrained?

He bent his head, breathed in her essence. She smelled of woman and something heady and enervating. Fear and trust and desire, they all swirled around him, pulling him closer to her, inexorably into the web she artfully and innocently and ignorantly wove.

Her fingers gripped his arms. He could feel each separate finger, but she did not push him away. He bent and nuzzled her temple with his lips, feeling the power surge through him. Only this moment. *Give me this moment, Louisa, and I'll leave you unaffected and myself ensnared in want and need and longing.* Only a moment.

His lips brushed against her temple, a kiss to her forehead. She trembled beneath his touch, but it was not as prey to hunter. She quivered, his intransigent Louisa, in wonder and delight. A virgin's trepidation.

Her lips were full. She thought them too much so, he felt them pillow soft and welcoming. A need unlike any he'd ever known urged him closer, until even their clothing could not hide their bodies' changes. She breathed quickly, a cadence that lifted her breasts against him time and again, testing his restraint. He had none where this moment was concerned.

A kiss was just a meeting of lips, was it not? A hesitant breath exchanged, a tentative foray of tongues? That was all it was. Not a gateway to a forbidden place, a dark garden perfumed with sweet flowers and the heady lure of passion. She was an innocent, he could tell by the way she sighed into his mouth, by the way her heart beat over the joys of a simple kiss. She surely did not have the power to lure him closer, to instill in him both fear and blossoming desire. And yet, that was what he felt. As if he was not taking from her, but that she was granting to him, and the gift was too plenteous to absorb so quickly. He was drowning in need.

The surge came so suddenly, so forcefully, that he stumbled back under the power of it. It was as if lightning had joined them for a second, then severed that unearthly bond. She slumped in his arms, drained. In a moment tinted with horror, he believed her dead.

Some uttered prayer left his lips, but he did not release her, only carried her to his bed, to that solitary alcove that had been witness to too many nights sleepless and alone. Here he placed her, swept off the downy blanket and covered her with it, placing a barrier of cloth between them. He felt like fire burned his entrails, sparked each single place that beat with pulse, enlivened his heart. He felt satiated and filled with energy. As if he'd consumed her and quaffed her, quenching this long-held and barely-restrained need.

"Louisa?" *Please, I'm sorry. She was so tender and sweet and warm and heavenly and I am so damnably alone.* It had been so easy, too much so. He bowed his head on the side of the bed, wishing he could relive these last moments, refrain from taking from her.

Another moment, another chance. Would he have stopped? Would he have had the power to step away from her? *Idiot. Fool. Please, don't make me a murderer. Again.*

She lay like one dead, utterly pale. Her hands lay limply on the covers; she did not stir. Perhaps he should unlace her bodice, but he did not want to take the chance of touching her again. He was guilty of enough destruction.

When he fed, it was with conscious thought. He opened the mind of the person whose strength he drew, drained only what he needed and then left his victim tired but not destroyed. Why had this happened? Because he had not been centered on anything but that kiss. It had taken his reason and stripped him of every conscious thought but the need to possess.

He wished she had never come to him, never looked at him with those eyes of hers, so filled with innocence and trust. She'd called them hazel; the color hadn't mattered, only the emotion they betrayed so artlessly. Little innocent. For a moment, just a moment, he spared a thought of compassion for such as she, the unadorned, the naked, those who go through life with their wishes trumpeted for all to see. It did not take one versed in the seeing arts to know how lonely she was, to hear her heart plead. What did she want? Oh, too clear. Too appallingly simple. To be loved.

She had a delightful smile, one without pretense. And a wit that lampooned her own situation. She had made him laugh, called him names, reduced him to mortification and embarrassment.

He had never felt more alive than he did at this moment.

He touched the back of her hand with one finger. She was warming. A finger twitched and then her hand moved, grasping his before he could pull away.

"Douglas?" A weary word.

"I have never lain with a woman," he said without preamble. "By the time I was old enough, I had already learned that I could hurt others. It would have been the greatest intrusion, the most horrible of acts." He leaned back, stretched out his hands, widened the distance between them. It was an ancient act of supplication, one that showed there were no weapons, no defenses.

"I did not realize that passion could be so powerful," he said, his smile self-mocking and repentant. "I did not consider that you would prove so utterly desirable."

She raised her hand and found him, teased her fingertips through his hair, placed her palm against the side of his face. He pulled away.

"Do not, Louisa, I would not have you harmed."

Nonsense, Douglas, I can boast of kissing a vampir.

"And nearly died of it."

"You have very little faith in my abilities, if you think that is true. I felt a bit strange, but I am fine now."

"I will not have you on my conscience."

"And I did not ask you to."

She sat up slowly and dangled her legs over the edge of his bed. He could feel her embarrassment, her confusion. She would benefit from a little time to herself, he thought, as he stood and left her alone.

He could feel her thoughts, even from the outer room, sensitized to her in a way he'd not been to another person before. Had it been the kiss? A moment of pairing with another soul, however fleeting. Had it changed them in some way? *Nonsense, Douglas, you simply wish for an end to your solitude with such desperation that you see absolution in a kiss.*

Although he was curiously reluctant to wipe her memories clean, he would do it in order to protect her. Must do it.

Even now, she was not afraid. She should have been, of course. If not by the knowledge of what he was, then by the darkness, by the hint of mystery he unwittingly betrayed. Or by the power of that kiss, the heart-stuttering power of passion itself. Oh, dear merciful God, what a pair they were. He, with the power of death in his presence—she, with the longing for love in her eyes.

He whispered a command in his mind. An entreaty that did not filter through his thoughts with the alacrity it should have. It had been such an odd experience to be so close to another being without fear or disgust or despair marking his path that he had allowed himself the luxury of touch, permitted himself to kiss her. Better she should be gone before he could do her more danger.

"You will not remember me, Louisa." How strange that it should be such a difficult command. "I am but a dream." The words seemed to sing on the air, lilt through the breeze as if carried there. He sent more force behind the command. "It has only been a dream, sweet Louisa. A charming fantasy, but only that." He watched as she glided past him, an odd introspective smile upon her face, her gaze not on him but on the opening to the cave. He knew, if he thought to test her mind, that there would be no thoughts of him residing there. Nothing but a taste of mystery, a hint of darkness, and longing, perhaps.

In a moment, she had gone from him, leaving him alone again, protected from discovery and, oddly, more alone than he'd felt in all his life.

Seven

"Don't believe I've ever seen you looking so well, child."

"Thank you, grandfather."

"Heard you haven't been sleeping well." Arthur Patterson leaned on his cane and surveyed her. She knew better than to try to cozen him. Her grandfather was one of the most astute people she'd ever known.

"In truth, sir, I seem to have less need for sleep than before." She smiled at him, which made him frown. An odd reaction, but one that she pushed to the back of her mind.

"Going riding, then? It's a gloomy day for a picnic."

"The consensus seems to be that if we ignore the weather, sir, it shall become better."

"You're taking a suitable escort, I suppose."

"I have no less than five eager suitors accompanying me this morning, sir."

"Good decision, girl. Won't have a grandson who can't be mounted. Decidedly un-English."

"Rest assured, grandfather, I shall not countenance a suitor without a plethora of acceptable talents." She stood and brushed a kiss against his cheek.

He gazed into her face and his own seemed to soften. Louisa knew well enough that he did not see a resemblance to anyone beloved among her features. There was, simply put, no familial resemblance. "Know it's a hard time for you, child. But what I do, I do for you. Time enough that you married and filled your nursery. Won't be here forever, you know, and want to see you settled."

"I know, grandfather," she said, hugging him. He did not often submit to such gestures, but he did on this occasion. He even reached out to enfold her in a hearty hug of his own, one that lasted only a few seconds. Then he harrumphed and drew back, patting her on the back awkwardly with one hand and with such force that the feather on her riding hat jiggled.

"You made your mind up yet?" he said gruffly. "Given you a year, child. Seen more young bucks in Dorset than in London."

"I know, sir, and I thank you for your patience. I will choose soon."

"Give you one more month, child. That's all. You don't choose, I will. Two of my friends have eligible sons. Wouldn't mind you being paired with one of them. Make good stock, either of them."

Louisa forebore to mention that she was not a broodmare. The sad truth was that was exactly what she was. She was Arthur Patterson's hope for incursion into the nobility. With his funds he could buy a dukedom for

himself if he wished, but he had pinned his hopes on
her. He held fast to his vision of the Patterson fortune
nurturing countless generations of a noble family, never
mind that his granddaughter was not at all attractive.
The amount of money he was willing to offer her bride-
groom simply made looks superfluous.

She pulled on her gloves, adjusted the veil on her
hat, and waved her crop jauntily in the air. Louisa could
not muster a smile; she felt utterly wretched.

"I truly believe that we shall see the sun in just a matter
of minutes, Miss Patterson. This fog will disappear by
the time we unpack our viands." The Marquis of Bridge-
ton seemed fixated upon the climate, especially since
it was his idea that they all come on a picnic despite
the dreary day. Louisa nodded and smiled, which only
seemed to encourage him further. "And the breeze so
balmy for this time of year. It brings back memories of
the East Indies."

"By the King's nose, Percy, don't go hammering on
about that trip again."

"I but wished to entertain Miss Patterson with tales
of my travels, Damon. No need to get your feathers
ruffled because you've not been outside of England,
but for your Grand Tour."

"I am charmed by stories of your adventures, sir,
and am certain Miss Patterson is also. Pray tell us, do."
Margaret Rocher was half French, the daughter of an
émigré count and his English-born wife. She had
appointed herself peacemaker between the two men,
mainly, Louisa thought, so that she might be seen as
gentle, sweet, and polite to the bone. Not because she

wished to attract either man. Margaret was desperate to attract the attention of Lord Sheraton, who was also in residence at Bainbridge Hall. Lord Sheraton, it was rumored, was planning on a career in diplomatic circles, and Margaret Rocher had decided that this was one instance in which her half-French heritage would not be held against her and might possibly be of benefit. The fact that Lord Sheraton was immensely appealing to young ladies and had recently inherited an uncle's fortune only stood as proof that her instincts were correct. Louisa silently blessed her for her intervention since it made the chore of responding to her suitors' comments unnecessary.

She frankly was not in the mood for an outing, but it was either this or suffer through countless notes sent to her chamber, all of which must be responded to lest she seem rude. Another task she felt unsuited for today.

It was the lack of sleep, that was all. Only that. And the dreams, Louisa?

"Don't you think this is just the loveliest place, Louisa?" The comment from Ann Martin, the Earl of Cheswick's second daughter, cut short the necessity of an internal reply. Louisa was grateful for the respite.

Ann was so filled with eternal good humor that it was difficult being in her company at times. Especially today, when her laughter seemed to trill through the forest like an errant wind, catching hold of Louisa's composure and chilling her with its breath. Even a smile seemed beyond her, but she forced one onto her lips just the same, glancing around her at the clearing with what she hoped could be taken as approval. She was the oldest female among them, at an age acquitted too advanced to be called girl and too young to be called spinster, but slotted somewhere in between. At this moment, she felt as aged as her grandfather, yet lacking his determination or ambition.

The only determination she felt was to outlast this day, the only ambition to select one of their guests for her husband. To cause her grandfather and the selected suitor to wear similar looks of relief.

And to end it, once and for all.

One more night of this, that was all. Tonight she would announce her choice to her grandfather. Who shall it be? Peter Gregory? He owned a brewery that was badly run, needing funds to make it profitable again. He was a widower, balding slightly, with an amiable disposition and a habit of sucking on his bottom lip. Or Matthew Higginbotham, who had never been married before, but who had five sisters he was desirous of helping scale the social ladder. There was no better way than with the coin of the realm. Or the Earl of Somerset, who was quite a nice person, actually, except that it was rumored he was desperately in love with a vicar's daughter. However, he had to marry for money because of the Somerset properties that must, at all costs, be maintained. There were at least three others who might suit. None of them, of course, being the odious Harold Minter and his friend Charles Wilcox. That pair had decided to leave Bainbridge Hall and its attendant festivities once it was determined that Harold was no longer in the front running for her hand.

She was so eternally tired of the rounds of parties, balls, outings. It didn't matter anymore, any of the posturing. She must select one of them and with any luck, her choice would be a man with innate kindness, who would leave her with child and then alone. If she were blessed, he would go off to spend the Patterson millions in a luxury of excess.

If it were not for the dream, it might have been possible. But she was being taunted with what might have been. Dear God, that it was only a dream. That seemed the cruelest thing.

Dreams were only that.

Someone stretched a cloth over the ground, and someone else produced a wicker basket. Louisa could remember the scolding she'd received from Cook for returning home without a similar basket. Cook saw nothing wrong in a little pious humility, no matter that Louisa was reputed to be one of the wealthiest young women in England and could have purchased thousands of baskets and never minded the cost.

She shook her head. Cook had never scolded her. She had never taken a basket from the kitchen. Never packed it full of pastries and apples, or a stone jug filled with tea.

Love is not merely based upon appearances, Miss Patterson.

A line from a dream. Uttered in a voice she had imagined.

I am a hermit because I choose it, not because someone forced me to seek seclusion. I nurse no broken heart nor battered pride, Louisa.

Should she be able to recollect him so completely? As if she'd cut him from a cloth of wishes and imaginings, fashioned him into a man, and blown her own breath into his lungs that he might be all things she wished of him. Amusing and compassionate. Kind and filled with strength. Arrogant? Oh, yes, he was that.

You will not think of me, Louisa. Only a dream. How odd that she could still hear his voice, could recall it as well as she could hear the legendary bells of Bainbridge chapel, pealed only on days of family significance. This voice was like that, musical and low and holding such portent that she could not help but remember each and every word spoken.

"Louisa?"

A voice called her back to the present, to the grove and clearing, where several pairs of eyes were all directed at her. She still remained mounted, while everyone else was on foot. She accepted the assistance of Major Bentley, brushed her skirts back into place, and allowed him to tether her horse with the others. She was aware of eyes upon her as she sat upon the blanket, accepted a glass of lemonade, and forced herself to smile.

The conversation seemed to swirl around her, interspersed with Ann's soft laughter and Margaret's solicitous comments. A baritone voice mingled with a feminine one, a lower voice, a jolting sound of laughter.

He stepped back behind a tree, the sudden movement appearing no more furtive than the shimmering air above a cook fire; a breath of breeze, that's all he would seem. An insubstantial mist before the eyes, that was all.

Instead of contributing to the conversation, she seemed alone, a soul's island, inviolate and untouchable. She did not even seem part of them, as if there was something in her very nature that set her apart. It was not her appearance. In truth, she did not reflect well among the young beauties that accompanied her. But it was her heart he was concerned about, the state of the mind that seemed to shout its confusion even to where he stood. How could her companions not hear her heart? It seemed so loud and filled with entreaty.

She stood and, amidst the chattering, walked to the top of the hill, stood there watching the scenery before her. She seemed to take it all in, study it as if it were a picture set out for appreciation and judgment. *Foggy Day in Dorset* by the artist, The Great Creator.

What was she thinking—then damned that thought even as it whistled through his mind. He should not wish to know.

But, oh, he did.

It was a sad-looking day, filled with mist and odd memories. She heard the laughter and felt as though she belonged to the fog, not to the lively group behind her. But then, she felt almost invisible most times. Most people were content to allow her to be their hostess and then to ignore her completely, as if her presence were no more important than a footman or a maid. She recognized her alienation at the same time it occurred to her that she welcomed it. At least now.

She gripped her hands in front of her, staring at the rolling hills and the valley filled with fog. It appeared as if she were adrift in a cloud, and without much conscious thought, she could pretend that she stood alone on the edge of the world, but for the mist slowly approaching.

What whimsy. It was only that she was tired. Too many nights without sleep, afraid to be immersed in a dream that felt more real than this moment.

She had become used to only sleeping a few hours per night, then lying awake and restless until dawn. One night, she'd wandered to the library and the major-domo, thinking it an intruder, had roused the entire household. And now they all knew and speculated and pondered. Did Louisa dream of a lover? Was she heart-sick and lost in love?

More lost in confusion, and longing for something she'd never known. She wrapped her arms around her waist and stared into the silvery mist. She felt as though she were sleeping when she was awake; as if the dream-ing hours were the ones that were real. A dream, that is all it was. Only a dream. But, sweet Heavens, what a forbidden one.

If she were asked what the single most momentous event in her life was, she would have had to respond that it had been encased in a dream. How sad that admission. A kiss. One filled with emotion, not simply the touch of another's lips on hers. But a hint of passion, a word she'd not ever thought to know of, an emotion she'd never expected to feel. She had dreamed of a man kissing her, and it had seemed so real that she occasionally touched her lips to see if they were still bruised.

Even exhausting herself did not seem to stop the ache. As if this exact loneliness was real, a spear to her chest, a knife between the ribs. Could you die of this?

No, of course you could not. But you might wish to.

What kind of mind fashioned something so forbid-den? Was she evil? Was she blessed with a wanton's nature? Or too vivid an imagination that she should feel such things only in her sleep? Did men and women actually feel that way about each other? Or did such a thing only occur in a shadowy world of dreams? And what kind of person was she that she had crafted an imaginary partner with a secret so vile? A vampir, Louisa? Not a duke or an earl, not a baron. Not even a knight mounted upon a white horse, St. George on a quest, armor shiny and face radiant with righteousness and a passion to be on God's errand. A man of darkness, Satan's tool, a man who whispered of his own innocence, who had the power of life in his hands, who made her wish to be naked and writhing with his touch. What kind of woman conjured up a hero like that, a dream lover?

A shocking one, perhaps even depraved.

Could loneliness make you mad?

Douglas backed away and closed his eyes.

What had he done?

He wished she would stop. Either that, or cease condemning herself. It hurt to hear her, was almost agony to taste each tear that remained unshed. He sent a thought to her, knowing that it would be useless. She was so bound up in her own despair that she would not hear him.

If she only knew that she was not alone, that he shared equally in her longing and the hint of shame. He blamed himself for what happened in the same instant that he would willingly replicate it. That was culpability, Louisa. Not your innocence.

Not yours.

Eight

"You're a willow on the dance floor, Louisa."

"Thank you, Mr. Adams."

"I cannot say when I've enjoyed myself so much, in fact," he said, wiping his brow. The poor man was sweating heavily and looked to be more in need of refreshments than another turn on the dance floor. When she declined his invitation, he almost sagged in relief.

"I cannot imagine what has happened to my son," he said, anxiously searching the crowd. The ball was well attended. There were crowds throughout Bainbridge Hall; even the ballroom was filled to overflowing with people. Almost everyone who'd been invited had come, either to claim they'd seen the reputed wonders of Arthur Patterson's palatial estate, or to study the heiress.

Louisa fanned herself, wondering how she could possibly escape yet another overt attempt at matchmaking.

Everyone knew that Mr. Adams was a delightful man, a fair squire, a quite able tenant of Mittleborough Farms. The fact was, however, that cash was always in short supply. And Mr. Adams had an eligible son, who was unfortunately a boorish lout. He stood a foot taller and two feet broader than Louisa and wore a habitual smile that looked more cruel than pleasant. She had said two words to Jeremy in her entire life, and they were "excuse me," when he had attempted to waylay her in the card room this evening. If she never had occasion to see him again, she would not miss the lack. He disturbed her. No, he frightened her a bit, with his habit of watching her, and that odd smile.

You are an odd woman, Louisa, in that you fear what you should not and show courage where there should only be terror.

"I am sorry, Louisa, did you say something?"

A dream again? Louisa, you are awake.

She shook her head, managed to smile and murmur some excuse before slipping away. The ballroom, with its vaulted and painted ceiling, inlaid wood floor, and ornate gilt panels occupied most of the first floor. She passed several couples on her way down the grand staircase. It was an architectural feature of Bainbridge Hall that was distinctive to the house. There were two landings, as the staircase curved around to meet itself on the second floor and then soared upwards for an additional story.

She took the steps too rapidly for proper decorum, but was in too much of a hurry to truly care. All she wanted was to ask Cook a question that had been in her mind all afternoon.

Cook was supervising the midnight supper, a huge repast that was offered to all the guests and was tantamount to a six course meal. The kitchen staff did not seem unduly surprised to see her, even attired in her lovely white and silver ball gown. She had been a frequent visitor since she was a child.

"Of course I remember the basket, Miss Louisa." Cook turned and slapped a hand down on the bread board. Flour misted in the air. The dough beneath her fists seemed to cower in surrender. "One of my very favorites. Had little rings woven into the inside of the top for napkins and such. You haven't gone and found it?"

"No," Louisa said. "Can you remember, did I happen to ask for a picnic that day?"

"Well, it wasn't but a fortnight ago, was it? I've memory enough for that, I'll reckon. Apples and pastries you wanted. And my meat pies, but I'd not finished baking them. You took slivers of roast beef instead." Her eyes were sharp and all-seeing. "I'll want it back if you've got it. It's not like you to be going and forgetting things. Even if you are in love." There was a twinkle in place of the sharpness now, and a titter from the back of the room seemed to accompany her all-knowing gaze. The people of Bainbridge Hall desperately wished for a love story, for her happiness.

And what could she offer them? A dream that might not be a dream after all.

Instead of returning to the ballroom, she slipped around to the back of the house, to the Morning Room, where the floor to ceiling doors opened onto the terrace.

The wind seemed to greet her, sending a scattering of leaves across the cobbled path. Louisa placed her hand on the flank of one of the stone lions that crouched upon a pediment facing south to the gardens and beyond to Hodge's Hill. It was nearly midnight, much too late to even consider venturing away from Bainbridge Hall. Even to investigate a cave that might not be the figment of a dream after all.

And to see if a hermit resided there?

"Douglas?" The name seemed like an invocation, a whispered entreaty. Retrieve me from this madness. Let it be real. Let you be real.

"You were not supposed to remember, Louisa."

She turned, and he was there, dressed as splendidly as any of the men upstairs, in dark colors that seemed to offset the snowy whiteness of his shirt and cravat, only his face in shadow.

"I did not, for too long a time." She walked toward him, and by the light from the candles arrayed in the morning room, she could tell he tensed. She reached out a hand to touch his sleeve, then pulled it back, trapped in the essence of herself in a way she'd never been before. She did not touch others because of propriety. She did not touch him because of his self-imposed isolation. The barrier was there, so palpable that she could almost see it. Yet the wish for it was there and she knew he could hear it. She wished she could see his face, wished she could discover if his smile was as tender as it sounded when he spoke, or if his gaze was as soft.

"Did you put a spell on me, Douglas, that I would not remember you?"

"One that you have too much stubbornness to accede to, evidently."

"Then why are you here, dressed so splendidly?"

"You're still too fixated upon appearances, Louisa," he said.

She laughed, surprising herself. Merriment had been lacking in her life for too long it seemed.

"What transfixes you with mirth?"

"The fact that it was not a dream, after all. I remember your telling me that, on too many occasions. As if you held little appreciation for good looks."

"Would you be happy if you were beautiful?"

"Is that within your power?"

He laughed, but she felt as if he laughed not at her, but at the circumstances, at the society that had crafted her and brought her to this point of asking nonsensical questions with such hope.

"No, Louisa, it is not."

I would wish to be beautiful, just to be your equal.

"Oh, Louisa, you cannot see me. You only believe you can, because I've allowed the thought in your mind. You see what you want to see. Not what is real. In actuality, I'm more shadow than substance."

"Unless you feed."

"I should never have told you that."

"Why did you?"

He smiled. "Because you have the uncanny ability to listen, Louisa, and there are few enough people who do that. A heady lure indeed, especially for a hermit who has had little enough of companionship."

"And yet, you hear the thoughts of others so easily, I would not think your self-enforced isolation to be that onerous."

"And that, too, you recall with too little difficulty. If you had any sense, you would cherish your ignorance and wear it like a cloak about you."

"Very well, Douglas. I shall consider you a stranger, come upon me in a moment of reflection. Stranger, what is your purpose?"

"Instilling some sense in you, I believe. You are totally lacking in propriety, Miss Patterson."

He was right; she was not thinking correctly. If she had been a proper maiden, she would have fled from him the moment she'd first met him, not returned the second time, captivated and enchanted by a voice in the darkness. Nor would she be so appreciative of his presence now, for the paradoxical normalcy of him. There was no falsity about Douglas; he did not proclaim her accomplished or lovely or tell her that her voice was so beautiful it seemed to rival that of any bird.

The musicians were playing a lovely ballad. It scented the air with sound, seemed to match the play of leaves upon the stone, the wind that rushed through the branches of the elm and oak trees.

"I cannot help it, Douglas. I am happy."

He said nothing, only seemed to study her. She smiled, so widely that the smile seemed to be borne in the direction of the tip of her toes, spreading up and through her with a warmth that banished even the chill of the late summer breeze.

"I have come to ask a question of you," Louisa said. "One that is easily answered."

At his silence, she smiled at him. "Not fair, Douglas. You can divine my thoughts, but I have no inkling of yours."

You can hear me, Louisa. But he did not say the words aloud, and it was almost as if she imagined them.

"Will you dance with me, Louisa?"

"Do you dance, Douglas?"

"To the delight of my dancing master, I can assure you it is so."

She held up her arms, welcoming him with a smile.

He tapped her lightly on the nose with his fingertip. "You should not be so improvident, Louisa. You should at least ask if such an action is safe."

In that moment, she remembered everything.

"You would not hurt me."

"And you are too trusting."

"Then, is it safe, Douglas?"

"For a short while. One dance, perhaps."

"A waltz?"

"You do challenge fate and custom, don't you?" He extended his left hand; she laid her right upon it. Even so, gloved as they both were, each could feel a tingle as their palms met.

As if he commanded it, the musicians began a waltz, the lilting tones so pure in the near darkness that it was as if sweetness itself were given voice. Her skirts billowed around his pant legs as he whirled her in the darkness to their left, then back again to the right. Even the sound of the leaves crunching beneath their feet seemed an accompaniment to the perfection of this moment.

Neither spoke, intent upon the music, the silence, and the peace of the night, oddly partnered and chaperoned by two stone lions. Did the lions smile? Or did they keep watching over any intruder who might disturb this moment? Or was it all just whimsy, unsettling and charming, and utterly wonderful?

"Someone is coming," Douglas said, bringing them to a stop by the stone banister. She didn't question how he knew. He was something she was not, blessed with powers no one else possessed, versed in a world that was imagination to her. And for a few moments, she'd allowed herself to forget.

Her grandfather stood on the other side of the doors, staring out at the terrace.

"Leave me, Douglas," she said, even though he'd stepped between her and the terrace doors. She did not want him to have to explain himself, answer questions that would be too pointed and difficult.

He glanced down at her.

"You really must refrain from thinking me one of your causes, Louisa."

"Douglas." She thought about all the difficulty that would come if her grandfather discovered her alone on the terrace with a stranger. Douglas stifled a smile and walked to the steps where the shadows seemed deepest.

"Very well, Louisa."

As he left, melting into the shadows in the blink of an eye, she had the most absurd feeling that he had meant to say something, to warn her, or perhaps try to convince her again that he was but a dream. But it seemed as though he had changed his mind at the last moment, and the thought hung in the air like a sigh. One of resignation. Or perhaps simply acceptance.

Arthur Patterson wiped the moisture from his eyes. He was not so much stricken by the grief that had rushed over him at the sight as he was now by anger. For too many months, he'd let Louisa call the tune. She'd evaded his questioning and murmured excuses each time he'd attempted to get her to select one of the infernal young men who were forever milling about the place.

There they were, upstairs, drinking his liquor and dancing to the musicians he'd hired, burning over a thousand candles, laughing and enjoying themselves thoroughly at his expense, and what was she doing?

Careening around the garden terrace dancing by herself. Her arms uplifted as if she actually danced with a tall man, a silly smile on her face that made him want to cry and shout at the same time.

Well, he'd allowed her enough time. The decision had now reverted to him. He would be the one who selected her mate, and choose he would.

He slipped away from the door and walked to his library, where he slammed the door so forcefully that a bust of some obscure Roman emperor crashed to the floor.

"Leave it," he said, and waved his hand at the ever-present footman who'd opened the door and was even now attempting to clean up the mess. Money purchased many things in his life, he thought, not the least of which was the eternal companionship of paid flunkies, who insisted upon being at your beck and call even when you'd just as soon be alone.

He poured himself a measure of brandy, sat heavily behind his desk, and started scribbling names on a sheet of paper. By the time this week was over, Louisa would have her husband. No more foolishness.

Nine

Was it possible to feel enchanted?

For the next few days, Louisa slipped away as often as she could from Bainbridge Hall and went to the cave. If Douglas had any reservations, he kept them to himself. It was a perfect interlude, one in which it seemed that even time ticked by with blessed indolence. While the guests at Bainbridge slept their mornings away, she slipped away to the cave. While they danced during the night, she waited on the terrace for him, sometimes dancing again, sometimes only sitting in the darkened garden or showing him places where she'd played, the boxwood hedge that had been her hiding place, the tree she'd ached to climb.

"Shall you do it now?" he teased one night.

She had answered the smile in his voice with one of her own. "I am much too prim and proper now, sir."

"Are you really, Louisa?" And when he asked, just that way, she wondered if she was.

The days became almost magical, a separate existence as beautiful and as rare as a yellow diamond. She learned that he truly abhorred meat of any kind, and even eschewed fish and fowl, that apples were his favored fruit. He would, he claimed, have done anything for an apple cobbler and so she brought him one the next day, having lied to Cook to obtain it and feeling not one shred of remorse that she'd done so. He relished reading and learning and she brought him some of the newest novels and some scientific works included in the latest shipment from London. Her grandfather did not even open most of the large crates anymore, complaining that his eyes bothered him and the script was too small. Louisa had filled a straw carryall with books and brought them to Douglas.

Sometimes they spoke of art, sometimes of literature. He accused her of having plebeian tastes. She countered by saying he was too arrogant by half. She discovered that he was remarkably knowledgeable about politics and world events. She brought him the first copies of the new *Observer* and he delivered the news that the motion for abolition of the slave trade had been carried through Parliament. They discussed Shakespeare and Bacon, Mozart's *The Marriage of Figaro*, one of her favorites, detested by him.

It was time out of time. A special interlude in which neither of them discussed their mutual past or their separate future. It was as if they were frozen in the moment, ghosts of themselves, sent to revel in a world they had created from the mists of dawn and the magic of dusk.

"Tell me what you were like as a boy," she asked one day, and he smiled at her.

"Like any other boy, I think. I loved to fish, had a set of tin soldiers I played with incessantly, hid from my nurse when I could."

"Did you have no playmates, then?"

He smiled again, a tender, reminiscent smile. "There were no children around my home, and I was an only child. I think, sometimes, that my childhood prepared me for an adulthood spent without people. I do not mind it as much as someone might who has been long used to company."

"And yet, you even eschew those who are like you."

He stood, walked to the fire, poked it with the branch he'd brought inside and trimmed for just such a purpose. The fire outlined him, left him less a shadow than he would have wished to appear. For that reason, she did not tell him. "I do not like to think we are alike, Louisa. They cultivate myths about us that would make a rational person blanch."

"Like being undead?"

"Or worse. Like having the power to convert someone to vampir by biting them. Or being able to travel in time."

"How utterly silly."

He glanced at her. "Do not dismiss such silliness, Louisa. People will believe what they wish. Even if it bends every law of nature. It is simply easier than attempting to understand."

"Have you ever considered, Douglas, that there are others out in society just like you?"

He frowned, stirring the stick. More embers flew, but he seemed oblivious to them.

"Or even more wonderful, Douglas, what someone like you could do in society?"

That comment prompted an even greater frown. "Think about it," she said, enlivened by the thought. "To be able to discern an enemy's mind would be most helpful in war. To move so quickly might be very beneficial, do you not think? And to be able to control someone's thoughts could be perfectly wonderful in the right circumstances."

"You are a romantic, Louisa, to even think such a thing might be possible. Have you considered the deleterious effects my presence brings?"

You do not hurt me.

And each moment, I promise myself I never will.

"I cannot say that I am not disappointed, my child."

"I am sorry, grandfather."

"Because I am," he said, as if he hadn't heard her. "I am not considered a patient man, Louisa." He sat in his claw-foot chair with his gold-topped cane choked in his right hand, an emphatic thump on the carpeted floor accentuating every other word. "I do not begrudge the care and feeding of half of London while they parade up and down for your perusal, child."

Thump, thump.

"But I have lost all hope of your selecting one of them for your husband. Especially—" thump, thump, "—since you gave me reason to believe you would do so imminently."

"I thought I could decide, grandfather." The decision had been easier postponed than made. She hadn't wanted to think about marriage.

"Therefore," he said, again ignoring her, "I will choose for you." He continued with his announcement, enumerating all her future husband's attributes as if she were not sitting there, stunned.

"We shall make the announcement this evening, Louisa, and the banns will be read in three weeks."

"And I have no say in this, grandfather?"

"I gave you near a year, Louisa. And in all that time there was no one you selected. Dash it all, girl, I gave you every opportunity!"

She stood, no longer content to remain seated in front of her grandfather's desk much as she had as a child, terrified and waiting to be disciplined.

There was nothing she could say. He was right, of course; he had been more than patient. It was not his fault that she had not found anyone who wanted to look beyond her face to the person she was. Who wanted to talk with her or listen to her, who discussed politics or asked her opinion. Not like Douglas.

He said nothing when she burst through the door and escaped.

For a long time, it had not seemed like a cave at all to Louisa, but a dark and sweet-smelling home barricaded against the intrusion of the sun, shielded from the elements, even the seasons. Somewhere, the sound of water, and then the whoosh of air as if the cave itself breathed deeply.

"Douglas?"

"Why are you crying?" he asked from behind her.

She whirled and he was there, so motionless he might have been part of the darkness.

"I am not."

"I can feel your tears, Louisa. Even see them."

She brushed them away with the back of her hand.

"What is wrong?" he asked, as he brushed past her. There was the sound of something and then faint light. To reassure her, to make her feel more comfortable. He was continually doing things like that.

"I am no saint, Louisa. Do not make me one in your thoughts."

She looked away, and he bent to light the fire. A sense of unreality crept over her, as if each separate action had already been done. Rehearsal for this moment, this day? He stood and brushed his hands against his trousers. She could not see his face, but she sensed he was not happy about her presence. Or perhaps that was not correct after all. Perhaps he had picked up her thought, her unruly and wild idea, and even now braced himself against the asking of it. It was not emotion she was feeling from him, but a tense wariness, as if he were a caged animal seeking an opportunity for escape. An odd thought. Did he think her jailer, then?

"Are we not jailers for each other?" he softly said, without turning. "We put such restraints upon ourselves in an effort to be civilized and in doing so, we curb all originality of speech, action, even dress. A woman is praised for being an Original, but only if she is the most spectacular of a certain type of beauty. A man must emulate a certain style or he is considered not quite *on dit*. And yet, we mourn for our heroes, for those who dare to be different, to rise above the pack."

His mood seemed oddly sad, but then, she'd often thought that about him. And sometimes, she actually felt that she might be able to dispel that sadness, coax a smile forth, and she had. For too brief a time.

"And where would you have us find our heroes, Douglas?"

He turned and drew near; his fingers brushed aside the tendrils of hair from her temple. A tender gesture, one too intimate and arresting. It seemed to stop her heart and send it fluttering again, all in one breath. "In men of letters, perhaps. Or men of science. Or perhaps one from each realm of life. A lord, a lady, a saint, a sinner. Can we not all be heroic from time to time?"

"I have never been."

"Do not sound so disconsolate, Louisa. You are the greatest of heroines, to breach the gorgon's den. To invade the vampir's home and seek him out for sanctuary. Why are you here?"

"I am to be married."

He continued to study her. She looked away. Of course she was to be married. It was the way of the world. But she had hoped for so long to put the moment away, to delay the inevitable. The man her grandfather had selected was not a bad person; of all her suitors he was perhaps the most eligible. He was in his thirties, studious it was said, a man who had ventured only once to Bainbridge Hall and then not come again. He was a neighbor who had known her father, and even herself in a faraway time, when she was just a child and he not much more than that. He had no faults, her grandfather said, none that would deplete her capital, and it was said that he treated his horses and his servants well, a sure and certain sign that his wife would no doubt be treated the same.

Douglas turned away.

"It seemed the best place to come," she said simply.

"And it was the very worst place, Louisa. I cannot change your future for you. Is that why you came? So that I might change your bridegroom's mind for him? Or your grandfather's?"

"I would not ask that of you."

"Then what do you ask of me?"

"Have you given no thought to marriage?"

"We played with disaster, Louisa, as two children will dance around a bonfire, aware of the danger and thrilling in it, never seeing that the consequences for doing so might be immolation. The time for playing has come and gone, and we've both outgrown our childhood."

She felt a spurt of anger, then quickly tamped it down. Not quick enough, however, because he sensed it. Felt her momentary and fleeting rage.

"What is it, Louisa?"

"I thought you were my friend." She spun away, the skirts of her dress swirling around her ankles as she strode to the cave opening.

"Louisa!"

The shout was both a command and an entreaty. She clenched her fists tight, then turned and faced him.

"I cannot marry anyone, Louisa. You of all people should know that."

"Why not? We do well together. We laugh and talk."

Unbidden, the memory of a kiss and dances in the dark.

"Do not be foolish."

"I am not a child, Douglas. I know my place in the world, my obligation to my grandfather. I know that women such as I must marry. Even as ugly as I am. I can be a chatelaine of a castle, organize and prepare a dinner party for fifty. I am prepared to birth however many children God sees fit to give me, to love them and nurture them and release them when it's time." She could hear the stridency in her own voice and forced herself to take several deep breaths. "I had thought, however, that there might be someone who would value me for who I was and not what I owned or could grant to them."

"I value you, Louisa."

"Then marry me, Douglas. Please. So that I can say my friend is also my husband. So that perhaps, in the dark, you can forget about what I look like and think only that I am amusing, or intelligent, or kind."

"Have you forgotten what I am?"

She advanced on him, all thought of retreat gone. "I know you are a man who does not seek the company of others, because he fears he might unwittingly harm them. Who believes himself cursed because he is different. But who is intelligent and witty and kind."

"A vampir, Louisa. Cursed from my cradle."

"Take your energy from me, then, Douglas," she said, extending her two hands, palms up. "I will gladly be your sustenance if that is what you require."

"Do you wish to escape marriage so desperately that you would choose death, instead?"

"No harm has come to me."

"Because I have been careful to make it so."

"And could you not be as careful if we were wed?"

He shook his head and turned from her.

She lowered her hands to her sides, standing so straight it felt as if she had been laced to a backboard. She blinked rapidly, allowing her eyes to roam over the cave, dim except for a flickering candle. It was not that she was humiliated. She had sunk far deeper than that paltry emotion. She was so immersed in shame it seemed to cover her. She could not breathe because of it.

"It is not what you are thinking, Louisa," he said, turning. "It is not your appearance. It is the sheer lunacy of your suggestion. I can never marry. I was born different. Do you think I would bring another child into the world like me?"

"And I am certain it is your loss your mother grieves for, Douglas, not your birth." *And how do you know it would be so? Have you no hope?*

You have too much for both of us, Louisa.

He stretched out his hand. She fled from it, and from him, wishing she could blank her mind as easily as he seemed to read it.

Ten

"Oh, Miss Louisa, this shade of peach looks just too lovely on you. Don't you think?"

She nodded, then forced a smile.

"And this lace. Why, I think it must have taken the nuns nearly a year to tat it. It is so exquisite, like a web a very delicate spider might weave." Hester Marston held it out. It was nearly translucent, showing the well worn palm beneath it.

"It is quite lovely," Louisa said.

The seamstress glowed with achievement. Louisa did not doubt that this ball gown was quite exquisite. In addition, the matronly spinster had been commissioned to provide Louisa's trousseau, the equivalent of a year's income. Her village shop was small and barely capable of handling the influx of business, but on this fact Louisa had been adamant. She did not want to send to London for her new gowns. Nor did she want to hire one of the refugees who were rumored to have catered to the deposed French monarch and his court. Something plain and simple was all she needed, and if Hester Marston benefited from her wish for restraint, then that was all for the better.

Tonight, her engagement would be announced. Twice, she had met with Mr. Dunston. He seemed very polite. She had no doubt they would get on acceptably. They may even become amiable after a time. She would, perhaps, ask him if he liked poetry, and he might surprise her by saying yes and quoting a few verses from a poet she did not know. Or perhaps she might ask him of his opinion of the troubles in France, and he would, of course, speak of how he felt, giving her enough information so that she could understand his point of view, while never forcing her to agree with it. Perhaps. It was possible. Anything was possible—even a myth that existed in the shadows and laughed at her fears and spoke French and German and teased her provinciality.

The silence was deafening. The sounds, not in the room, as Hester and her apprentices knelt at her hem, pinning, measuring, pinning. Not even from outside, which she could see quite well from her perch upon the seamstresses' small elevation. Another carriage rolling up. The end of the season in London. A final ball at Bainbridge Hall. The heiress has chosen. Who shall it be? Poor rich fool, that he would gain both a fortune and a millstone at the same time. No. The sound she missed was the companionship of her mind. An errant thought she could sometimes catch from a far off hill and a cave nestled behind a rock. An admonishment, a wry bit of humor, a quizzical comment. They were gone, as if she'd never become alert to the sounds of his thoughts. When had she begun to notice that it was true, that she could hear him as well as he could hear her? It didn't matter now. It didn't matter now. Say it again, Louisa, and it might be true.

She felt something lurch in her chest, as a picture of him seemed to slide into her mind. Douglas, so strong, so sure, so alone. He was going away. She was certain of it. She clutched at the bodice of her gown, began extracting the headless pins.

"Miss Louisa!"

"I am sorry, Miss Marston, but you must simply get me out of this." Her fingers flew, and one of the apprentices ducked while the other scrambled for the precious pins.

"But the fitting!"

"I don't care. Please help me."

"But we're running short of time, Miss Louisa. The ball is tomorrow night!"

"I really don't care, Miss Marston." She bundled up the skirt in both hands and yanked it over her head, dropped down from the stand, and opened the wardrobe door. The seamstress and her two apprentices simply stared at her, mouths agape. She supposed she was acting oddly, but she had to get to Douglas.

One of the apprentices stepped forward and laced the back of her favorite day dress. She thanked her, hesitated at the door, and wondered if she should try to explain the urgent need for haste.

Laughter overwhelmed her at the thought of the story she could tell them, of the absurdity of trying to explain Douglas, the cave, or hearing his voice wishing her farewell in the most tender of whispers. Which one would they disbelieve the most? It didn't matter, because she had no intention of telling them, of telling anyone.

* * *

She lit the candle he kept for her at the entrance to the cave. But she did not call his name or announce her presence. She didn't need to announce herself; he knew she was here by the sudden alertness she felt. The candle cast ominous shadows upon the cave's domed ceiling. A breeze sent through the chimney hold nearly extinguished the small, brave flame. It was enough to see the open trunk, the scattering of books upon the tables, the stone ledges where he held his treasures. Two more trunks sat bound, their leather straps pulled tight over bulging contents.

"So, it's true."

"You've grown adept at hearing me, Louisa. It is a talent I'd not thought so easily transferred."

"Where are you going?"

"Away. Somewhere. Anywhere. Does the destination matter?"

"Yes." She could tell she surprised him with both her answer and her vehemence. "I want to envision you someplace in my mind, Douglas. So that I might say good morning when it's dawn and good night when the moon is full."

He turned. "I wish you had never remembered me."

Was this cruelty? No, only truth.

"I, too, Douglas. It would have been so much less painful."

It was as if her words hurt him, but that could not be so. Vampirs do not feel pain, or grief or loss or regret.

"Or hope or despair or loneliness, Louisa? You put me in mind of Shakespeare, Louisa. I am no Moor, but I bleed as ably."

"Choose which you would be, Douglas. You cannot be both, part of mankind and yet apart from it. You want to be something more and yet shun it altogether."

"What do you know of it, Louisa? You dabble in my life. You venture here for a short while and then return to your home as if it were an adventure to visit the vampir. Why, Louisa? Is your own life so blessedly dull that you crave adventure, the edge of danger? Or only because you wished to call me friend, to have a novelty no one else has. The heiress with a new diversion." For the first time, she saw his anger, the fury he'd spoken about but never shown.

"Why are you doing this, Douglas?" His anger freed her own. "So that you can walk away and not feel anything? So you can assure yourself you do not deserve to be treated as anything but an animal? Animals live in caves, Douglas. Is that what you want to be, truly? Free to feed on anything you wish? Free to bathe in blood? And all the time, crying aloud to the heavens to show mercy for what you are."

"You cannot know, Louisa. Keep silent about those things you know nothing about." His arms were outstretched upon the stone, his head bowed between them.

She should not have come, that was evident from his welcome.

She looked at the fire, rather than at him. How odd that he'd expressed displeasure to her, was angry, yet she did not feel as horrible as she had when escaping Bainbridge Hall. Perhaps because he had been honest in his emotions, had treated her as if she were a person, not simply an ugly face. At least he accepted her, without wanting to change her, without telling her to alter her posture or her dress or her manners. At least Douglas saw through what she looked like to the inside of her, to the wishes and dreams and wonderings of her, the real Louisa.

The light from the fire warmed the cave, lit his outline, cast shadows upon his face. Even without seeing him, she could feel his scowl. How odd that she should not be discomfited by such a look.

"Why are you here?"

There were too many lies she could tell him to explain her presence here.

"Are you the only one, Douglas? The only one who ever wished to walk among others? Or are there others, who have mastered themselves, and taken the harder road, who wake each day uncertain of their capabilities, but wishing to try all the same?"

One more step, and his hands reached out and gripped her shoulders, shaking her, until she dropped the candle and it rolled away, extinguished.

"You cannot be the only one, Douglas. Have you ever considered that?"

"What do you want from me, Louisa? I cannot be your husband. I am no longer content to be your friend. Would you make me writhe upon a spit for being what I am?"

His fingers trailed across the shoulder of her day dress, stroked the nape of her neck. His palms reached up to caress the sides of her face, cupped her cheeks as thumbs brushed against her lips. All in anger, in grief, a kind of helpless wonder.

"Douglas?"

"Yes, Louisa?" A soft whisper, a breath of air upon her temple.

"You are touching me, Douglas."

Did time stand still for a moment? It seemed as if it did. There was no sound from him, no movement, but she could sense the change in him, as if all the anger had softened and sweetened to become joy. His hands trembled. She could feel the movement as if the ground rocked beneath him. She reached up and covered his fingers with her own. Only a slight tremble, a sharp tingle that felt as if a bee had been trapped within her cupped hand and then released. That was all.

Did he breathe? His harsh indrawn breath proved it. His fingers slid beneath hers; he stepped back, away. Not until that moment did she realize how much warmth had come from his presence.

"Douglas?" She turned and he took one more step back, holding his hand up in the air as if to forestall her approach. She knew better than to touch him now. It was as if in the last few moments he had changed, become someone she should fear. And yet, there was something else, something she could not decipher in his expression. Or there had been—a sense of joy so profound that it had stilled her heart for a moment.

He did not move as she approached him; he remained as still as stone when she reached up and touched his cheek with one finger. A testing, then. Nothing. Only the feel of warm skin beneath her fingertip. He was a statue, completely motionless, except for the slow rise and fall of his chest. Shock, or something else? Her palm flattened against his cheek; her fingers trailed into the hair at his temple. No surge of pain, no feeling of being drained. Nothing. But for the sensation of being improbably daring, of being shocking, she might have believed herself numb and insensate. But she felt something, a warmth deep inside her, as if a tiny sun resided in her stomach, warming everything around her, creating an oasis so bright that it could not help but be seen and felt. Or was she feeling what Douglas felt, as if something had dissolved and melted in his heart? Something that had kept him from another human being, that had denied him the touch of another person.

She took one step forward and although he did not welcome her, neither did he forestall her advance. He only remained as he was, still and accepting as if not daring to believe it true. She curved her hand around to the nape of his neck, feeling the softness of his hair, the corded muscles of his shoulders beneath her wrist. Another tiny movement forward and she raised her lips, stepped on tiptoe, lifted her mouth until it was only an inch from his. She tasted his breath on her lips, the soft outrush of a gasp, or moan, or release of dammed-up despair.

He reached out both hands and with a suddenness that shocked her, gripped her arms and pulled her forward, bending his head and enveloping her lips in a kiss that was different from the first. This kiss did not seem to care that she was ignorant of the feelings that coursed through her body. It did not bestow, it stole. There was heat and fear and surprise and wonder all wrapped up in a bright gold box and tied with scarlet ribbons. A present, then, of nature's inattentiveness, or Heaven's kindness, or a miracle so rare that it had never before been spoken of or written.

Or, an aberration in time, a lure to the unwary.

"What is it?"

"You must leave," he said, his voice harsh and without its usual melodious note.

"I must?"

"Do it, Louisa." She heard the cacophony of his mind as he seconded the command with his thoughts. *Go away, Louisa. Leave me. NOW!* It was as forceful as a shout and she reeled from it, confused.

Don't you see, you stupid little idiot? Don't you know what kind of danger you're in?

You would not hurt me, Douglas.

You little fool. You have no idea, do you?

"Not by taking your life's energy, Louisa," he said aloud, "but by stealing your innocence."

"You cannot steal what is given freely." She gripped her hands tightly together, hoping her voice did not sound as tremulous as it felt.

"Oh, Douglas, do not turn away from me." Her words followed him into the darkness, into the stygian black of the cave. But he did not turn, nor did he return.

It seemed too great a feat to remain standing, and she crumpled to the stone floor in a cloud of skirt. She'd been a fool, an utter idiot. She swallowed back her tears, blotted those that did not obey from her cheeks. It had not been true, none of it. She had not found sanctuary in this place. He had not, truly, cared. There was none of the camaraderie or friendship she'd imagined, and he did not care to learn what was inside her heart or the thoughts of her mind. He did not need to cut out her memories or dampen these days in fog. She would excise them herself. They had been little more than whimsy. And humiliation too great to think about, to even bear.

"You are too stringent in your thoughts, Louisa. You are rarely kind to yourself."

It was her turn to avert her head, but he would have

none of it. He knelt in front of her, grasped her hands, held them tight in his own. It was the first time he'd ever been able to do such a thing. The thought came to her in waves of feeling, so sweet it seemed to pierce her heart. His head bent and he covered his face with her palms, his breath warm against her skin, his tears hotter.

I but wished to protect you, Louisa. Not hurt you.

Please don't leave me.

There was no answer from him. She could hear nothing of his thoughts, and he did not speak. She raised up on her knees, slipping her hands from his grasp, extending them until she felt his face, his cheekbones. Her thumbs found his lips, acted as guide for her own. It was only the third kiss of her life, aided in expertise by a heart so full it spilled over into tears. She was no longer a novice when she pulled back, retreating from the power of that kiss with a pounding heartbeat and ragged breath.

She was no longer an apprentice but a woman in love.

Please, Douglas.

The sound of his heart was all she heard, beating loudly enough to drown out her own. She trailed her fingers down his neck to shoulder to chest, planting her hand against where his heart beat. Not steady, not sure, but fast and with enough strength that his skin seemed to vibrate against her palm.

Please, Douglas.

He seemed to sigh. Expulsion of all his grief? Or resignation for the extent of his sins? Because he stood and drew her up into his embrace, cradling her in his arms as if she were the most tender of burdens and the most fragile of packages.

Only when he reached his bed, in that antechamber

he had crafted from stone, did he stop and lower her upon the down-filled mattress. Hedonism, even here. Luxury in a stone cave. An errant thought, but one that he caught and sent back to her with a smile. *The better to catch an heiress, Louisa.*

And then, in that next moment, he cautioned her, all levity forgotten. The words he spoke were echoed against the rock that cradled them, that hid them from disturbance and discover.

"Be sure, Louisa." *Tell me now, if you are not.* And into her mind came a multitude of vignettes, small snatches of memory often recalled and even more poignantly relived. All of them of Douglas. Always alone, eternally adrift, forever solitary.

"Yes, Douglas," she said, "I am sure."

There are moments in each life that are so perfect, they are recalled unto death. That time in the black cave, with darkness both a hindrance and a blessing, was such. Douglas seemed to be content with a slow exploration of her, while Louisa was consumed with hunger. Not for fruition, or even for understanding, but for a touch, a reassurance, a kiss, and more. Yet each cared little for propriety or morals or the disgrace of one ugly heiress. She felt like a diamond, unearthed and muddied, being shined to her own perfection. And it was Douglas's hands that readied her for the beauty of it, who blew on her skin and suckled her and stroked her where she was forbidden to touch by her nurse's admonitions. It was Douglas who held her when she cried from the pain of it, then the beauty of it. And, finally, it was Douglas who sank into her arms and held her, as he whispered words until her heart quieted and her skin cooled.

Eleven

London was filled with people. Too many people, Douglas thought, as he felt jostled on the thoroughfare. It was as if the city were a great breathing beast that nearly suffocated him.

It is just that you are used to being alone, Douglas. With only yourself for company.

Louisa.

He brushed the thought from his mind, irritated that she should surface so quickly. How many times had he told himself to forget about her today? Ten, twenty? More like a hundred, Douglas.

She did not vanish with the ease he'd hoped she would, always there on the fringes of his thoughts. But then, she'd always been intransigent, even from the first time he'd met her.

I'm very good at hiding from others, which is probably why I knew you were here. And now, Louisa? Do you hide your thoughts from others with more ease than you hid them from me?

No. He was not here for that. He did not wish to think of Louisa Patterson. Not now, not for the foreseeable future. Perhaps once he had made it to the Continent, he would allow himself to remember her, like a sweetmeat he held out to reward himself for diligence. Not now, especially not now, when he needed to feed.

He hated this part of himself, hated the necessity of it. It would be easier to allow himself to simply slip away into nothingness, become that which he most feared, a shadow, a wisp, a frail and insubstantial memory of himself. An absurdity in truth, but the hunger was there, the need was there, that odd ache that could only be appeased by stealing something that did not belong to him.

Louisa.

No, damn it! His outcry was mental, but strong enough that several passersby stopped in the act of journeying from one place to another. They looked about, as if seeking the source of the pained cry, then traveled on, shaking their heads.

He should not have taken her innocence, but it would be a memory to sustain him for the rest of his life. And guilt. That too, would last the extent of his mortal years. Perhaps beyond, if his kind were the stuff of ghosts. In truth, his knowledge of himself came from spurious sources, the hideous tales of those who had been tinged with madness, and those stories imparted with much glee from Adrian.

Are you the only one, Douglas? The only one who ever wished to walk among others? Or are there others, who have mastered themselves, and taken the harder road, who wake each day uncertain of their capabilities, but wishing to try all the same?

She would not be gone, was incapable of being silenced. This, then, was the payment for stealing from her what she should never have shared. An innocence, a hope, a belief in him.

Have you ever considered, Douglas, that there are others out in society just like you? Or even more wonderful, Douglas, what someone like you could do in society?

Damn you. And it was not Louisa he cursed, but himself.

"Miss Louisa?"

"Yes, Annabelle?"

"Could you not eat a bite, miss? Cook will box my ears for sure if I return your tea tray to the kitchen without a bite been taken. And your grandfather gave me strict orders to see you eat."

"I'm truly not hungry, Annabelle." She turned from the window seat, smiling at the young maid. "But please, take some of those pastries yourself. That way, neither Cook nor my grandfather will plague either of us."

"Oh I couldn't, miss." There was a look of horrified wonder on the maid's face. Louisa held the plate out for her. Annabelle grabbed two of the berry tarts and put one in her commodious apron pocket. The other was eaten slowly and with great appreciation.

"Is it the dreams again, miss?"

Louisa only smiled. No dreams, only an influx of emotions that had her sleepless, and near tears every minute of the day.

"Well," Annabelle said, picking up the tray, "they all

say down in the kitchen that the sleepless nights might be something to cultivate, miss, what with the change in your appearance.'' The young maid looked stricken. ''Oh, I beg your pardon, miss.''

Louisa was only mildly curious. ''My appearance?'' Her nose had not decreased in size, nor had her teeth receded back into her mouth, and the last time she'd cared to look, her forehead was just as broad and high.

''It's just that it looks like the sun is right behind your skin, miss. Some women use lead but then they get those awful-looking spots because of it. I told Cook I knew you wouldn't use beauty paste. Begging your pardon, miss.'' Annabelle curtsied out the door, as eager to leave as a fox at the start of a hunt.

Louisa stared after her, a bit discomfited by that impromptu speech, enough to be lifted from her lethargy and walk to her dressing table. She picked up the silver-backed mirror and stared into it. Her face looked back at her, still as misshapen, still as difficult to look upon, but it was true that her skin looked particularly luminous.

She laid the mirror back upon the dressing table, turned and walked to the pier glass, where she studied her gown, habit keeping her gaze carefully away from her face.

She studied her appearance. The pale peach gown was quite lovely, really. A little low in the front, but no more than the fashion. She wore her mother's pearls, suitable for an unmarried woman, if not quite a maiden.

Once, she would have been willing to trade all the money she had for a pretty face, to catch a man glancing at her, perhaps even smiling. To see someone stop in the act of talking to another to follow her progress across the room with his eyes. Not in surprise or revulsion or mockery. But with masculine appreciation.

And now, it didn't seem to matter at all.

Louisa heard the whispers as she crossed the ballroom floor, and she discounted them. She could not, however, ignore the curious looks sent her way. She glanced down at her bodice, surreptitiously running her hand down the back of her dress. Nothing was amiss. Then why was everyone staring at her so? Did she look as distraught as she felt? No, she did not. She had practiced her smile in the mirror for almost an hour.

She truly wished they would not stare, almost as much as she wished this night were over so that she could return to her room. Then, she would spend the rest of the night crying. It seemed the only thing she really felt like doing.

Despite it all, he had left. Despite yesterday afternoon, the wonder of it, the sheer exultant joy of it, he had left her. But she refused to think that what she had done was shameful or disgraceful.

Please, Douglas, do not leave me. An entreaty that had drawn no response from him. Nothing. He might have been a shadow in truth for all the emotion he'd shown. He would never return, and she would always be left with nothing but memories.

"Are you ready, child?" Her grandfather smiled fondly at her. Louisa echoed the smile, wondering if the assembled guests had any idea of the tumult in her heart, or how difficult it was to pretend for this moment.

Her grandfather motioned for attention. The musicians caught his signal; the melody lingered for a few minutes, then gradually faded to silence.

"It is my great honor, my dear assembled guests, to announce that my granddaughter Louisa is about to become a bride." A flutter of voices, a small laugh, a surge of people forward to catch the name of the fortunate and newly wealthy groom. Mr. Dunston moved out from behind her grandfather, and Louisa sent him a bright and utterly false smile. He was not to blame for the circumstances, and she could not bear that he be ridiculed for his bride's lack of enthusiasm.

"Therefore, I would ask that you join me in announcing the very best wishes for Louisa and her bridegroom." He reached over, grabbed Alan Dunston's sleeve, and pulled him forward. At that moment, the crowd lost interest in what was before them, instead transfixed on what was happening in their midst. It was the oddest thing, Louisa thought, but it was like the biblical parting of the Red Sea; they simply all stepped back against the wall, leaving the way clear for the most wonderful creature in the world to be viewed in all his sartorial elegance.

He stepped out of the shadows, into the light given by the thousands of candles. He was taller than most men, dressed in dark colors. His face was pale but no more so than those who cultivated such pallor and labeled it aristocrat's disease. Nature, having bestowed a myriad of generational mistakes on her, had picked only those attributes of beauty and strength for him. His face was that of a man who had lived and experienced life, whose emotions shone in his eyes. High cheekbones, features that complemented each other, hair as ebony as the darkness.

She knew who he was instantly.

You are utterly beautiful.

And you are still too fixated upon appearances, Louisa.

If that were true of her, then it was just as true of the others, especially the women who seemed to stare at Douglas as if he were a sweetmeat and they orphaned and starving children. She smiled, this time a gesture of delight. She could feel his embarrassment, the wish that they would look elsewhere. For a moment, his thoughts entertained her, supplanted curiosity and wonder that he should be here at all.

He did not answer the questions framed in her mind, did not speak until he reached her grandfather's side.

"Sir?" he said, as he sketched a short bow, then extended his hand to Louisa. She, bemused, took it, allowing him to pull her close. One hand motioned to the musicians, who obeyed in silence. Then, upon the breath of a waltz, he danced with her. Back and forth, in a gentle pattern that widened the ballroom floor, creating an oasis for them lined by the curious.

"What a striking couple."

". . . could be love?"

". . . never would have guessed it."

"I'm sure I don't know, but she's done something."

"It's a new face paint."

"Never noticed that smile of hers before."

"Have her eyes always been that shade of green?"

Louisa heard the murmured comments, the whispers. Something like laughter blossomed inside and formed her lips into a broad smile. Her gaze met his, an answering gleam in his eyes mirrored her own mirth.

"You are never going to leave me alone, are you,

Louisa? Your thoughts are going to be forever in my mind, whether I want them there or not, aren't they?"

She blinked, then gave him the truth. "I hope so, Douglas. With all my heart, I hope so."

"I could hear you from London, you know. And I could probably have felt you from Venice."

"Perhaps."

"And you would never have ceased bedeviling me with your questions, or challenging me, would you?"

She lowered her face so he would not see her smile. His tone was decidedly annoyed, but beneath the irritation was another, blessed, emotion.

"No, Douglas," she admitted, "I do not believe I will ever cease."

"It is better to surrender," he softly said, "when you are outmatched in weaponry."

She blinked up at him. "I can hear your thoughts, Douglas, but I cannot see in the dark. Nor can I move as quickly as you."

"But you've gained the ability, Louisa, to control my actions with but a smile. Will you marry me, Louisa?"

Yes, Douglas.

And more than one of the assembled guests wondered at the smile they exchanged.

Twelve

"You did not tell me you were an earl." She fanned herself with the betrothal document.

"Was that why you decided to accept my offer, then?"

She smiled. "Of course. Grandfather has always wished to be aligned with the nobility."

"My cousin will not think highly of me for reappearing, especially since I was supposed to have died in Italy."

"But think of how joyful your mother will feel, Douglas."

He brushed his finger across the tip of her nose.

"And is that the only reason you wish to marry me? Because I am the only person you can touch?"

"Your eyes are so solemn, Louisa. Are you terrified of my answer?"

"Quite frankly, yes."

He stood, came around the desk that had witnessed

the signing of their betrothal contract, and placed his arms around her. "Did you not see me shaking your grandfather's hand?"

"Well, yes," she said, not demurring when he bent his head and placed a kiss on her temple.

"And did I not slap your Mr. Dunston on the back with all good cheer, commiserating with him on the loss of such a great prize for a wife?"

"Frankly, Douglas, you made me feel as if I were a boar that you had been the first to bring down."

She could feel his laughter, and he was not being at all subtle about his smile. It took her a moment to realize what he was asking her.

"What has changed?"

"I'm not sure, Louisa," he said, pulling back, "but it's as if I can control it in greater degree. Perhaps you were right, Louisa, and I can use my talents to greater purpose than holing up in a cave."

And perhaps you are right, Louisa, and I have not had enough hope. Perhaps there are others like me and things I might do with those talents I have.

She leaned her cheek against his chest. *Tears, Louisa?*

Instead of answering, or even acknowledging the thought, she escaped from his embrace, gripped her hands together, and then turned. This question was too difficult to ask, too difficult to hear its answer. If he lied, she would know.

"Why me, Douglas?" *You could choose anyone of the group outside this door, anyone of the guests and any woman would count herself fortunate.*

"Louisa," he said, the sound of his voice so filled with kindness that she closed her eyes to it.

Please, Louisa.

"How is it that you think yourself ugly, Louisa?" His finger brushed her shoulder. He bent and brushed a series of kisses across the curve of her nape.

"I do not think, I know. I see myself in the mirror every day." *Despite wishing to. It is not a sight I welcome.*

"But what you see is only what is measured by other people, Louisa. You see your nose as too large. Why, because the fashion is for dainty bumps, barely visible between rounded cheeks? And your teeth are white and perfectly formed." He brushed back the curls artfully arranged upon her forehead. "A profile such as yours was much prized in ancient Greece, where a high forehead was deemed a sign of great intelligence. And eyes such as yours, especially when they snap and snarl at me like they're doing now, are to be treasured more than simple blue or brown. They can take on a different color according to their mood."

She pulled away finally, feeling more irritated than embarrassed. "I have made a full inventory of my parts and pieces, Douglas, I do not need one from you."

He turned her so that her back was to him. Only then did she see that they faced the window and the night beyond acted as a mirror. She would have pulled away, but he would not allow her to, holding her shoulders fixed and in place while both of them stared full face into it. It seemed almost unbearable, her face next to his dark beauty. She closed her eyes against the sight.

"I think you do, Louisa. Look at yourself," he said, his voice too close to her ear. "Open your eyes and truly look at yourself." There was something in his voice, something rich and filled with humor and somehow promising. She blinked, then squinted, then opened her eyes, viewing herself without surprise or eagerness.

"See yourself as I see you," he said, pulling her back against him. It was neither proper nor maidenly, but it was ardently desired, such proximity to him. She allowed herself to sink back against him as he stared over her shoulder at her, daring her with his eyes to even glance away.

"Your eyes, Louisa, are kind. I've not seen avarice in them, or selfishness, or anger. Only compassion and forgiveness. Even for such as I." She blinked, glanced at him, then away. "Your lips have never spoken lies, except for the ones you've told about yourself." Another glance, another frown. "Your hair is not merely brown, Louisa, but has at least five colors in it, from gold to red to a color that reminds me of the oaks near my home. It shines in the sunlight, I wish you could see how much." She could feel the flush lighting her cheeks, the warmth from her toes to her collarbone. She focused her attention on his beautiful eyes, not the shape of his mouth as he framed the words. To do so made her think of things she should not be thinking. Thoughts not at all maidenly and reticent. "And your skin, Louisa, is the color of a peach, delicate and radiant and soft."

She glanced at her reflection, and for a moment, a brief and shining moment from the corner of her eye, it looked as if another woman stood there. A woman with a soft glow about her, with sparkling eyes, and a smile that was as radiant as the sun. A man stood behind her, a man whose beauty only mirrored hers, who basked in her warmth and reflected it.

"And love, Louisa? Cannot you see that?" He turned her, looked down into her eyes, now misted with tears.

"I cannot promise you a future untainted by difficulty. If I had any sense at all, I would run from you and your open heart. But I've discovered that I would rather believe in a better future than hide myself away and tell myself it was not mine to begin with. Perhaps there are others like me. And perhaps there is a way I can live in this world. Help me find it, Louisa.''

And this time when they kissed, it was not only in longing and anticipation and desire; it was in joy, shiny and polished and real.

Epilogue

Unlike fairy tales, in which happy ever after is a constant, living a life he'd always wanted was not an easy task for Douglas. There were times in which he despaired of being as he was, descending into a black mood from which only Louisa could tease him. But there were always compensations for the dark times. The first time he held his son in his arms, for one. The discovery of another like himself, a man benefiting his country by being active in the foreign office, was yet another.

Douglas chose to become indispensable to his nation in time of war, primarily as an aide to Arthur Wellesley. Louisa, a devoted and ardent wife and mother of their three children, was never separated from her husband, using her not inconsiderable resources to create a warm and welcoming oasis of peace for her family wherever they traveled. In addition, the Patterson wealth was often spent to provide a temporary home for all those people left adrift in the middle of war. People forgot about her appearance, primarily because her smile was so warm, her capacity for love was so great. She was forever to be known as the Angel of the Battlefield, while Douglas, not to be undone, was considered the Angel Earl. Both sobriquets amused their recipients and their children greatly, only one of whom had the ability to discern his father's secret talents.

But that is another story.